MAGGIE'S FORK IN THE ROAD

Montana Bound Series Book 2

LINDA BRADLEY

SOUL MATE PUBLISHING

New York

MAGGIE'S FORK IN THE ROAD

Copyright©2016

LINDA BRADLEY

Cover Design by Syneca Featherstone

Published in the United States of America by
Soul Mate Publishing
P.O. Box 24
Macedon, New York, 14502

ISBN: 978-1-68291-207-2

ebook ISBN: 978-1-68291-147-1

www.SoulMatePublishing.com

The publisher does not have any control over and does not assume any responsibility for author or third-party websites or their content.

Praise for **Maggie's Way**:

"Linda Bradley's fresh voice will keep readers riveted from beginning to end. Bradley delivers a heart-warming story full of disarming honesty and beautiful drama . . . This one stands out!" —Jane Porter, New York Times and USA Today Best Seller, Author of *Flirting With Forty* and *It's You*

"Maggie's Way is a heart-warming tale of love and loss, fear and friendship. With charming characters and a moving plot, Linda Bradley's lovely debut gently reminds us that it's never too late for second chances." — Lori Nelson Spielman, International Best Seller, Author of *The Love List* and *Sweet Forgiveness*

The Romance Reviews, Readers' Choice Awards Finalist — Summer 2016

Greater Detroit's BookSellers Best Award Finalist — 2016

For Scott.

All forks in the road lead home.

They say, home is where the heart is.

And when I'm with you, I am home.

Acknowledgements

Special thanks to Debby Gilbert for working with me on *Maggie's Fork in the Road*. Thanks to Pam for continuing to be my beta reader. Thanks to my readers and family for your continuous support. Your encouragement and love for the *Montana Bound Series* means the world. I'm excited to share the the next chapter of Maggie's life with you.

Chapter 1

John's news knocked the wind out of me leaving me breathless, speechless . . . paralyzed.

Breathe, I told myself.

The dim room grew foggy as my eyes searched John's face. "Really," I said. "Why now? And why here?" What was it about delivering bad news in a restaurant? First, Beckett, now John. For the love of God, I wondered if breaking a woman's heart in public got them into a secret men's club.

Letting my guard down proved one thing. Hurt was inevitable. John and Chloe's absence would leave a hole in my heart, a gorge of sharp edges. We were more than neighbors. We'd become friends that navigated life's ups-and-downs together. And now they were moving. I'd have new neighbors and I didn't want new neighbors. I wanted John and Chloe. I *needed* John and Chloe. We bonded last summer when I dealt with breast cancer. Their craziness made mine seem normal. John and Chloe weren't any ordinary neighbors; they were family, eccentric misfits, like myself that conformed to the beat of life while traversing the bumps in the road.

Massaging my temples, I caught my breath. The throb pierced my skull. Since John and Chloe's arrival, there'd never been a dull moment. Mom came around more often. And Chloe's mother, Brook. Jesus, she flitted in and left like a summer storm leaving sky-high humidity and heat that scorched everything in its path.

Broken-hearted, Chloe had wept over false promises, her bags packed, her hopes magnanimous. And God, Beckett.

My ex-husband found his footing with a *new* lifestyle that didn't include me, or any other woman. I'd heard through the grapevine that he *was* dating and wondered if his better half was as handsome as he was.

I searched John's face for an answer.

"I didn't know how to tell you. I'm sorry, Maggie. I don't belong here," he said, lowering his voice. "I can practice medicine in Montana and my dad could really use the help."

Montana was one hell of a long ways away. I swallowed the sting of disappointment. John's eyes searched mine. His news left a bitter taste at the back of my throat. "You can't leave. I love you," I whispered.

The pressure behind my eyes burned something fierce. How was it possible that I felt so much for someone I wasn't romantically involved with? I certainly thought about it enough and the few recent kisses we shared established a deeper connection spurring buried promises that I'd made to myself. Moving forward in the wake of waiting for perfect timing proved difficult.

The corners of John's mouth drooped. His jaw clenched.

"I can't believe I said that." I stared into my half-empty glass of Merlot, my cheeks smoldered from the realization that he didn't return my sentiments. My chin quivered as he touched my hand from across the table.

"I want to put the house up for sale when Chloe's school year ends."

My forced smile hurt. It was the kind that everyone knows is fake and by John's expression, my attempt to lighten the moment had failed. He squeezed my hand. I sipped my wine trying to avoid eye contact with the waitress. Her return with the dessert tray came at the most inopportune moment. After listening politely, John asked for the check. I wrapped my shawl around my shoulders trying to hold myself together. "I'll meet you outside," I said, fumbling with my purse.

"I won't be long," he said. "Maggie—"

The leg of my chair got stuck on the carpet. I shook it loose in disgust, studying the face of a man that I thought just might be a permanent fixture in my life. His eyes sadly apologetic.

"Damn, you're beautiful." With a heavy sigh, he paused. "I'll be out in a minute.

The cool spring breeze sent shivers down my spine as I exited the restaurant. I caught my breath. How could I have told John I loved him? Why now? I wrapped my arms around myself. If I could survive cancer, I'd survive this. Hearts mended. Beckett taught me that lesson the hard way, but this *was* John and Chloe. Our attachment was the seam that mended that wound, made it invisible.

John opened the car door for me. I climbed in. His stare rustled my nerves. Pretending to rummage for something in my purse, I rooted around inside my bag and finally decided I was searching for my sanity. It wasn't there. I even checked the hole in the satin lining. Nothing. How could I be so upset over something I didn't ever really have? John reached over and buckled me in before shutting the door.

"I know you're not okay." He turned the key in the ignition. "This wasn't an easy decision," he added.

I studied his profile. "I know it wasn't easy. I know you're unhappy here in Michigan." My heart skipped a beat. Saying the right thing tasted bitter. I wanted him. I wanted him before, but couldn't admit it. I wanted him now, but he was leaving. "Thanks for dinner," I said, trying my best to be grateful.

"I know this wasn't the evening out you were expecting." He checked the mirrors and backed out of the parking spot.

The jazz on the radio couldn't fill the silence between us. The ten-minute car ride by the lake seemed like an eternity. The sliver of moon like a dagger in my heart as its white glow washed over the glassy lake. I loved the lake. The lazy cove in Grosse Pointe was the place where my only son,

Bradley, grew up. It was a place of solace, a place for meeting new friends like Judy and her two boys, Harry and Walter. It was the place I first saw that horseshoe tattoo on John's left shoulder as he strolled down the beach holding Chloe's hand. It was the place where Bones peed on Brook's leg, the place where Brook and I bantered over Chloe, and took photos in an effort to prosper from our differences. It was the place where I held the snarky seven-year-old when Brook broke her heart and went back to Hollywood, California, after promising her daughter a life together.

John coasted into his driveway. "I'll walk you home."

A thin grin passed over my lips, lips that he'd kissed just before telling me that he was moving to Montana. My empty stone house waited for me, along with a wrinkly-faced Bulldog. I'd still have Bones, thanks to Mom. Maybe that's how it was meant to be.

John parked the car then gazed into my eyes. He longed for something, something I secretly hoped would keep him here, close to me. He got out and walked around to open my door. As I swung my legs out of the car, my skirt cascaded over my freckled shins. He linked his arm with mine and led me home. "All seems quiet. Chloe must have been good for the sitter."

"We'll see. Only time will tell," he said. "She's older and wiser now."

"She's eight, and being in third grade doesn't make you necessarily wiser, it makes you taller with bigger teeth."

We sauntered up the stairs to the porch. Digging in my purse for the key to the front door of my house, I stood like a pillar of salt waiting for John to say something, to tell me he'd changed his mind on the way home. "I'm not sure what to say," I whispered. John caressed my cheek. I shut my eyes, memorizing his touch. I nuzzled into the palm of his warm hand. *Please don't leave,* I secretly wished. I had no right to ask. He stepped closer, his breath in my ear.

"You're not making this easy. You never do, Maggie Abernathy. Look at me," he murmured.

Afraid to open my eyes, I swallowed away emotion. John was always doing stuff like that, telling me I was beautiful, telling me I had a hold on him, but not a strong enough hold to keep him here. I gazed into his Irish eyes. I heard my heart shatter as it broke all over again, leaving me with a pit in my stomach. John led me inside, his hand on the small of my back. His eyes gleamed with intent. He tugged at the fringe on my shawl making it drop to the ground as he kicked the door shut. John picked me up then carried me upstairs. As much as I knew I should have stopped him, I couldn't. I didn't want to.

Moonlight flooded my bedroom. John took off his shirt then unbuttoned my blouse exposing my lace bra. He ran his fingers along the edge of the cup, tickling my skin, leaving me with goose bumps, wanting more. His mouth covered mine. Laying me upon the bed, I closed my eyes, and let him in.

Moonlight washed over his skin. It caressed every muscle and curve of his brawny body. I snuggled in behind him, tracing his horseshoe tattoo with my finger. "Did this hurt when you got it?" My lips grazed his skin as I whispered into the darkness. "Maybe if I got one, I'd have better luck." I closed my eyes then crawled beneath the covers. John's square jaw and simmering eyes held my stare. He crawled back to where I'd settled in and peered down at me. Lowering his head, his lips met mine. I squeezed my eyes shut damming the deluge. My heart pounded against my rib cage, telling me it was time, time to let go. John was leaving and this would be our perfect goodbye. "Chloe's probably wondering where you are," I said, caressing his whiskery cheek. "So, you've decided to grow a beard?"

"No, just a little scruff. I hear women like that."

He leaned over me and kissed my lips as he brushed strands of stray hair away from my face. His Adam's apple twitched when he swallowed. I waited for the words, the words I wanted to hear, but they didn't come. "You're so damn beautiful," he said, caressing my cheek. "We should have done this a long time ago, Maggie Abernathy."

Nervous knots filled my belly as I listened to his deep coaxing voice. My eyelids fluttered. Fierce emotion mounted beneath my calm surface. Reaching up, I wrapped my arms around his neck. "Yeah," I whispered. "We probably should have."

Chapter 2

My cup clunked against the saucer and tea slopped over the side. "Shit," I mumbled, staring at the mysterious cane with my father's name etched in the black paint hanging on the hall tree in the corner of the room. Tiny brown drops splattered across my desk catching the corner of my latest cow photograph. I wiped it off with my sleeve. Bones ran through the foyer and sat in front of the door.

The bell rang. I knew it would. Bones always knew when Chloe was coming. I stood up, took my glasses off, and hung them from the collar of my shirt. Bones' tail wagged, his rump swayed side-to-side, his pink tongue waggling just waiting for his buddy from next door. I opened the door. The pink ribbon she'd made for me before the Detroit Race for the Cure hung in remembrance of those Judy and I jogged for, including ourselves. We were breast cancer survivors, but the notion it could rear its ugly head again lingered. "Hi, Chloe," I said with a smile. She wore blue jeans with holes in the knees, her pink Chuck Taylor tennis shoes, a jean jacket, and the purple knit hat my mom made her last summer. Her T-shirt had a purple peace sign on it. Her backpack dangled from her fingertips.

"Hi, Maggie, I need help," she said, fingering the word *survivor* she'd written on the satin bow in silver glitter. "Can I come in? I have to do this stupid book report and I don't know what to do."

"Where's your dad?" I asked, thinking she really didn't need help since her reading had improved since last summer.

I'd taught Chloe to read better and she taught me how to train Bones. The deal sweetened both our pots.

"He's on the phone with my grandpa. They're talking about the ranch."

"Ah, so this is an escape," I said, not wanting to hear about the ranch in Montana. It'd become a big part of John's life since Christmas and he'd gone there several times since January to see his dad. I should have known. "How's your Grandpa?"

"Good, I guess," she answered, bending down to scratch Bones' belly. "Hi there, boy."

Bones jumped up on Chloe to lick her face. She fell backward and bonked her head on the door. Rubbing the spot, she groaned. "I'm okay, I'm okay." She blinked away the sting.

Chloe's hair had grown shoulder length, and wispy bangs hung in her eyes. She needed a haircut. I held out my hand to help her up. She grabbed it and I tugged. Bones trotted into the kitchen, his nails clicking against the smooth floor.

"Smells good in here. Whatcha making?" Chloe inquired, following in Bones' footstep. She dropped her backpack in the hallway.

I noticed a purple string sticking out. "Won't Voodoo get hot in there?" I asked, picking up the worn bag. "Do you even have a book in here?" The backpack was light as a feather.

"Oh, I must have forgotten it." Chloe peeked in the oven. "Yum, cake," she said, peering back over her shoulder. "I can do the book report later."

Chloe scooted out a chair at the kitchen counter.

"Dad's talking about moving."

My gut twisted. "I was wondering if you knew."

She shook her head. "I don't want to go. I want to stay. We've moved enough. I'll miss Harry and Walter."

Her eyes connected with mine. Sad pools of green stared at me. I knew she'd miss more than that.

"And you," she added.

I mussed her hair as I walked past. "Yeah, I know what you mean." In some strange way, Chloe helped fill Bradley's void. He was grown and on his own in Boston. The buzzer on the oven dinged. I rummaged through the cupboard for toothpicks to check the center of the cake. A blast of hot air covered my face when I opened the oven door. "I think it's done."

"Can we frost it?"

"Not yet, it has to cool. Why don't you take Bones for a walk? Maybe when you get back, it will be ready."

Chloe jumped down from the stool. "Sure, why not." She patted her leg and called Bones' name. "I'll get the leash and a poop bag. That sounds funny, poop bag," she said, shaking her head. "I love this new leash. Skulls and crossbones, so cool."

Following her and Bones to the front door, I wrapped my sweater tight across my chest. May usually brought promises of warmer weather, but this spring it delivered an unexpected chill in the air. "Chloe." I grabbed a scarf from the hall tree then hurried out the front door. Wrapping the scarf around her neck, I smoothed blond wisps of hair from her face. "You really should have on a warmer jacket."

The wind caught loose dishwater-blonde tresses as it rushed by. Chloe shook her head. "You sound like such a mom," she said. "You must have done a real job on Bradley." She spun on a heel, skipped down the stairs, and scurried along the walk with Bones by her side.

"Get your book on the way back," I called before going back inside and shutting the door behind me. The doorbell rang shortly after returning to my library. "What did you forget?" My breath caught in the chilly air. John's emerald eyes smiled at me. Heat rushed through my veins. A shiver of shyness caught me off guard. "Hi," I whispered.

"Can I come in?" he asked.

I couldn't help but grin. "I'm not so sure that's a great idea." Flashbacks filled my mind from our night together. A warm sensation crept over my skin like his fingertips in the dark.

He snickered and drew his coat tighter around his neck. "Sure is brisk out here, ma'am. I promise I don't mean no harm," he said, sounding like a bad spaghetti western.

"Fine, shut the door behind you." I went into the living room and sat on the sofa. "I'm thinking about getting a chair."

"Thought you didn't want clutter yet. You said something about filling this place with memories," John replied, sitting at the other end. He unbuttoned his jacket then wiggled out of it.

Two days ago, we filled my bedroom with memories, memories I wasn't sure I could bear to think about now he'd planned to move. My heart twitched with the onset of that familiar ache. I felt alive when he and Chloe were around. "Might need a chair for Bones to curl up in."

"You sure have become fond of that dog," John said with a crooked grin.

I'd become fond of lots of things in the past nine months. "Yeah, he's kind of grown on me. My mother knew what she was doing." Bones' stare from a black-and-white photo on the mantle warmed me. My heart pounded. Sadness crept up my throat as I swallowed away the truth. I tucked my hair behind my ears. Hot waves washed over me. How was it possible to feel ablaze in this unexpected May chill?

"Maggie," John said.

"Yeah," I said with caution. I knew the expression, the furrowed brow, and the apologetic tone. I preferred his smile. I loved the laugh lines around his eyes, his strong jaw, and rugged chin. John really didn't look like a pediatrician, but then again, what does a pediatrician *really* look like? Maybe he was ready to abandon his career, too. He'd mentioned giving up his practice, but I never thought he'd make good on the banter. Similar thoughts surfaced when I pondered my career. I knew I'd retire should the right opportunity present itself, but that kind of luck usually escaped me. I was in it for the long haul. With all the changes in public education, I found myself counting the few years I had left.

"I don't want you to think I don't care," he said. His chest rose and fell with a deep breath. "You've done so much for Chloe—" He stopped and reached for my hand. "And me."

I'd been such a fool to blurt out that I loved him the other night. "I know you care," I said, lowering my gaze. Letting my hand slip away from his, I tucked my knees up into my chest then wrapped my arms around them. Staring into the dark fireplace, I wished for enough heat to make John stay. I just wanted to hang onto him for a little bit longer. The photo of Judy and I crossing the Race for the Cure finish line caught my eye. If I could survive cancer, I could survive John's revelation to move to Montana. If I reminded myself enough, maybe I'd believe it. Judy and I were decked out in pink running gear and had jogged the whole five kilometers. The electricity between us as we held hands at the finish still lingered.

"You don't have to sound like that," he said.

"Sound like what?" I asked, meeting his gaze.

"So cold. The other night was—" John rubbed his chin and his eyes grew dark.

"You said you were putting the house up. You're leaving. The other night was just two people saying goodbye." He narrowed his eyes at me when I leaned back to rest my neck on the pillow of the sofa. "Let's not do this." John stood up, wiggled his way back into his coat then buttoned it as he took two steps closer to me. I liked it better when he was crawling over me in bed, staring down into my eyes with something else on his mind.

"You are one aggravating woman, Maggie Abernathy. I didn't come here to fight. I came here to tell you—"

We both glanced toward the foyer when the front door slammed. Bones ran through to the kitchen as Chloe skipped behind him. "Hey, Dad, can you help me with my homework after I help Maggie with this cake? It smells yummy."

John leaned closer to me. "We are not done here," he whispered.

I wasn't sure about that.

Chapter 3

The phone rang. "Let it ring," I told myself, checking the caller ID. Talking to John was the last thing I wanted to do. I swiped the paintbrush across my colored palate letting fate choose the color of the next cow. I wanted it to reflect a lost soul, like me. *Damn him.* Everything was going so well. Being on an even keel suited me fine. John contemplated leaving his practice, but why now? I thought he'd wait until Chloe got older.

Who could replace them? No one.

I touched my paintbrush to the black-and-white photograph. The gray-blue hue transformed the heifer into the perfect specimen of melancholy. The evening sun lowered in the sky sending fragmented jets of light into my library. Yellow and orange hues warmed me, leaving me anxious for summer. But what would it offer me now that John had decided to sell his house? I shook away the thought while anticipating late night chats on the porch swing, cookouts, the beach with Chloe, and our everyday routine that I preferred even if it meant picking up sticky Popsicle sticks, slamming screen doors, and Mom on my heels. Summer dreaming was my prescription for survival the last few days of school when the to-do list grew longer and the students shut down, but now those images blurred like a hazy morning at the lake.

For now, Saturdays were my break in hectic expectations, but Sundays were laced with the hint of Mondays. Ugh! Staying organized and on top of state requirements took its toll not only for me, but also for my colleagues who understood that education was morphing rapidly into a beast none of us seemed to be familiar with. The days of painting and rest time faded into the hypocrisy of politics. I loved the students, but the new-and-improved delivery of curriculum stifled my philosophy.

Bones barked then trotted to the front door. I poked my head out of the library to see what the commotion was. He sat and stared at the wooden panels. With a quick glance back at me, he wagged his tail. I opened the door before Chloe could knock. "Hi, Chloe." Anxious to get back to my project, I rambled. "What's going on?"

"Can I hang for a while? I'll take Bones for a walk. I won't bother you. I just need a place to hang out for a while."

She sounded like a fugitive on the run. I crossed my arms over my waist. "Why? And how much trouble is this going to get us into?" She peered back over her shoulder with caution. I suspected she was expecting her father.

"Dad's just busy. He's on the phone with Grandpa, again, and I'm bored. Please," she begged.

Like a sucker, I let her inside. "Sure, but I'm kind of busy."

"You painting your pictures for cow books?"

I nodded. "Yes, and I'm kind of on a roll. You're not gonna be mad if I ignore you, are you?" A dark cloud drifted across her emerald eyes. She resembled her father more and more every day. "Who am I kidding? I could never ignore you." I rolled my eyes.

Chloe shut the door behind her then followed me into the library. She flipped her bangs out of her face then blew the last few stray hairs away with a huff.

"You ready for a haircut?" I asked.

"Nope," she said, staring up to me. "I want it long like my mom's hair," she said. "And you. These colors sure are pretty."

"Yeah, they are." My mind focused on the array of hues I'd spread out on my palate like Van Gogh's *Starry Night*. Putting my glasses back on, I dunked the tip of my paintbrush into the cup of water. Chloe's eyes watched intently. "You like to paint?" I touched my brush carefully to my photo.

"Yup, but I don't get to do it very often and usually in art class we have to follow the rules," Chloe said.

"Yeah, darn teachers." I snickered, and she smiled at me. The gap between her big two front teeth less and less with each passing day. "Wanna paint with me? Who knows maybe you'll inspire me to think outside the box."

Chloe laughed. "You have a blue cow on your paper. You're pretty much already *way* outside the box, but I like it."

I peered over the rim of my glasses then smirked at her youthful disposition. "I'll let you in on a little secret." I paused, taking in her inquisitiveness. "I was the only child in my kindergarten class to paint my Indian princess face blue." I pointed to the plaster masterpiece on the wall behind Chloe. "And there she is." I beamed with pride. My sculpture reminded me of a relative youthful uniqueness that all children possess.

"You made that. That is so cool." Chloe stepped closer to it to get a better look. "A blue face, classic!" With two thumbs up, she bowed. "I love it."

My teacher's expression, fresh in my mind like it was yesterday. I stood by her side and stared into her careworn face, digesting her disappointment. My lack of understanding direction and conformity, dissatisfying. "Yeah, well, my teacher was speechless and we all know what that means. The boys made fun of me all day, but when it was all said and done, I knew which princess was mine in the sea of uniformity." I smiled at Chloe's furrowed brow.

"Um, some kids can be mean and boys are kind of stupid anyway. It's perfect. I'd probably paint mine blue, too."

"Thanks." I winked at her and marveled at her insight, dead-on. Boys could be stupid even if they were handsome and wore a stethoscope.

I rearranged my desk so Chloe had a spot to paint. Handing her a pile of rejects, I said, "Pick a photograph. They're all prepped and ready for paint."

She searched through the stack on the chair. There were no photos of her mom hanging around. They'd been sent to Brook last summer or I had already given them to Chloe. She picked out a photo of Bones sleeping on a mat in front of the French doors in the kitchen. "Good choice," I assured her. "Here, use these brushes. Let's try to keep the paint neat so we don't have smudgy colors." She wrinkled her nose at me. "You know, when you're in art class sharing and that annoying kid next you sticks his brown paintbrush in the yellow paint?"

The corner of her mouth curled up. "That annoying kid is *usually* me. I get so excited I forget what I'm doing sometimes."

I smiled. "Whatever, I won't get mad, but try to be careful," I whispered, choosing my next color. Chloe's bright eyes caught my attention. She was inches away inspecting my deliberation and staring with comical intent. "What?" I asked.

"You must get *egg-zausted* with all that thinking. Just pick," she said in true Junie B. Jones fashion, then she dunked her paintbrush into the pool of yellow paint. "Bones likes the sun so the windows will be yellow. His fur feels so toasty after he's taken a nap in the sun." Chloe's tongue poked out of the side of her mouth as she carefully filled in the square panes of glass in the photo with the color of the summer. "It's cool how the paint sticks to the little bumps you sprayed on this paper."

"You mean exhausted?"

"Yeah, whatever, super-duper tired. My dad does the same thing. Geez, just pick already what you're gonna do? It makes me tired just watching you people," she said, concentrating on her brush strokes. She dipped her brush into the puddle of yellow paint again without looking up. "He's going to Montana next week. My nanny fell through."

I stopped mid-stroke. "What?" I asked, my eyes focused on her steady hand, her neatness better than I expected.

"She met me. We tried it out that night you two went to dinner. I'm not sure what did her in though."

I dipped my brush into the gray-blue paint again thinking about Van Gogh's genius. "What do you mean? You were bad on purpose?"

"Promise not to tell," she mumbled without looking up from her project.

My right eyebrow shot to the ceiling. "Do I want to know?"

Chloe shrugged. "Probably not, but it involved blood, fake blood, that is."

I narrowed my eyes. Chloe batted her eyelashes at me with an expression of genius in her own right.

"It wasn't real blood. It was ketchup with a little soy sauce mixed in to make it look like real blood. Harry taught me how to do it. Harry used the trick on Walter. Said it worked like a charm so, I pretended to hurt myself. I can't help it if she was wearing a white sweater. Gotta be prepared for anything." Pride exuded from her grin. "Who wears white around an eight-year-old?"

"What did you pretend to cut off?" I asked, envisioning a valiant act of third grade grossness. I began painting the third cow a lighter shade of midnight then stopped as the gears in my brain ticked louder. Finishing the cow, I mixed a bit of brown paint in with the blue to pay true homage to my own inspiration. I added short swirly brush strokes across the dusky sky and smiled at my creativity.

"Nothing," Chloe said, inspecting my new technique. "Oh, I like that."

"Thanks." I glanced over to Chloe. "Well what did you do with the blood?"

"Remember when we whacked heads and you had to get stitches?"

"Yeah, how could I forget? I have a scar on my left temple to remind me," I said, continuing to paint.

"I just thought about what your head looked like and made myself look like that and then laid down on the sofa, and started to cry."

"Maybe you'll be an actress when you grow up," I said, thinking about her mother in Hollywood posing for the camera.

"Dad was pretty mad. I stained the sofa. Special cleaners are coming to get it out. He says it's coming out of my allowance. I don't care, though. It was worth it. She was a dope. That's what you get for spending all your time on your phone. I probably did Dad a favor, saved him a real trip to the hospital for when she was there the next time not paying attention to me."

"Hmmm. But now there's no one to watch you. It's hard to get babysitters." When I glanced up, Chloe grunted, her eyes thin slits.

"I am *not* a baby!" Chloe huffed before swishing her paintbrush around in the jar of water with vigor.

I rolled my eyes. "Lighten up, will you? You know what I meant." Ignoring the irritation in her squeaky voice and my poor choice of words, I went back to work. Chloe was more grown up than some adults I knew.

I handed Chloe a paper towel to wipe her wet paintbrush on. She carefully dangled the tip of her brush in the water. Her intense eyes searched mine. She sparkled with a twinkle of more contemplative genius. I assumed the same genius that concocted an accident to test the next new hire. "What?" I slowly stopped working.

"Dad's not going to be gone for too long. How about I stay here with you. I promise, I'll be good."

Chloe cocked her head and clasped her hands in front of her. She wrinkled the bridge of her nose making her brow furrow.

"Oh geez," I said, "I think I hear your dad calling you."

Chloe quickly painted dark-green spots on the rug in her photo. "Pleeeease. I want to stay here. I don't want to go to the ranch."

How could she not want to go to a ranch? How could she pass up a trip to Montana that meant missing school? What was she thinking? I leaned back in my chair. "I don't think this is for us to decide. Your dad will figure it out." I sighed. Chloe's sad expression resembled Bones' face when he pouted. A twinge of ingenuity brewed in her eyes.

"I'm sure he will," she added.

Chapter 4

"What?" I said with a squeak. My mother stood in my kitchen explaining the opportunity before her. Was she crazy? She shushed me with that all-knowing pointer finger that mothers possess.

"He's in a pinch. It's only for a few days. I raised you just fine. Besides, it will be fun."

I poured myself another glass of wine and headed to the table. "You're really going to watch Chloe?" Mom followed me.

"Sure, it will be fine. When she's at school, I'll do my regular things and when she's home, I'll be there with her."

"You mean over here with me, with her?"

"Why the sour face? You love Chloe." Mom sipped from her glass as she sat down across from me. "Mmm. This is tasty. I should drink more often."

"No, you shouldn't," I said softly.

"Oh pish. Give your momma a break. Why do you care so much?"

Sipping my wine, my chest bubbled with angst. John was always saying I was the one making it so damn hard. He wasn't making it any easier. Mom's phone vibrated across the table. She picked it up and smiled as she checked the caller identification screen. She put her finger up letting me know she had to take the call. She scooted out of her chair and strolled out of the room.

I sat.

I waited.

I eavesdropped the best I could without leaving my spot. She was making arrangements with John. She sounded sure of herself and happy to help out while I sulked. I inspected her smug demeanor as she rejoined me at the table. "I just don't know why he called you. There are lots of services out there," I said.

"Did you want him to call you?" she asked.

"No, why would I want that?" I stared into her hazel eyes. "Seriously, I don't think that would be a good idea."

"What's going on between you two?" she asked.

Avoiding her gaze, I got up when her eyes sparked with curiosity, then went into the kitchen and buried my head in the refrigerator pretending to search for a snack.

"Nothing." I heard Mom's chair scrape against the kitchen floor.

"All in good time, all in good time. You may not want to share now, but there's something between you two. You're not fooling anybody. I've said this before, Marjorie Jean, give it a whirl, you never know."

I pressed my eyes shut. "He's leaving his practice. He's moving to Montana to help his dad." I shut the fridge after grabbing an apple. I bit down hard and snapped off a mouthful. The juice squirted in my eye and my head jerked backward.

"Oh, that is a predicament, isn't it?"

I cocked my head to the side at the lack of the concern in her voice. "Really?"

"No need to be snooty with me. Things could change," she added.

I bit off another mouthful barely able to chew it. Resting my belly against the kitchen counter, I stared out the window into the backyard. The plants were fighting to come alive in the cool springtime air. I imagined lilac bushes and yellow daffodils bowing to me as I welcomed them in the warm days ahead. "How are they going to change?" I mumbled to myself. I was stuck. I had a career in Michigan that I needed to finish. My home was here, Grosse Pointe, Michigan, always had been, and always would be. I didn't have family in Montana. The hefty breath of Mom's sigh nudged my imagination. My shoulders slumped from the reality that nipped at my conscience. I finished my apple and tossed the core into the sink, then burped aloud.

"You survived a divorce. You survived Bradley moving away. You survived cancer, for crying out loud. You'll figure this out, too. I didn't think you cared so much about him," Mom said.

Mom fiddled with her wineglass. My eyes stung from the sour aftertaste of the Granny Smith apple. "Well, I do," I said, holding her stare. I rubbed the stabbing pain in my temples. "Good grief, this is too much."

"You'll figure it out. I'm sure there's a plan even if you don't know it yet."

I detested these parts of life. I hated not knowing what was in store. Mom always seemed confident, strong enough to go with the flow, and unwilling to cave to uncertainty. "Why did you stop over tonight?" I asked, forgetting her original intention.

"Just to see you," she said with a smile.

"Oh." I twisted my hair into a knotted bun at the nape of my neck. "I'm not very good company."

"Oh, you're very good company," she reassured me. "Well, I should be going. I have to get my house in order before I come stay with Chloe."

"Chloe's lucky to have you," I whispered. Glad for the smile on my mom's face, I walked over to where she stood and wrapped my arms around her, then hugged her.

"Thanks, but we're the lucky ones and don't you forget it."

Mom rubbed my back as she spoke. "We have you. Life would be pretty boring without you, Maggie."

A thin smile crossed my lips. "Thanks, Mom," I said, leaning back to gaze into her eyes. "I think."

She tapped my nose like I was a child, her pointer finger getting more crooked with the passing of time.

"I better get going. A mother's work is never done," she said.

"You're right about that," I added, helping her with her coat. "Bradley doesn't need me much now that he's grown and living in Boston."

Mom buttoned her jacket. "He may be far away, but he's close at heart. You're with him whether you realize it or not. Babies always need their mommas and mommas always need their babies. You're the voice in his head when he's making a decision, my girl."

"Thanks, Mom." I kissed her cheek. I touched her knitted hat. "I like your hat. Did you make it?"

"Yup." She tugged the knobby thick design over her ears then headed for the front door with a smile. "We're not done talking about this John thing."

Hastily, I opened the door and eyed her with warning. "Goodnight, Mom, be careful driving home," I said, pecking her on the cheek. "I think you're shorter."

"I'm not falling for that," she said with a smile. "This is going to be great living next door for a few days."

I rolled my eyes.

"Don't roll your eyes, Marjorie Jean," she said with a tone. "It's not polite."

I gave her another peck on the cheek. "Okay, Glad." I closed the door to the May chill then strolled to the living room window to watch her go. She was spry as ever even if she was shorter and a little more wrinkled. She was still my mother, and I loved her even if she did get under my skin.

Chapter 5

"Your mom's all settled." John glanced down at the paper in his hands. "I know you're not happy with me for calling her, but I was stuck, really stuck and Chloe wasn't helping." He held out the list of phone numbers in my direction. "I hate to ask, but can you keep an eye on them?"

"Oh, geez." I sighed. "You're as bad Chloe. Of course I'll keep an eye on them." I took the paper that John handed me then scanned the names in case of emergency.

"Glad has a copy, but I just want to make sure you have one, too."

"Did you ask Brook to help?" I regretted the question as soon as it left my lips. John's stare questioned my intention. "Sorry, I just thought maybe she might help."

"Not that lucky, not in her genes. I don't think Chloe needs her mother her right now anyway," he said. "Chloe was a mess after Brook left her behind last summer. Don't need to test the waters."

I took a deep breath remembering it took months for Chloe to get back to her old self after the last disappointment. He was probably right. If Brook was my ex-wife, I wouldn't call her either. "Just curious." I shrugged, trying to appear indifferent.

John stepped inside the house, checked over his shoulder, then rested his hands on my shoulders, proximity his secret weapon.

"Have a safe trip." I crossed my arms in front of me as I peeked up at him through my eyelashes.

"Maggie."

"What?" I asked softly. He didn't answer immediately, but held my stare. "What?" I pressed my lips tight trying to hold in anything cutting that might slip out.

John leaned in and held my face in his hands. I stifled the quake rumbling through me. His lips kissed my forehead. I closed my eyes like I'd done before not wanting to forget how it felt to be close to him.

"Don't go," I whispered as he turned to leave.

His eyes filled with question. "What did you say?"

I held his gaze. "Don't go." I shifted my weight with conviction.

"Maggie, this is what I have to do. I'll be back in a few days." He shoved his hands into the pockets of his jacket. "You really don't want me to go?"

"Jesus, John, you're just as irritating as I am," I said. "I told you I loved you the other night and you didn't say it back. I'm asking you not to go. We slept together for crying out loud. You're always prodding me to admit my feelings. Now I have and you're not sure what to do with me?" I tilted my head to see through the blurry tears. "Figures," I murmured.

"Maybe it's just bad timing," he said after a long pause.

"Or you're a big fat chicken, too." I waited for a reaction. With a heavy breath, my heart pounded against my chest walls. "Have a safe trip," I said before walking away.

"Maggie."

"What?" I snapped, glancing over my shoulder feeling the sting of abandonment.

"Nothing," he said.

Why so many tests? The sooner he went, the better. I had a friend who used to say that there would always be someone else, no matter the circumstances. What if I didn't want someone else? Maybe, I only wanted him. Maybe, I didn't want a man after all. My head pinged in every direction. "I'll check on them. Don't worry. Enjoy Montana."

"Thanks, Maggie. You're a good friend."

His words burned like the kiss of death as he shut the door behind him. Angry, I cursed myself for allowing him to get closer. Scrolling down to Brook's phone number in my list of contacts, I poked out a message then deleted it. I went to my laptop and logged into the retirement website for teachers. My teaching years equated to almost twenty-seven years. I had more time in than I realized, not remembering substitute teaching counted for something. My eyes scanned home page. To the left of the screen there was text stating the rules for buying additional years. Eager to understand the options, I scoured the information.

The rumble of John's Harley knocked at the window. I got up and peered next door. Shocked by the sight, I put my hand on my chest, squeezing my sweater shut. John kicked up the stand, rolled his bike backward, and then pointed it toward the road. With a rev of the engine, he slowly picked his feet up then rode away. A thin smile crept across my lips even if it felt like he was taking my heart with him. "Damn you," I muttered.

"Sometimes you have to let go."

I jumped with surprise. "You could at least warn me when you come in," I scolded my mother, trying to catch my breath.

"You should be used to it by now," she answered.

"Thought you were next door."

"Almost. John's going to get Chloe. She's with Walter and Harry," Mom said.

"On the bike?"

"Yup, she has a helmet and everything."

"Guess those classes really paid off." I shrugged, wishing I were the one holding tight with my arms wrapped around John's waist peering over his shoulder at the open road.

"He's leaving at seven."

Mom's eyes flickered. I ignored the jest. Bones barked wildly at the front door. I padded softly to see what the ruckus was all about. There was nothing. Pulling the phone out of my pocket, I checked for calls and texts. I thought about John's ex-wife, Brook, thinking she should be the one taking care of her daughter. With Mom next door, I may as well have said Chloe could stay with me. I thought about sending Brook a text again, but what would that accomplish? Nothing. I tucked the phone back into my pocket. "So, you know what time Chloe needs to be dropped off at school and what time she needs to be picked up?"

"Yup. We leave at eight sharp and I pick her up at half past three. I've been to the school, know where I can park, and have been put on the emergency card."

"Wow, John was thorough."

"Oh, stop looking at me that way. It's only three days. He'll be back before you know it."

I gnawed at my thumbnail as I plopped down on the sofa. "Yeah, long enough to put the house up and be on his way." I leaned back, my eyes glued to the majestic beamed ceiling, wondering why I didn't have the guts to leave too, follow a different dream now that I was alone. "What if I decided to move? How would you feel about that?"

Mom's face wrinkled with question. She plopped down at the other end of the sofa, wedging herself in the corner to get a better look at me.

"Seriously, you need more furniture in this room. I'd like to sit across from you so I don't have to crane my neck. I'm getting too old for this."

"What if I moved?" I put my feet up on the table I inherited from my grandma. Images of the the ocean or maybe a cabin in the middle of nowhere drifted in and out of my mind.

"Not sure. I'd miss you, that's for sure, but what about your job?"

"I'd make sure I had my ducks in a row. Just thinking. What's really grounding me here?" Mom cleared her throat as I rambled. Her eyes glimmered with hurt. "I didn't mean it that way," I said, raising my left eyebrow. "What if you came with me?" I wanted to retract the statement as soon as it left my lips. I'd lived within a five-mile radius of my mother all my life, with the exception of college. Obviously, I'd missed any opportunity to break free. Maybe John had the right idea. Maybe it was my time to go. Mom sighed. He was moving back to his childhood home while I wanted to run away from mine. The seasons were changing and not just outside my picture window.

"Really, you need more furniture in here. I don't see you going anywhere. It's not your style."

My gut twisted with irritation. She was right, it wasn't my style to pick up and go, but I yearned for the inclination. "Yeah, you're right. I hate that," I whispered.

"I'm sure you do, Marjorie Jean, I'm sure you do." Mom giggled and fiddled with her hair.

"What are you middle naming me for?"

"Because I can, my darling."

The front door slammed. I rolled my eyes at my mom then peered over my shoulder. Tension seized my neck muscles as Chloe bounced in wearing a purple motorcycle helmet.

"Hey, people, I'm here," she announced, throwing her hands in to the air.

"Nice helmet."

Her head bobbed as she grabbed the sides of the helmet and forced it off her head.

Bones barked.

"How heavy is that thing?" I asked.

Chloe brought me her helmet.

"Here," she said, pushing it toward me. "It's heavy. I'm surprised my head can hold it up. Crazy." Chloe shook out her helmet hair. "You should try it some time. It's fun! Dad wouldn't let you crash."

I handed the helmet back to her. "I like the skull-and-crossbones sticker on the back. Classy." Mom leaned over, her shoulder touching mine.

"Yeah, that's nice," she said.

Chloe wrapped her arms around Mom's neck. She squeezed. "Hi, Glad," she whispered. "I can't wait to get this girl-fest started. What are we going to do first?" Chloe asked.

"Yes, Glad, what are we going to do first?" I asked.

"Watch your tongue, young lady. I can still scold you." Mom focused on Chloe. "And we will be doing homework first."

Chloe wrinkled her nose. I smiled at the possibility of a clash of the titans. "Yuck, can't you show me how to knit some more? Maggie can learn, too."

I lifted my eyebrow. "I'll watch. Knitting makes my eye twitch. Too much thinking, knitting, and pearling for me."

"Party-pooper," Chloe grunted.

"What's for dinner?" I asked Mom, thinking she would be cooking for Chloe. She crossed her arms as she hemmed and hawed. "Not sure. What are *you* making?"

"Yeah, what are you making, Maggie? Let's have dinner together." Chloe tucked her hair behind her ears.

"Oh brother." I huffed as Chloe stood with clasped hands begging. I got up, stretched my arms to the ceiling as if the day hadn't been long enough. I checked the clock on the mantle then ran my fingers across the silver frame that held the photo of Judy and me raising our fist in victory. John was leaving in little over an hour. Bones faced me and barked. His front legs came off the ground with excitement. When the doorbell rang, Mom answered it, and I meandered into the kitchen. Chloe's voice filled the air as I rummaged through the refrigerator wondering about dinner.

"I'm sure Maggie wouldn't mind," Mom said.

John's deep voice followed. I slept with him, told him I loved him, and then he reassured me he was leaving. Hurt seethed within me. Getting tangled between the sheets didn't change the facts.

Chloe bounded into the kitchen. Bones nipped at her heels as she skidded to a stop in front of me. "What?" I snapped.

She wrinkled her nose at me. "That didn't sound very nice," she started. "I was just gonna ask if Dad could eat with us seeing he is leaving in a little while."

I swallowed my pride. Somebody had to be the adult here and I thought it should be me. It wasn't Chloe's fault her dad was being a jerk. "Sure," I said, seeing the flash of excitement in her green eyes.

"Yay!" It can be a going away party. "Dad, you can stay," she hollered with her hands cupped around her mouth.

Chloe stuck her fingers in her mouth and blew. A loud whistle pierced my ears. I grimaced as Bones skidded across the kitchen floor. He still respected Chloe more than me.

"Fine, take her side," I chided. Taking Bones to dog school last year seemed to help Chloe more than me, although I was getting better about making him obey. I wondered if I'd ever bloom.

"Dad taught me how to do that. Pretty cool, huh?" Chloe said.

"Way cool, but save it for outside." Secretly I wished I knew how to do that. It would come in handy during outdoor recess.

"I can do it louder," Chloe boasted.

"How about we grill hamburgers? It's quick."

"Hamburgers?" Chloe questioned as if I had offered her seaweed and tofu.

"I have cheese." Her dubious expression irritated me. "It's either that or cereal," I said, showing her the American cheese. "What do you say?"

"You really shouldn't ask her," John interrupted with a smile. "Beggars can't be choosers," he added, ruffling Chloe's hair.

His thin smile tugged at my heart.

Mom peeked into the kitchen. "Come on, Chloe. Let's run up to the market and get a cake. Make your dad's last night here special."

I shot her a look. Chloe clapped. She hugged her dad and scooted out of the kitchen as I busied myself at the counter. I raised my hand as John started to speak. "Just a second. Let me make sure we have propane for the grill."

"I'll get it," he said.

"Thanks." I watched him walk out to the patio. His shoulders seemed hunched, not straight and strong like usual. He was at a crossroads, too, but damn, it was at my expense. I continued working on dinner and John sat at the counter across from me fiddling with the saltshaker.

"You didn't have to have us over."

Deflated, I thought about the grains of salt hitting my wounded heart. It burned. "Just because we're at odds doesn't mean I have to ignore Chloe. We can be adults," I said, turning the faucet on to rinse the vegetables. I glanced at John. "What do you want me to do? You asked my mother to babysit while you go see your dad." His green eyes flickered. "If she's involved, you get me too. You know that." I turned my back to him and washed the carrots.

"I know," he mumbled.

The faucet clunked as I shut off the water. "I know, you know." My blood ran hot and my patience thin. "Look," I said, smacking the hamburger patties together. "I don't get it." I leaned over the counter and held his stare. "It took me long enough to trust you. Not to mention, I said that I loved you and where did that get me. Nowhere. You could have said something about leaving a little sooner."

"I'm sorry." His voice broke as the front door slammed shut.

Chloe trotted in. "Mission accomplished." She held up the cake she and Mom picked out together.

Not quite. I nudged the platter of uncooked burgers toward John. "Could you put these on? I'll get the plates. We'll have salad while the burgers cook. Should be quick," I said, avoiding John's gaze.

Mom filled Chloe's bowl with tossed salad. Chloe licked her lips and rubbed her tummy. "Yum. I love salad. Does Winston like salad?"

"You really shouldn't call him that. He's your grandfather." John handed Chloe a napkin to wipe her chin.

She popped a cherry tomato into her mouth. "But I like his name. What's his whole name again? You say it better than me."

John swallowed his bite. "Winston Ludlow McIntyre."

Chloe smiled. "I like it!"

"That's a fancy name," my mom said with a wink.

I listened to them talk about the ranch, horses, and cattle.

After dinner, John kissed Chloe. "You mind your manners while I'm gone, young lady. Glad has my number and she can call at any time." John held her chin in the palm of his hand.

Chloe grinned her toothy grin as she clung to her father's neck. "I'll be good. Glad is my friend. She's not like the others."

I couldn't help but grin, too as John stared through me. "She's right about that." I squeezed my mom's shoulder then kissed her cheek.

John stroked Chloe's messy hair. "You finish your cake while I talk to Maggie for a minute. In private."

I scooted my chair back and walked with John to the far side of the yard. Chloe cackled at Mom's silly jokes while I tried to focus on John's words. I shoved my hands in my pockets. He put his finger under my chin and I gazed up into his eyes.

"I'm sorry, Maggie. I never meant to hurt you. There's a lot to figure out here. I really do appreciate your help with Chloe. She needs you."

"What about you?" I asked barely able to speak. He caressed my cheek just like he had done to Chloe moments ago. My insides crumbled.

"It's time to go." He checked his watch, shifted his weight, then put his hands in his pockets. "You're the best thing that's happened to me in a long time. We can talk when I get back," John said, reaching for the gate.

He kissed my forehead then waved goodbye to Chloe and Glad.

Chapter 6

Chloe and Mom swung on the porch swing as I drove up the driveway. They belonged together. It amazed me how some people just fit. I parked my Equinox and got out. Bones ran up to me and nudged my leg. His tail whipped back and forth against my shins.

"Hey, boy," I said, reaching down to pat his head. Papers from my book bag flitted to the ground. As I knelt down to retrieve them, Bones snatched one from my hand. With his head between his front paws on the ground and his hindquarters in the air, he beckoned for me to chase him.

"You can keep Justin Knight's paper. He won't miss it," I said, walking away. Bones trotted alongside me up the stairs to the front porch with the paper between his teeth. Chloe stopped reading to Mom as soon as she saw Bones.

"Drop it," she commanded.

Bones dropped the paper at her feet then jumped up in her lap making the swing lurch. Mom dropped her knitting needles.

"Geez, Louise," she said.

I dropped my school bag, picked up her needles then handed them back to her. I inspected Justin's paper. It was sopped with dog drool and now had holes in it just below his name, thanks to Bones.

"That's funny," Chloe said. "You can tell your student that *your* dog ate his homework." Chloe used air quotes when she said the word, "your." She read the name aloud on the paper. "I know a boy named Justin and he's not very nice. He thinks he's funny, but really I wish somebody would clean his clock."

Her Justin and my Justin had a lot in common. Mom peered over the rim of her peony pink reading glasses. "Clean his clock?"

"Yeah, you know, give him a taste of his own medicine, beat him up a little so he'd stop picking on others. Clean his clock, that's what Dad calls it." Chloe scratched Bones' head as his eyes drifted closed.

"Speaking of your dad, has he called?" I inquired nonchalantly.

Mom continued knitting. "He called earlier. He arrived safely. His dad sounds nice."

"I don't want to move there. I want to stay here," Chloe said. "It's not fair, I'm the one that has to sacrifice because grown-ups don't know what they want. First, my mom with this modeling gig and now dad wants to move back to Montana. I know I haven't seen my grandfather in a long time, but now we have to move there? They didn't even bother to ask me what I wanted to do."

Mom's gaze met mine.

"I'm sure it will all work out," Mom said, yanking fuzzy purple yarn from the knotted skein.

"Right," Chloe said, rolling her eyes. "For who?"

Bones settled in her lap and snored.

"That's just what grown-ups say so us kids will think something good will happen."

"Can't argue with that," I said, picking up my things before heading inside. My phone chimed with a text. I inspected the screen, John's name flashed across the digital display. I kicked off my shoes and plopped down on the stairs. Blue sky and mountains filled my screen as I opened the multi-media message. The photo reminiscent of a classic *National Geographic*. I read the message. *Just checking in. This is what I'm talking about.* I closed the photo and marched upstairs to change my clothes. My phone chimed again. This time, Brook's name flashed across the screen. I sat at the end of my bed slumped over like a losing prizefighter. "Nothing good can come from this." I sighed then opened the text. *Just checking in. Chloe called today. Where's John?*

I typed my response. *Chloe's fine. Call John for the details.* "Oh for God's sakes." Lying back trying to fan away the hot flash, my phone chimed again. I checked the screen then read John's next text. *Do you know if Chloe called Brook?* I set the phone down on the bed. Irritated about being the monkey in the middle, I closed my eyes. "Oh for God's sakes, just talk to each other," I said to myself before stretching out and grabbing Luanne Rice's latest novel from my nightstand.

I thumbed through the pages to find where I'd left off. Immersed in the words the day's drudgery seemed almost tolerable. With additional cuts and demands at school, my energy was being zapped. Like today, I felt my fingers slipping from the lifeline. John knew what he wanted and I wavered in the land of indecision. The unknown sparked worry. I wanted a clear picture. Once upon a time, that picture was crystal clear, but like Beckett it had faded into the background.

"Five minutes' peace is all I want." I sighed as the phone rang. Brook's name flashed across the screen. That little voice warned me against answering it. I continued to read, hesitating to answer the call. "Hello," I said as the cover of my book flipped closed when I put it down.

"Hi, Maggie?"

"Hi, Brook. It's been a long time. How are you?" I rolled my eyes as her sigh prickled at my nerves.

"Let's get over the pleasantries. I'm fine. How about you?" she said.

"I'm great." I sat up. My hair fell into my face as I leaned forward to inspect my toenails.

"So, what's this about John going to Montana?"

"Um, I think you should really talk to him."

"I tried calling. He didn't pick up. Is your mother really staying with Chloe while he's gone?"

"Yeah, everything is fine. They're downstairs reading at the moment. I really think you should talk to John about this." I squeezed my eyes shut. "So Chloe called you?"

"Yes. I have to go. Please keep an eye on her while he's gone."

I rubbed my right temple as it began to throb. "Sure." I inhaled and held my breath thinking if I held it long enough I would pass out from the lack of oxygen instead of this conversation with John's ex-wife. "Quick question."

"Yeah."

"You sure you want me watching your daughter?"

"Chloe likes you. Thought maybe you could head her off at the pass if she decides to act up. She seems to listen to you."

My lip curled upward at her annoyed tone. Deep down Brook trusted me, even if I got under her skin. The clock read six. That meant it was three o'clock in Hollywood. "Brook."

"Yes, Maggie?"

"Why did you really call me? I haven't seen you since you left last summer. You never called to say you received your photos. And now you're calling me to find out about Chloe?" I heard her sigh, again. I pictured Brook pushing her newest pair of Channel glasses up onto her forehead in disgust.

"No reason. Tell Chloe to be good. Talk to you later." Brook's faint words trailed off.

Brook disconnected herself before I could say goodbye. "Whatever?" I said to myself. The thought of making dinner pained me. The thought of eating dinner exhausted me. I scorned my rumpled bed and forced myself to go downstairs after slipping on my sleeping pants and a T-shirt.

Mom peered at me as I lollygagged about the kitchen. I opened the refrigerator, inspected the contents, then shut the door. The cake from last night's dinner sat on the counter. Opening the box, I sized up the contents, broke off the corner, and shoved it into my mouth leaving a trail of crumbs.

"You're a sad state of affairs," Mom said.

"Yup," I murmured, trying not to lose any cake in the conversation.

"Rough day?" she asked.

I swallowed. "Rough everything," I answered.

"Chloe had a rough day, too."

"How rough could it be being in third grade at this time of year?" I asked, shoving another bite of cake into my mouth. I grabbed a napkin and wiped the frosting from my lips.

"She got into a fight. I picked her up early."

"What!" A few crumbs flew in Mom's direction. I swallowed then wiped them off the counter. "That doesn't sound right." I pictured Chloe scrapping with another child.

"Does John know?" I asked, reaching for another bite of cake.

Mom grabbed my hand before my fingers touched the frosting. "I'll make you two sorry girls diner dinner. Stop eating that. And yes, John knows. Go turn on the grill."

The cool tile floor soothed my tired achy feet as I walked across the kitchen toward the patio doors. It wasn't like Chloe to get physical. Her scrappy demeanor and quick wit seemed like the perfect combination to detour any jerky kid. Running my fingers through my hair, I rubbed my neck, and waited for the grill to ignite.

Bones scurried across the patio and out to the Dogwood tree. My eyes followed his path. So did my feet when I saw a pair of high tops peeking out from underneath the blooming branches. I knelt down to wiggle Chloe's toe. "Hey, Glad is going to make us diner dinner."

Chloe didn't stir.

"Hey, are you in there?" A hot flash warmed my cheeks and singed my nerves. I wiggled Chloe's toe again. "We're having diner dinner. You won't want to miss that."

Nothing.

"Fine, have it your way," I mumbled. Chloe wasn't the only one feeling sucker-punched. It was a tough time at school with the angst of unknown projections for the following year and the students' excitement for summer vacation.

"What's diner dinner?" Chloe said.

Bones gave a little woof then licked Chloe's shins. She wiggled her legs. I thought I heard her giggle.

"Stop that," she whined. "What's diner dinner?"

"Hotdogs, homemade fries, and milkshakes." It'd been a long time since we'd made a diner dinner. Mom made them for me a lot during my teenage angst years. I'd made my share of them for Bradley when he needed comfort. Glancing over to the house, the whirr of the blender purred through the open window. "You want a strawberry or a chocolate milkshake?"

Chloe didn't answer.

"You know, you aren't the only one that had a crappy day."

"You shouldn't swear," Chloe jabbered.

I rolled my eyes. "If you're gonna stay under that tree, I'll have your milkshake, too." My knees creaked as I stood up. The shaggy grass tickled my toes. I felt a thin grin creep across my lips as a ladybug waddled across the top of my bare foot. I touched my collarbone remembering my bought with breast cancer and the tattoos radiation left behind. The insect's tiny wings fluttered as it flew away. I envied its freedom to come and go as it wished. It flitted past my ear sending a shiver down my spine. I was pretty sure it was delivering a message. Mom yelled from the patio. "I need to help Glad," I told Chloe.

The lower branches rustled. Bones sat and waited at Chloe's feet. When she emerged, her face was smeared with dirt and tears.

"I want chocolate."

"By the looks of you, I think you're going to need whipped cream and extra fries."

Chapter 7

Chloe joined Mom and me on the patio after she cleaned herself up. I scooted out her chair then helped her get situated. Her eyes grew big as she scanned the table of junk food. Bones rested his head on my feet under the table anxiously awaiting his share of greasy morsels. His bristly whiskers tickled my skin and I was grateful for his company as well as Mom's and Chloe's. "Thanks for making dinner, Mom." I sucked the whipped cream from the top of my milkshake.

"It's the least I can do. You and Chloe are one sorry sight. Tomorrow is a new day. You can start over after a good night's sleep."

"It's still going to be the same old shit on a different day," I said, holding her gaze.

"I told you, you shouldn't swear," Chloe gurgled around a mouthful of milkshake. "Dad says it's not ladylike."

"Well neither is fighting," I said, connecting with Chloe's stare. I wasn't sure why I picked on her now.

"Hey, she deserved it," Chloe said. Her narrowed green eyes scorned me.

"Knock it off, you two." Mom handed Chloe the ketchup bottle. "Geez. What a bunch of sourpusses."

Chloe's scrunched her nose up. "Sourpuss?" Her lips curled upward. "That's a silly word," she said, squirting ketchup on her plate.

An air bubble caught in the bottle and spattered ketchup across her plate.

"Did you hear that?" she asked.

Mom and I stared at her.

"It farted." She shook the bottle. "That's not ladylike either."

"Nice," I said, biting off the end of my hotdog.

Chloe giggled. "Yeah, you're right, Maggie, this has been a crappy day!" she said, nodding in my direction.

Mom smiled. The grilled hot dog danced on my tongue with the tangy ketchup sending happy pheromones to my brain.

"I won't tell your dad you swore," I said.

Chloe winked at me. Things seemed to be better already. "I won't rat you out either." Chloe's cheeks bulged as she chewed too much food.

Mom smiled. "That's more like it. Now hand me that *farting* ketchup bottle."

Chloe giggled and settled in at the table. "That girl really made me mad today," she said. "That Hilary Barnyard thinks she is all that and a bag of chips, too."

Mom's eyes lit up. "Her last name is *Barnyard*?"

Chloe rolled her eyes. "Actually, no. It's Barnhardt, but I call her *Barnyard*, because she stinks."

I handed Chloe a napkin to wipe the mustard from her cheek. "What exactly did she do?"

Chloe swiped the napkin across her face then smacked her lips.

Mom sipped her strawberry milkshake, her eyes focused on Chloe. Obviously, knowing more than she let on.

"Well, serve it up. What was the fight over?" I asked.

Chloe shifted her weight in his chair. She dug into the pocket of her blue jeans.

"Those are some skinny jeans," I continued, curious if her hand would get stuck, wondering if we'd have to call 911, wondering what Randolph Mantooth looked like nowadays.

"Skinny jeans. Mom wears them." Chloe wiggled to retrieve whatever was jammed in her pocket.

"I bet she does," I said.

Chloe produced a folded piece of paper with tattered edges, her face intent on the importance. Her adult teeth almost fully grown in as she smiled at the worn advertisement. She seemed older, but just as scrappy with her wispy dishwater blond bangs hanging in her eyes. She handed me the advertisement ripped from a glossy magazine. When I saw the image of Brook, I began to understand.

Mom peered over as I showed her what Chloe harbored. Her eyes flickered as her gaze met mine. I looked back over to Chloe. "Your mom is beautiful," I said, smoothing out the photo. Brook's ultra-blond hair was like a halo of light framing her face. It was lighter than last summer. She was dressed in Ralph Lauren head-to-toe. Her lanky body and smoldering blue eyes captivated my attention. "What did that girl say that made you angry enough to hit her?"

Chloe chewed furiously then swallowed. "She said she wasn't my mother." She pointed to the photo. "I said she was and then *Barnyard* said there was no way I could have a mom like that on the count of what I looked like."

Chloe's eyes flashed with hurt so I decided against giving the motherly speech about walking away. "You're beautiful in your own way, Chloe. Don't let some girl take that away from you. You know the truth. You know where you come from," I said, letting my eyes flit toward my mom then back to Chloe.

Chloe nibbled at the end of a fry. "Well, that's all fine, but she had no business telling me that wasn't my mother. And cause my mom's not around. No one has really seen her. Harry and Walter know because they saw her at the beach last summer."

My heart ached for her. "Your true friends know you're not making it up," I said, wiping the sweat from my old-fashioned milkshake glass, my finger fitting perfectly in the fluted edge.

Chloe grunted, "Of course they do. They're my friends."

"Exactly, they are your friends. This girl doesn't sound like a friend. She probably doesn't have many friends."

Chloe rolled her eyes. "She has plenty. The kids follow her around like a puppy dog. And if you ask me-" She paused taking a deep breath. "She is a dog, a *barnyard* dog."

I ignored her snippy comment. "Did you leave a mark when you hit her?" I asked, reaching for another hotdog. "These are so good. I haven't had a hotdog in ages." I loaded it up with ketchup and mustard this time. My thoughts drifted back to Tiger Stadium, Ernie Harwell, and time with my dad.

Chloe swallowed. "I punched her hard. She has a black eye." Remorse rimmed her eyes as she glanced over to Mom. "I'm sorry, but she was just being so mean."

Mom patted her hand. "It's all said and done now. Your Dad seemed to be pretty calm when I spoke to him last."

Chloe let out a sigh and slumped forward.

"Chloe will be home for a day. John said he'd handle it when he got back."

Part of me admired Chloe's nerve. I wouldn't have the guts to punch someone. "So, you'll be home tomorrow. Did you bring homework to do?"

"Plenty." Chloe lower lip jutted out as she pouted.

"Sorry, but it's probably for the best." I raised my eyebrow as Mom held my gaze.

"Whatever." Chloe's chin quivered, and she wiped away a tear at the corner of her eye.

Mom tried to hold her hand, but she pulled away. "It won't be so bad."

Chloe wasn't buying what Mom was selling. Chloe sucked in a breath of air. "You don't understand. Career day is coming. Almost everyone has someone coming to represent them."

"What do you mean?" Mom asked.

Chloe sipped at her milkshake. "It's in the gym. It's a big deal around here because everyone has a job, apparently.

You have to make a poster of your person's career. And your guy sits by your poster and answers questions as us kids walk around interviewing them. After we ask our questions, we have to write a paper on what we want to be when we grow up. It's a big deal."

"Your dad's a doctor. That's nothing to snivel at," Mom said. "You know," she continued, "it's nothing to be ashamed of. That's a very important profession."

"Whatever," Chloe said. "Lots of kids have doctor and lawyer parents around here. Of course, Dad could come, but when we started talking about our parents and their jobs, I told the kids what my mom does. I've been carrying this picture around for a while just waiting for the chance to tell them." She sighed. "Whatever." She folded up the advertisement and jammed it back in her pocket. "Stupid Hilary *Barnyard.*"

"When's the career fair?" I asked.

Chloe shoved the last bite of hotdog in her mouth, "May, sometime."

"It's May now, a little more than halfway over," I reminded her. "Does your dad know about it?"

"Yeah," she mumbled. "I was just really hoping my mom would come." She looked over to Glad.

"I know," Mom said.

"I think we did an awesome job cleaning our plates. I think I feel better already," I said, standing up.

Chloe dug the photo out of her pocket again. She unfolded it. My heart ached for her. Kindred spirits with broken hearts made for a stronger bond between us.

An impossible notion crossed my mind. I warned myself about getting involved, but it was worth a shot. "You done with that?" I asked Chloe as she licked the last bits of salt from her plate.

"I vote for more diner dinners," she said, batting her

eyelashes my mom.

Mom smiled then handed me her plate.

I piled up as many dishes as I could carry. The pile tipped, but I caught it before plates crashed down.

"Whoa, there." Chloe's squeal roused Bones from beneath the table.

I smiled. "What's life without a little excitement? Good thing I'm not a waitress," I joked. "How long you guys staying?"

"Not too much longer." Mom paused and winked at Chloe, "She's got work to do then bed."

Chloe scowled. "She's tough, no wonder you're like you are," she said, reaching down to pet Bones. Chloe patted her knee. Bones jumped up in her lap and settled in. His pink tongue licked ketchup from the side of the table.

Chloe and Mom chatted while I cleaned up the kitchen. Weighing the consequences, I opened the cake box and broke off another hunk then gobbled it down.

"You gonna share that with me?" Chloe asked, hopping up on a stool at the counter.

"Sure," I said, scooting the box closer to her.

She took the fork from me. "Aren't you gonna give me a plate?" she asked.

"Nope. You can eat out of box."

"Really?"

"Really," I said, getting another fork for myself. I sat beside her, moved the box so it sat between us, and took another bite.

Chloe smiled, eyed the cake, and took a bite, too.

Mom came in. Bones' nails clicked against the tile floor. His leash hung from his mouth. I looked at Chloe and Chloe looked at me. Mom snapped the leash on his collar.

"I'll take him," she said, groaning. "You two finish off that cake."

Chloe and I went back to polishing off the last bit of chocolate cake. Mom tied two poop bags on Bones' leash then she hooked it on his collar. Bones' nose twitched at the treats in her pocket then he licked her shin.

"Did you call your mom, Chloe, and ask her about the career fair?"

"I left her some messages. She hasn't called back. You know her, she barely ever calls." Chloe sounded exasperated.

Mom patted Bone's head then they both strolled out the door. I couldn't imagine my world without her. Chloe's expression made me sad.

I put my fork down to stroke her head. "Sorry." Her hair was soft, soothing, and refined. She was just a girl trying to find her way, just like me. "Your hair is getting long. It's past your shoulders."

Chloe's eyes gleamed with purpose. "I want it to be like my mom's."

Chloe mumbled so I leaned closer. "What did you say?"

Chloe's eyes were wet with tears. She pursed her lips then sucked in a deep breath. "I said, maybe if I'm more like my mom, she'll pay more attention to me." She put her fork down. "I think I'm full."

Wetness trickled down Chloe's cheek. I wiped it away and put my finger under her chin so I could look her in the eyes. "I'm sure she loves you very much," I said, despite my feelings for Brook. "Not all mommas stay home and bake cookies, but they have love in their hearts even if it doesn't seem like it." An image of Bradley popped into my head. "When Bradley was about your age, he got super mad at me. Said I needed to stay home like his other friends' mommas', said I didn't care, but you see, I did care very much." I took a deep breath to push through my speech without crying. "I wanted Bradley to see that you can follow your dreams. I wanted him to know that hard work was necessary to support a family."

Chloe's eyes softened. "You miss him, don't you?"

I nodded. "Very much." I paused. "But children need to grow up and do their own thing."

"Maybe Mom does miss me." Chloe's eyes lightened.

Tucking her hair behind her ears, I couldn't imagine Chloe being anything different than what she was, a sassy youngster with spunk, more like her dad than her mother in many ways. "I'm sure she does." I hoped like hell she did because if she didn't, that just wouldn't be right. "I've had enough cake too," I said, taking our forks to the sink.

"Yeah, probably shouldn't eat stuff like cake if I want to be more like my mom," she said, patting her belly.

"I think you're perfect just the way you are." I threw the box of cake crumbs into the trash.

"Thanks, Maggie. I can always count on you," Chloe said.

John was right. There was no way getting around loving his daughter.

Chapter 8

Hope streamed through the library windows in the midday sun. Longer days helped me fight through year-end stress. Coloring photographs diluted the constant reminders of what needed to be accomplished. My painted cows were spread out before me with an entire set of holiday scenes. My *New Year's* cow sported a diaper in the moonlight while the other heifers mooed to the heavens. Submitting them to a publisher would require research and a new level of courage. More rejection would come I reminded myself. Breaking free of old habits seemed formidable. Fear was crippling, but I couldn't escape it. The notion of not following through with my cow whimsy frightened me more.

Thoughts of Chloe drifted by. A thin grin passed over my lips as I imagined the girl with the black eye. I checked my phone knowing it was a gamble. Hesitantly, I picked it up, leaned back in my chair, and ran my finger down the scroll. Brook's name popped out. It seemed darker and bolder than the rest. I held the phone to my chest and said a little prayer as I dialed her number. The anticipation of actually speaking to her made my hands sweaty.

"Hello?" Brook answered. "Is everything okay with Chloe?"

I took a deep breath to calm my jitters. *Brook is just a person like you.* Leaning forward with my elbows on my desk, I mustered up my teacher assertiveness and spoke. "Yeah. Everything is okay." I knew it wasn't, but the words slipped out. "I just wanted to touch base since you texted after our talk earlier. Did you get a hold of John?" I asked, killing two birds with one stone. Clever. My confidence blossomed.

"Yes. He reminded me that Glad was watching Chloe and that he'd only be gone a few days."

"Good. I'm glad you two talked. I'm just calling with a question. Has anyone mentioned the career fair coming up at Chloe's school?"

"Yeah, Chloe left me a few messages. I figured John would cover that."

Like he covers everything else. I rubbed my temple sending her subliminal messages to cooperate. "Well, it came up at dinner tonight and I was wondering if you could find time in your schedule to fly back to Michigan to be Chloe's special guest." I waited, leaned back, and closed my eyes as silence grew between us.

"Did Chloe ask you to call?" Brook asked.

"No," I answered truthfully. "She doesn't know I'm calling you." I paused knowing intervention might prevent Chloe's heart from shattering completely. "I just thought—"

"You thought what?"

Her bristly tone surprised me. "Maybe I shouldn't have called," I said. "I'm sorry. I didn't mean to bother—"

"When is it?" Brook's vibrant irritation resonated in her clear, sharp tone.

"I have the flyer right here in front of me. It's the Friday before Memorial Day, May twenty-third," I answered.

"I don't think I can. I have a shoot in Chicago around that time. Big campaign."

"I understand. I know it's short notice. I won't tell Chloe that we spoke."

"Okay," Brook muttered.

"Well, I hope everything goes well. Talk to you—"

Brook interrupted again, I thought she had a change of heart. Frowning, I silently scorned her as I listened to her excuses. A nasty lecture flashed through my brain. "Are you going to call Chloe and talk to her about this?" My voice had an unusual edge.

"I will. And Maggie . . .?"

"Yes, Brook?"

"Chloe looks up to you. Maybe you could be her special guest."

My blood boiled. Chloe's third-grade class didn't want to interview a teacher. They had that opportunity day-in and day-out. That was the last straw, Brook totally missed the fact that her daughter wanted her, not to mention, needed her. "Like you said, John can be her special person." I emphasized the words *special person.* "But, I think her classmates would be more interested in you." I picked at my thumbnail. My eyes scanned the cow photographs. The day's last light brought promises of fairy dust and daydreams. "I'm sure that she'll figure it out."

"I'm sure she will. And Maggie . . .?" Brook said.

"Yes?"

"I love the photographs of Chloe that you sent me last summer. Thanks."

I rolled my eyes. That was just like Brook. Just when I thought I couldn't like her, she threw a shred of decency into the game making me feel guilty. "You're welcome. Please call Chloe."

"Okay. Bye."

"Bye." I ended the call.

I blew a strand of hair from my face. "Oh my God."

Bones exhaled with a grunt as he settled in his dog bed. His furrowed brow and wise eyes were telling me, *I told you so.*

I set the phone on the desk thinking about my life, thinking about Brook's life, and I wondered if the stars really decided a person's destiny.

The computer screen caught my attention. When it opened from sleep by itself, I thought it was my dad sending me a message. It was my opportunity to take a few minutes to converse with him even though he wasn't in the physical world anymore. Searching picture book publishers, I jotted down a list of contacts as I scrolled. Curiosity led to reading articles about getting published. Intrigue spurred me on into the wee hours of the night.

My phone buzzed. The time read midnight, but I didn't care. John's name flashed across my screen. I opened his text. *Brook called. She's thinking about coming to Chloe's career fair. This has your name all over it.*

I tapped out a response. *How mad are you?* I waited for a response. Nothing came. I went back to reading. My gaze flitted between the monitor and my phone screen. I forced myself to shut off the computer, pick up my phone, and switch off the light. Bones' tags jingled behind me.

"Come on, boy, let's go outside one more time."

Bones snorted as we headed for the back door then he ran out.

The glow on the patio caught my eye. As much as I wanted to believe it was a fairy watching over my house, it wasn't. "Chloe, what are you doing over here?"

She flashed the light in my eyes. "Reading." She shined the light on her *Stuart Little* book. "I'm really good at reading now."

"That's swell," I said, sounding like my grandmother, "but does Glad know you're over here?"

"No, she's asleep." Chloe giggled. "This mouse is a crack up. I bet he and Junie B. Jones would have fun together."

I couldn't help but grin. "Yeah, that would be a hoot. Seriously, what are you doing out here?" I sat on the end of the chaise lounge. Bones trotted under the dogwood tree then joined us. His tail whipped my shins before he jumped into Chloe's lap to lick her face. He was always so happy to see her. I understood.

"I saw your light on in the library. You were up, so I decided to stay up since I don't have school tomorrow on account of punching *Barnyard*. She really did deserve it." Chloe turned the page. "I can see right into your library with my binoculars. I like your cow pictures."

My eyebrow arched at the thought of Chloe with a pair of binoculars. "You really shouldn't use binoculars to spy on somebody, let alone look into their homes."

"I know. Dad caught me once and took the binoculars, but I found them and snuck them back into my room. I'm really not spying on you, Maggie."

I drew my sweater shut as the cool breeze kicked up. "Then what are you doing?"

"Truth?" she asked with a wrinkled nose.

I scooted closer to see her better. She held the light below her chin. Although it cast a creepy shadow across her face, I couldn't help but grin at her silly behavior. "Yeah, truth."

"I just check to see if you're home. It makes me feel better when you're around."

I rubbed Chloe's knee. "Want to know something?"

"Yeah, what?" she questioned, switching off the flashlight.

"I'm used to you spying on me." Dad had probably sent her on his behalf.

Chloe giggled. The flashlight fell to the ground as Bones licked her face. "I better get back so Glad doesn't worry."

"That's very thoughtful. I'll walk you home," I said, reaching for Chloe's hand. Bones jumped down and followed us to the gate. "You stay here," I said. He sat. I waited for him to try to escape. "Stay. Down," I commanded. Bones went down with a grunt.

"Hey, you're getting better," Chloe said. "Night, Bones. See you tomorrow."

"Chloe, you really shouldn't leave the house without asking."

"I know," she replied. "Please don't rat me out."

"I won't this time, but I couldn't live with myself if something happened to you because I didn't say something. This is serious. It's fine that you want to come over, but not in the middle of the night. Got it?" Her brow wrinkled as I politely scolded her. I waited for a rebuff, but none came.

"Okay."

I escorted Chloe home and waited for her to go back inside. I didn't leave until I heard the bolt on the door lock. She was going to be a real handful in her teenage years. Shaking my head, I headed home to get Bones from the backyard. My phone buzzed as I locked my own doors. John's name flashed across my screen. I opened his text. *Why do you always think I am mad at you?*

I shut off the kitchen light, checked the front door, then headed up to bed. I responded to John's text after I brushed my teeth. Bones curled up at the end of the bed while I settled in. *Because I'm not so sure I'd like an outsider butting into my personal life, my child's life if it were me,* I texted back.

My phone rang. "Hello," I whispered into it.

"What are you still doing up at this hour?" John asked.

"I'm not so sure you want to know." I thought about Chloe reading in the moonlight, so glad she was reading on her own now.

"I'm thinking I shouldn't ask," John said.

I smiled. "Probably not, but everything is fine."

"I'm not mad at you. And, Maggie, not everyone is like you."

"Thanks, I think." I nibbled at my thumbnail in the darkness.

"Truth is—" He paused. "I'm not so sure Brook would have even consider it if you hadn't called her. We've talked about this before, Brook's not exactly a doting mother."

"Sorry," I said.

"Sorry for what?" John asked.

"Sorry, for Chloe. To be honest, it's not fair," I muttered, feeling Chloe's dilemma.

"Maggie, you of all people should know, life's not fair."

I chuckled. "You're right about that. Hey," I said, staring at Bradley's old Batman clock beside my bed. If I couldn't have him home, I'd have his favorite things scattered around. "What are you doing up?"

"Obviously, Brook has no sense of time. Shocker. And Maggie—"

"Yeah," I replied, closing my eyes, thinking about how John's skin felt against mine. His midnight voice seducing the memories. I swallowed away the knot at the back of my throat.

"I'm really not mad. I may not understand at times, but we all have to move forward."

"That we do, my friend, that we do," I whispered.

"Maggie."

"Yeah, John," I said, his name hot on my lips, his image alive in my head, his breath in my ear.

"I hope you know, we're more than friends," John said.

I closed my eyes tight, painfully aware that I was lying alone.

"Maggie, are you still there?"

"Yeah, John, I'm still here." The words caught in my throat.

"Sleep tight," he said. "And let me remind you, you're not an outsider."

"Right back at you," I said, "See you soon."

"Yes, you will. I'll be dreaming of you."

"Night," I said as I ended the call. My head and my heart were at odds.

Bones grunted and snuggled in against me.

I patted his head. "Night, friend."

Chapter 9

The phone rang at seven o'clock. I spit out a mouthful of toothpaste, wondering what trouble Chloe had found at such an early hour. I checked the number. School. I answered it without saying hello.

The automated operator greeted me. "Due to a water main break, school has been cancelled for staff and students today."

Excitement prickled within me. This never happened. I turned off the bathroom light, undressed, put my pajamas back on, then crawled back beneath the covers. Light streamed in through the slats of the shades as I read my Jennifer Weiner novel.

Bones barked relentlessly. I tried to ignore him, but he jumped up on the bed then nudged the book out of my hands. He dug his front paws into my stomach as he stood over me. "That's just like you. I was almost to the end." I grunted at him. He barked then licked my nose and I reluctantly crawled out of bed. "Come on," I said as I made my way downstairs.

Chloe stood at the front door ringing the doorbell. She was the only one I knew with a trigger finger that could make the chime continue without pause.

"Coming," I yelled, "stop ringing the bell." The door stuck as I tried to yank it open. "What's going on?"

Bones' tail waggled. He looked from Chloe to me as if he was urging us to open the door.

"Is everything okay?" Chloe asked.

"Uh, yeah. Why?" I asked, checking to see if my mother was on her heels.

"Cause you're home and you're never home during the day. You never miss work," she said.

Peeking out at my Equinox, I cursed myself for parking in the driveway last night. "My school was cancelled. Water main break."

"Sweet. We can hang out now that I'm kicked out of school." Chloe bounced as she spoke, her perky behavior scared me.

"Um, I think you have work to do."

"I'm finished. I did most of it last night after dinner. I finished my math this morning," she replied as I wondered where she got her energy. "Why are you still in your pajamas?"

"I was reading in bed. Didn't feel like wearing my teacher clothes all day."

"Yeah, I can see why. You gonna open the door for me?"

I rolled my eyes at her. "Don't even say it," I said, unlatching the screen door.

"Okay, I won't, but it's not nice to roll your eyes. I think we've been over this," she lectured.

"Bad habits die hard," I said.

She scrunched up her face at me.

Mom trotted across the yard waving a piece of paper. "Chloe," Mom sang, "you have chores."

Mom held the rail as she climbed the stairs to the porch. She appeared older today, but then again weren't we all? Silver threads beamed in the sunlight that washed over her, fine wrinkles seemed more defined. My mother was growing older, and I didn't like it.

Chloe's shoulders drooped. "Come on," she said with a whiny intonation. "I already did my work."

Stepping out onto the porch, Chloe gave me the stink eye.

"What? I didn't do anything to you, you did it to yourself," I reminded her.

"Thanks for being on my side," Chloe mumbled.

My left eyebrow shot up. "I'm more on your side than you think," I said, Brook's words still fresh in my mind. John's comment about being more than friends, even fresher. I ruffled her hair. "What's on my mom's list?"

Mom caught her breath. "Boy, I'm not as spry as I used to be."

Chloe wrinkled her nose when she didn't understand or pretend not to understand. "Spry? You sure do use a lot of weird words."

I tucked a long strand of Chloe's hair behind her ear remembering how it felt to be a child. "You know, young, in shape," I explained.

"Whatever?" Chloe replied. "Yeah, *Glad*, what's on the list?"

Mom peered over the rim of her yellow reading glasses speckled with orange flecks. "Don't get sassy with me, young lady."

Chloe and I gazed at each other in surprise.

"Sorry," Chloe said.

A thin smile crossed my lips as I watched Mom and Chloe spar. It was nice being a wallflower, but after yesterday's interference, I was putting myself in danger of becoming much more than that.

Mom handed Chloe the list.

I peered over Chloe's shoulder as she read the chores aloud, "Laundry, empty the dishwasher, clean under your bed, and pick up dog poop."

Good one, I thought, hiding my grin.

Chloe glared at Mom. "*Pick up dog poop*. Yuck. I'm not the one with a dog."

"But you want one and you're with Bones much of the time. Get going, young lady." Mom put her hand on her hip as she leaned against the rail. "Maggie has a shovel and a bucket in the garage. You'll see it."

"You mean I'll smell it." Chloe stomped down the front stairs.

"Probably," Mom said as she sat on the porch swing.

I sat next to her, caressed her hair, and inspected the dark circles beneath her eyes. "You look exhausted."

She rolled her eyes.

I smiled. "More than you expected?" I knew what Mom was feeling.

"Uh, yeah," Mom answered. "You can wipe that smile right off your face Marjorie Jean. She is much more difficult than you ever were."

I nudged the porch floor with my foot to get the sway of the swing started. "You're welcome," I said smugly.

"Thanks for walking her home last night," Mom said.

"How did you know she was up?" I asked.

"I heard her go downstairs then I went into her room. I used her binoculars and watched her from the window. You know you can see right into your backyard from up there?"

"Apparently, you can see everything from up there."

"I figured she wasn't going far so I watched for a bit then read my book until I heard your voices outside. She was kind of noisy climbing back into bed."

"I told Chloe I wouldn't tell. Told her not to do it again. She's going to be *some* teenager." Mom stared at me.

"Why are you home? You're not sick again, are you? And if you are, you better be honest this time. I don't want any daughter of mine going through cancer or anything else by herself."

Her eyes scorned me. "Um, no, water main break at school. And why are you barking at me? I wasn't the one who got in trouble at school or kept you up all night." Mom narrowed her eyes and scowled at me. "Not this time, anyway," I added, giving her an exaggerated toothy grin.

"I had it easy with you. You were a good girl."

I grunted. "Yeah, that's me, the good girl, always trying to please others by doing the right thing."

Mom patted my knee. "Nothing wrong with that."

"Some days—" I put my finger up in jest. "Most days now that I'm older, I'm not so sure." Maybe Chloe knew something about being a kid I never did. "Where'd the list of chores come from?"

"Me. John said he'd deal with her when he gets home."

I smiled.

"Marjorie Jean, why don't you just admit you're sweet on the man?"

If only Mom knew. "I've got some chores of my own to get to," I said, stretching.

"Fine, avoid the subject," she replied.

"Okay, I will," I said, giving her another exaggerated toothy smile.

"You're not funny." She narrowed her stare.

I patted her head then pressed my lips to her forehead. She smelled like vanilla and love. "You're doing a good job. Don't let Chloe give you any crap," I whispered in her ear. When she chuckled, her soft cheek brushed mine.

"I'd better go check on the juvenile delinquent," Mom said.

"Hey, I'm not a juvenile delinquent," Chloe protested, scrambling out of the bushes.

I peered over the railing. "See, bad habits die hard," I reminded her, waggling my finger in her direction. Her hair stuck to the fine branches that hid her. Glancing back at my mom, I scowled. "Like I said before, you're welcome."

Mom sighed then tucked Chloe's hair behind her ears. "Let's go, kiddo. You know what I meant. I was just trying to be funny."

"Well, it's not funny." Chloe planted her hands on her hips in protest.

"Maybe not to you, now let's get to picking up dog poop."

"Some days it's smellier and thicker than other. Have fun." Chloe didn't think my shred of wisdom was funny so I went inside to answer the phone. "Hello," I said, checking myself out in the foyer mirror.

"Hi, it's Brook."

Bothered by her tone, I headed upstairs for privacy. "Hold on one second," I said, trotting toward my bedroom. After closing the door behind me, I went to the window.

Chloe searched the perimeter of the backyard for dog droppings. Bones followed her with a tennis ball in his mouth. Mom yanked weeds out of the garden. The blinds opened wide as I pulled the string to get a better view of the yard.

"You still there?" I asked reluctantly, not sure what she could possible want.

"I've been thinking about this career fair thing."

"Uh-huh. Did you call Chloe?"

"No. She doesn't have a phone."

"John still has his landline."

"Oh, I forgot," she said.

Yeah, you did.

Chloe put the poop bucket down. Mom gestured for her to join her in the garden. At the rate Mom was going, John wouldn't have much left to do in the way of punishment. Chloe stood with her hands on her hips then plopped down beside Mom. Mom pointed to the different plants. Chloe blew hair away from her face then lifted her chin to the sun. Mom handed her a silver pail then Chloe started plucking weeds.

"Anyway, I was wondering if you could do me a favor." Brook paused. "Well, I need something."

I'm sure you do. I wanted to be outside baking in the sun with Mom and Chloe even if it meant dirt beneath my nails and a sore back from bending over weeding the garden.

"Can you tell Chloe I won't be able to make it to career day after all?"

"What? Are you serious?"

"It'll be better coming from you."

"What?" My heart pounded with rage. "Call her yourself," I urged. "You can't—"

Brook interrupted. "Yeah, I can't, and John's not around."

"He'll be around tomorrow," I said.

"I want you to tell her."

"Listen, Brook. You can't possibly be serious. Be a mom and tell your daughter the truth."

"This is not my decision. I have to work. You know how it is? At least you get the holidays and the summers off."

I pressed my lips together holding back harsh words. She was not going to make this about me no matter her misconception. What did she know about staying after school to check papers, making lesson plans, making phone calls to upset parents, and putting the world back together one child at a time? "Yeah, Brook. I know what it means to have demands. And your daughter is demanding your presence. I'm not going to do your dirty work."

"Sorry," she said, "I didn't mean to make you angry. I just thought you could help me out. I promise I'll call her after you tell her."

"When's the last time you spoke to Chloe?" I asked. "You owe it to her to call. You owe it to yourself."

"It's just like you to say something like that."

Silently, I listened to her jest without hesitation, my nose practically pressed against the windowpane watching Chloe and my mom work side-by-side. I unlocked the window and pushed it open. The spring breeze carried their words up to my bedroom as Brook rambled on about herself. Would she ever realize it wasn't about her? Brook said my name. "What?" I said quietly.

"Do you understand where I'm coming from?" she questioned.

I swallowed away my hopes for Chloe knowing the ache I felt for her wouldn't make it any less. "Yeah."

"Great. So you'll tell her. I knew I could count on you. Chloe really looks up to you."

What just happened here? Brook ended the call. I stared at my phone screen in disbelief. Bones craned his neck, his eyes looked through me from below. His bark filled the air. "Shit," I said to myself. "This is turning into some day off."

Flipping up the covers, I pretended that I actually made the bed. "Who cares?" I said to myself. "You do," I scolded. I couldn't even have a one sided conversation with myself. "Shit, shit, shit."

I fastened my walking sandals and tied my hair up. Chloe met me at the front door. Pissed off, I stormed out with my camera in one hand and my car keys in the other.

"Hey," she called after me.

I hurried to my car.

"Hey," she yelled louder. "What's wrong with you?"

I unlocked the car. With one hand on the door handle, I turned to face the girl following in my tracks. "You don't even want to know."

"Must be bad. Your forehead is one big wrinkle."

"Thanks," I said, getting even more perturbed. Chloe tugged on my arm. Her eyes filled with worried curiosity. Frustration boiled. "You really want to know?" I knew better. I stopped myself.

"You're scaring me," Chloe said.

"Nothing can be scarier than my mom and a list of chores," I said. "Chloe, your mom is irritating." Her emerald eyes grew dark like a spring storm on the edge of summer.

"What did she do to you?" Chloe asked.

I glanced down. Brook's attitude bothered me beyond belief. "Nothing. She didn't do anything." I opened the car door. "Actually, she did do something. And it wasn't very nice. And I'm not going to discuss it with you."

Chloe shoved her hands into the pockets of her jeans. Her eyebrow arched as she scrunched her face up at me. "What?" I huffed.

"Now you know how I feel," she said. "She does it to me all the time."

Chapter 10

While Chloe was back home being ordered around by Glad, I stewed at the beach. Staring out at the water, I snapped a few pictures, boring pictures. It was quiet, too quiet. My thoughts pounded in my head. What could I do to make this better? Or what could I do to disturb Brook just enough to make her feel guilty about abandoning her daughter? Nothing.

I scrolled through the contacts on my phone then dialed Brook's number. I tapped my foot waiting for her to pick up. Just as I lowered the phone to end the call I heard Brook's voice say hello. "Hi, Brook, it's me, Maggie."

"I know. How did it go with Chloe?"

"It didn't. I told you, I wouldn't be breaking *your* bad news to her, but I do want to let you know that she is at home today because she punched another girl in the face because of you, but maybe you already know that." I took a deep breath. A freighter drifted by on the horizon.

"What?"

"Let me repeat myself. She got expelled from school because she punched another child and gave her a black eye. She was trying to convince the girl that you were her mother. She had your picture," I explained. "Chloe carries your picture around. She misses you. Can't you just do this one thing for her?"

"Why do you care so much?"

Because that's who I am. That's what I do every damn day. Because Chloe is part of my family now, too. Because she's John's daughter and I love him regardless of his decision to move to Montana.

"Because I just do," I said, rubbing my forehead. Brook's heavy sigh filled the airway. I stared at the rock where she and Chloe stood last summer, the place Chloe sat and sobbed her eyes out after her mom left without her. "You know what, Brook? Never mind. Go ahead, break her heart." I didn't wait for Brook's comeback and ended the call.

My phone rang almost immediately.

Brook's name flashed across the screen.

I declined the call.

Swaying in the moonlight, the creaking metal links that supported the porch swing hypnotized me. It'd been a long day back at work. I sipped my wine, gazed at the stars, and wondered what Chloe and John were doing. Bones nudged the screen door open with his pug nose. His mischievous expression taunted me.

"Lie down," I commanded.

Bones sauntered to the edge of the steps, his stance that of a dog ready to bolt. He looked me square in the eye. His stocky shoulders hunched in protest.

"Lie down," I said louder.

He stood frozen in time momentarily as if he were weighing his options. When I snapped my fingers at him, he plopped down and hung his head over the top stair.

"Can I come up?" John said.

"Sure," I said. "Bones, stay put."

John stepped over Bones. "You're getting better at that. He's getting better, too."

"Yeah. I'm okay, you're okay, everyone's, oh screw it."

"Tough day?"

"Yup," I replied, trying not to stare. I crossed my legs and finished off my wine.

"May I join you?" he asked.

"Sure, whatever floats your boat, but I'm not very good company," I told him.

John's green eyes twinkled in the evening light. My stomach flip-flopped. A shiver drifted down my spine. I set my wineglass beside me then zipped up my fleece. John stared at me.

"What?" I asked. "Do I even want to know what?"

"I'm not sure what you said to Brook." John paused and held up his hand. "Don't roll your eyes at me, Maggie Abernathy, but Brook wants Chloe to come to Chicago to see her in the shoot."

The corner of my mouth curled up, and the muscles around my heart ached in a good way. It was the same kind of invigoration I felt when dewy mist collected on my cheeks while jogging when the sun came up.

"What's this about Brook inviting Chloe to Chicago? Is this for real or just one of her stunts?" I stopped, marveling at John's expression. "Can I say that?" He didn't seem disgusted.

"You just did. Anyway, that's not the kicker," John added, rubbing his jaw.

"What's the kicker?" I asked.

"You ready for this?" His words were slow and steady.

"Probably not, but serve it up."

"Brook wants you to bring Chloe to see her."

John's jeans hugged his thighs. I lowered my gaze. He leaned closer to me. "Seriously?" I asked. "You're lying. You're a mean man. That's not even funny." I said, trying to read his mind and protect myself from the power of his proximity.

"This has your name written all over it, Maggie Abernathy."

All my attention went to his lips as he spoke.

"What exactly did you say to her?" John fiddled with his keys.

I shrugged, pretending not to remember. "I think our conversation ended with me telling her she was breaking her daughter's heart. Are you mad?"

John chuckled as he rubbed his jaw again. His eyes flickered in the moonlight.

"Nope, but it's a strange feeling when the woman I'm hung up on scolds my ex-wife. You're pretty bold."

"I can't help it, it's what I do for a living." John scooted closer to me then rubbed his foot against mine, igniting the inferno.

I unzipped my fleece and noted his comment about being hung up on me, but that didn't equate to saying, *I love you*. I wanted to know who wrote the rules for men.

"You two are like oil and water, and you usually come out on top. I like that."

I stared into his green eyes pondering his secrets. *He was hung up on me?* The curl of his lip taunted me. "I don't want to do anything to hurt Chloe."

"Why would you say that?" John asked, resting his arm on the back of the swing.

John's fingers brushed my shoulder.

"I just don't," I said. "She doesn't deserve more turmoil."

John faced me. I wanted to rest my head on his chest, but resisted the temptation. "I won't say anything to Chloe until you decide if you want to go."

The thought of an impromptu trip to Chicago excited me, but the thought of hanging out with Brook made my insides knot. "She is nuts. What good could possibly come from this?"

John shrugged. "Really, I don't know. It sounds like a recipe for disaster, but as you know, somehow, I think you'll manage to pull something worthwhile from the experience. Chloe would love your company. Just think about it."

His hand touched my shoulder sending a shiver down

my spine. "What did you say about the woman you're hung up on?" I asked.

"I think you know how I feel about you."

"I'm not really sure I do," I said. "You're still set on moving."

"That doesn't mean I don't care."

"This is too hard," I said. "We probably shouldn't go there." A lump grew in my throat. I didn't want anything to change. I wanted him to live next door with Chloe. I wanted things to remain the same. "I know you care," I said, blinking back emotion. I wanted him to tell me he loved me back. That familiar pang surfaced. I hated myself for blurting out my feelings against my better judgment, but my impulsive nature got the best of me.

"Maggie," John said, "I love you, too."

My chest rose with the hitch in my breath. It was what every girl wanted to hear, but I wasn't sure I was that girl anymore. I was a middle-aged woman trying to figure out the rest of her life. John's hand covered mine. His tenderness flowed through me like a country stream trickling over century old pebbles that were once boulders. I wasn't sure if his words or his touch impacted me more.

"How? When?" I asked.

Laugh lines emerged at the corners of his emerald eyes as a thin smile crossed his lips. He chuckled then shook his head. "Not exactly sure. All I know is that when I was in Montana with my dad, you were all I could think about." John made a clicking sound with his mouth like a cowboy prodding his horse. He stared over his shoulder and pointed behind him, then put his pointer finger up to his lips.

The flash of light in the bushes gave her away.

John grinned wildly. "So you think I should punish Chloe more?"

"Sure," I said. "Maybe ground her for a few weeks,

have her write sentences then have Glad make another list of chores."

"No," Chloe cried out, darting up the stairs to the porch. "Haven't you punished me enough? I picked up dog poop for hours."

"No, you didn't," I said as she plopped down on the top step next to Bones. "Obviously, he is on your side. He heard you coming and didn't flinch a whisker."

Chloe smiled. "Good boy," she said, scratching his head. "How did you know I was down there?"

"I saw your light flicker." John pointed to her metallic flashlight and leaned closer. "I also heard the latch close on the side door when you came out. What did I tell you about sneaking around, young lady?"

Chloe swallowed hard. "Sorry, Maggie."

Relieved for John's bionic hearing, our conversation could have resulted in chaos. I glanced over. John stared at me. His eyes glistened with intent. This was about to get even weirder, but Mom's words popped into my head. Maybe she was right. Maybe it was time to choose a direction, commit to a path, and embrace the journey.

Chapter 11

"Maggie, you said it yourself. I'm not the only one capable of breaking my daughter's heart."

I winced as Brook used my words against me. "No, I can't."

"So what do you say? It will be fun. It won't be career day, but Chloe can see what I really do. You could use a break, too, right?"

I held the phone away from my ear. My little voice sputtered inside my head. *Yeah, from you.* I covered my face with the pillow and screamed. Bones cocked his head and wrinkled his brow when I threw it across the room. I heard Brook say my name.

"What was that?" she asked.

"The television," I sneered at Bones as he licked my shins with his pink tongue. I swatted at him to stop, but he hunkered down to nibble on my toes. "Sorry, I'm a little distracted. I'll let you know later what I decide." Deep down, I knew I was going. That familiar queasy feeling consumed me. I held my stomach and hoped like hell it would go away. John's Harley purred in the distance. I went to the window, but couldn't see him. How was it Chloe could clearly see me and I couldn't see anything over there?

I dropped the phone on the chair, slipped into my flip-flops, and marched next door. John cut the engine on his motorcycle when he saw me coming. "Hey, bet you can't guess who called me." I dug my hands into my pockets and made fists.

"Uh-oh." He folded up his bandana and stuck it into the back pocket of his jeans.

I crossed my arms. "She used my own words against me. Told me I would be the one breaking Chloe's heart. So not fair." John's smile flatlined. "What?" I asked, walking closer to him.

"I've been thinking."

I questioned the look in his eyes as his expression went from happy to see me to serious.

"There's something about you being with Brook that makes me, well—"

"And?" I prodded.

"It's weird."

"Yup, you're right about that, but then again nothing in my life has been normal since Beckett told me he was gay." I thought back to last summer when Brook pranced around at the beach in her bikini and cutoff shorts showing off her thin perfect, long legs. That twinge of jealousy gnawed at my raw edges.

"You asked my mom to watch Chloe, for crying out loud. We haven't talked since the other night on my porch. We go about our daily business knowing that our confidant is just across the yard. Chloe wanders back and forth like it's nothing. You said you have feelings for me. Nothing about this is normal." John held my shoulders. "I should have minded my own business," I said. The words took my breath away. "What do you want me to do?"

"Maggie, I won't tell you what to do."

This proved harder each waking minute. Wasn't it possible to have a relationship with someone new without headaches, without angst? Couldn't we just move forward? "I'm not sure what I want to do?"

"Everyone has baggage," John said.

At least some of my *baggage* was full-grown and lived independently. Bradley happily resided in Boston. Beckett was content in his condo downtown. Mom was Mom, and there didn't seem to be a problem there. Maybe I was my own baggage. Chloe's laugh echoed in the distance. I took a deep breath then let it out slowly. "I guess," I said. The facts were plain, but not so simple.

Chloe ran into the garage. "Maggie, did you hear? Did you hear? I get to go to Chicago to see my mom in a shoot."

Her toothy smile sent my heart wielding. John unbuckled the leather-studded bag on his bike then pulled out Chloe's matted purple cat, Voodoo.

"Voodoo!" Chloe squealed with delight. "I wondered where he went."

"I haven't seen him in some time," I said.

Chloe squeezed Voodoo tight.

"Hey," I said, "he has two eyes now. What gives?"

"Glad fixed him. Look, she sewed it so it looks like he's winking. Cool, huh?"

That was my mom, she liked to fix things, didn't matter who you were, she was always trying to help. Maybe I needed to remember that more often. Maybe we weren't so different after all. "She does good work," I said, feeling Voodoo's newly stitched eye. "So what's this about Chicago?" I asked, grinning at John's mischievous expression.

"Mom said I could come see her in Chicago. Will you take me shopping, Maggie? I want to get some new clothes. Dad, is it okay if Maggie takes me shopping before I go see Mom?"

John organized wrenches on his tool bench. "That's up to Maggie. She's a busy lady."

Chloe turned to me with question in her eyes. I completely understood. Mom sent Dad shopping for clothes with me once and let's just say it was the only time.

"Sure," I said, "we'll figure out a time."

Chloe bounced with joy.

"Maybe you two should hit the stores in Chicago while you're there," John said.

I raised an eyebrow at him. The roguish glint in his

eye sparkled as he raised his eyebrow back at me. Now I knew where Chloe got it from, but she didn't catch her dad's comment because she was busy putting Voodoo in the basket on her bike. She straddled the metal frame and carefully tiptoed over to where I stood.

"So you decided to come, too?" Chloe asked.

Surprised that she knew I was invited, but not really, I smiled. "Yeah, sounds like fun." Chloe scrunched up her nose as she clipped the snap of her bike helmet. "You knew all along?" I asked.

"Yeah, I'm getting better at keeping secrets. Mom told me. She told me not to bug you about it," Chloe rambled under her breath as she kicked up the kickstand. "She told me to be patient. That's hard for a kid, you know."

"I know." I tucked Voodoo's leash into the basket. Chloe grinned in her dad's direction. He tinkered with the Harley. She had his eyes and his heart.

"I'm going to ride around the block. I'll be back." Chloe waved over her shoulder as she rode away making motorcycle sounds and pretending to rev her Schwinn.

John stood beside me as we watched Chloe pedal down the driveway.

"I knew you'd cave," he said.

"How'd you know?" I asked, watching Chloe pedal faster. Her hair flowed like blond streaks of sunshine in the wind.

"Because you're you."

I stared into John's Irish sparkling eyes. "That predictable, huh?" I crossed my arms in front of me.

"Not really, but something told me you wouldn't want to disappoint Chloe."

John nudged me with his elbow then put his arm around my shoulder.

I rolled my eyes. "You just knew, huh?"

"Yeah, because I can always count on you," he said, kissing the side of my head.

Chapter 12

My bed was heaped with clothes, jeans, trousers, blouses, jackets, and scarves, but nothing seemed right. Changing my mind several times, I couldn't decide what to pack. I should've followed Chloe's lead when we were shopping. After an hour of trying things on, she finally settled on a new pink pair of Converse Chuck Taylor's high tops, a pair of looser-fitting boyfriend jeans, and two new T-shirts. I really liked the white tee she bought with the skeleton face made of lace. I thought about asking if it came in adult sizes, should have.

Leaving my suitcase open, I scrutinized my dull wardrobe. Heat flooded me as the frustration grew in time with the smoldering hot flash. Even though I tried not to compare myself to Brook, she kept popping into my mind. No doubt, she'd be dressed to the nines, but like Chloe, I was partial to jeans and a simple shirt. In frustration, I hung everything back up in my closet then found my skinny jeans, a few button-down shirts, and a few T-shirts. High heels weren't in my realm of fashion and wouldn't ever be so I packed my animal print ballet flats. My gaze scanned the remaining contents of my closet.

"Take the black jeans," I said to myself. Pleased with how my pile shaped up I added an Italian lace scarf Mom had gotten me in Positano, Italy, years ago. "Better take the little leather jacket, too. And the London Fog trench," I mumbled to myself.

"Who are you talking to?" Chloe said.

I poked my head out of my closet. "No one. Just trying to get organized."

"My dad talks to himself, too. You guys sure are weird sometimes."

"Yeah, I know," I replied, grabbing my brown Frye ankle boots.

Chloe ran her hand over my things. "I like what you picked," she said with a smile.

"Thanks. This is hard."

"Yeah, I know what you mean. I'm never sure what my mom expects. I don't want to let her down. I wanted to get some different things when we went shopping, but it felt weird trying to dress for her."

I sat at the end of the bed. "Yeah, I know what you mean." Chloe scratched the side of her head and sighed.

"You do?" she asked.

"Yeah, it's hard being something you're not. Been there, done that," I said, taking a deep breath. "Sometimes I still catch myself doing it."

"I just want Mom to like me," Chloe said. "She's so beautiful and I'm just a dork."

"I'm sure your mom loves you regardless of how you dress."

Chloe sat in the chair next to the window. "It's not just that. I don't think I'll ever be as pretty as she is."

My insides wilted. Chloe would never know it, but I felt exactly the same way.

Chloe fiddled with Voodoo as she leaned back and let out a big sigh.

"You are beautiful," I said.

She stared through me. Doubt filled her eyes. "You're just being nice."

"You are exactly the way you are meant to be, and that's pretty perfect."

She snickered. "Yeah, if I'm perfect then why don't things go my way?" she questioned. "That stupid Hilary at school thinks I'm ugly."

"What does she know? I replied, hoping Chloe would bite. "Unfortunately kids are mean sometimes and usually it's because they don't like themselves very much."

"Whatever, I'm still a dork and hardly anyone believes that my mom is really in magazines."

"Fine, keep thinking you're a *dork*, but some dorks grow up to be incredible adults," I said, standing up. "What do you say we blow this lemonade stand?"

"What?"

"Never mind. It's an old saying. It means let's get out of here," I explained. "Your dad will be home by six. We have some time to kill. What do you want to do?"

Chloe shrugged.

"You're not very helpful," I said. "Let's go downstairs."

She stood, dropped Voodoo to the ground, and dragged him behind her on his purple leash.

"Is Voodoo going to Chicago with us?"

"Yeah, but I'm not going to carry him around. I don't want my mom and her friends to think I'm a baby."

"I doubt anyone will think you're a baby."

Chloe trotted down the stairs in front of me. Voodoo clunked behind her. His scrappy face stared up at me as his head thumped along.

"You keep dragging that poor cat around like that and Glad will have to sew another eye on him, his front paw is torn," I said.

"I know. I like it like that. Keeps him real."

Chloe stopped on the bottom stair and faced me. I smiled. Bones greeted us with a muffled *woof* then trotted away.

"Want to see if Walter and Harry can meet us at the park?" I asked.

"Yeah." Chloe beamed with anticipation.

If I wasn't mistaken, I thought maybe she had a crush on Harry who was a year older and in fourth grade. I could see how she might with his dark-brown, almost black curly hair and sparkling brown eyes. His good nature made it impossible not to like him. "You take Bones outside and I'll call Mrs. Goldstern."

Chloe skipped into the kitchen. She called out as she went, "Can I have a snack?"

"Sure, whatever looks good," I said.

"Thank you," she sang.

I dialed Judy and made plans.

"Chloe." She didn't answer so I called her name again as I followed her trail. I grabbed the box of cookies she'd left out on the counter then headed for the patio. Chloe sat in the chaise lounge chair on the patio wearing Jackie Kennedy sunglasses that covered her face. She had her legs crossed wiggling her toes in the sun. I sat beside her. "What's with the glasses?" I asked with a grin, offering her a chocolate chip cookie.

"No, thanks. Need to stay thin. You like the glasses, huh?"

"Classy," I answered, disregarding her need to stay thin.

"Do they make me look older?"

I squinted as the sun peeked out from behind the clouds. "I guess. Is that what you're going for?"

"Totally. If you look grown up, people will take you more seriously."

"Um, I'm not sure that's true. I know plenty of people that are grown-up and, you know, I gotta say, they're pretty dumb."

"Dad says it's not nice to call people dumb. He makes me use the word silly."

"Whatever. Potato, po-tah-toe," I said in my best English accent.

"I didn't know you knew how to speak a foreign language. That's cool!"

"I hate to break it to you, kid, but I'm still speaking English." I munched on another cookie.

"Oh," she said, pushing her glasses up on her nose. "It still sounds cool. I want to learn French and go to Paris."

"*Oo-la-la, mademoiselle.*"

Chloe peered over the top of her glasses.

I smiled. "Okay, I know a little about French."

"Show off." She snorted when she laughed.

A piece of cookie went down the wrong way. I swallowed hard to try and stop the brewing cough.

"You okay?" Chloe asked.

Nodding, I waved my hand and covered my mouth. My words were barely audible, "Let's go, girlie-girl. Harry and Walter await."

Chloe jumped up. "Let me make sure I look okay," she muttered as she ran into the house.

"Take your time." I patted Bones on the head. He slobbered on my knee. "Gross, let's get cleaned up. You can go, too as long as you mind your manners." Bones wagged his tail and barked. "Come on." I wiped up his drool with a tissue from my pocket.

Bones jumped and twirled in the air. His paws hit my thighs.

"Whoa, that was cool." Chloe clapped at Bones' display "Let's go."

"Get Bones' leash," I said, turning toward the door. I couldn't help but notice Chloe's eyes. "Um, are you wearing makeup?" I wondered where she got the eye shadow.

"No, why?"

"What bathroom did you use?"

"Yours," she said matter-of-factly.

"You know, you really should ask before you use something that's not yours," I reminded her. "Not sure your dad will like that?"

"It will be gone before he sees me. Promise," Chloe said. "Quit looking at me like that."

I cleared my throat. "Fine, have it your way." I hooked Bones' leash to his collar. "Let's go." I grabbed my purse and keys off the kitchen table and headed to the garage. I peered behind me at my two passengers. "Buckle up." Chloe kicked the back of my seat. My head hit the visor, and Bones barked.

"Sorry, Maggie."

"No worries." I inspected my forehead in the rearview mirror.

"Better than the last time. At least there's no blood."

"Yeah, you're right about that." I thought back to when Chloe and I bumped heads in the kitchen. I wound up with stitches while she shook it off. Her resiliency, mind-blowing. Chloe could withstand bumps, mean girls, a mom that lived far away, a dad that worked nine-to-five and sometimes seven days a week. She was more than resilient, the girl possessed super-human endurance and stamina. She could roll with the punches better than anyone I knew. Checking the rearview mirror, I watched her put some lip balm on. The cherry scent wafted up to the front seat, definitely a crush on Harry.

Sun glared across the rear window as I backed down the driveway. I rolled my window down to get a better view behind me. Two girls stopped. I braked and waited for them to cross the sidewalk behind my car. One of the girls pointed in our direction. "There's Chloe. She thinks her mom is a model."

"She doesn't have a mom," the other girl said loudly.

The hair on the back of my neck bristled. My grip tightened on the steering wheel as I glanced in the rearview mirror, again. Chloe's eyes grew uneasy and her jaw clenched. Water brimmed at the corner of her eyes while her chin quivered.

"You want me to say something?" I asked. "Is that the Hilary you've been talking about?"

Anger flashed in her eyes, and Chloe shook her head. "Yes," she mumbled. "Just run them over."

"As much as you'd like that, I think we'd both regret it," I replied, glaring at the girl with long, dark hair. The girl's thin squinty eyes leered back at me, and I wondered what her problem was.

"Look, Chloe's hired a bodyguard or did she hire that lady to pretend to be her mother?" The other girl sneered with a smirk.

A worried expression consumed Chloe's face when I put the car in park.

"What a couple of snots," I muttered to myself. Hilary stared through me. I got out of the car, and Chloe sunk in her seat.

Bones sulked on the seat beside her as I slammed the car door. "Can I help you?" I asked.

The girls sized me up. Dialogue ran through my head. *I might not be Chloe's mother and I might not be her bodyguard, but I sure can kick your butts.* A woman came around the corner being walked by a St. Bernard.

"Is that your mother?" I asked.

Hilary's eyes shone with spite. Her friend surveyed the area, I assumed for witnesses.

"Is it?" I asked again, trying to remain calm.

"No. And even if it was, it wouldn't matter," she replied.

"Too bad, I'd like to talk to her."

"You wish," Hilary uttered under her breath.

"Nice." Sarcasm dripped freely as I spun on a heel and got back in the car.

Chloe let out a loud sigh. "See, I told you. She's a witch."

"Yeah, I guess so. Who is that other girl, the one with the blond hair, the one who actually looked scared?" I asked, putting the car in reverse.

"That's Maddie Carson."

"Snots," I said, stopping at the corner. I glanced in the mirror to see Chloe wiping at her eyes. "You okay?" I asked softly.

"Yeah, I guess so. I just get tired of it sometimes," she replied.

"I know. We all do."

Chapter 13

I opened the door, grabbed Bones' leash, and let him hop out. "You coming?" I said to Chloe, slumped in the backseat. "It will do you good. If not, I can tell Harry and Walter we're not going to stay."

Chloe unbuckled her seatbelt at a snail's pace.

I looped Bones' leash around my wrist to free my hands. "You mind if I wipe your eyes. I'm afraid your eye shadow is smeared."

Chloe stared up into my eyes and nodded. Her hurt lingered behind feisty green irises. Flashes of Bradley came to mind.

"You know," I said, "Bradley had a tough time sometimes, too. People can be mean."

"What he'd get teased about?" she asked, scooting her legs over the side of the seat.

"His reading and red hair. And look at him now. He's a great reader and he's pretty handsome. The girls love his red hair."

"I got a long way to go until I'm as old as he is. Please tell me life isn't going to be this hard all the time."

"You want Voodoo?" I grabbed the cat's purple leash.

"No, that's just one more thing that someone can pick on me about. He can stay in the car."

I shut the door. "I'd like to say that it gets better, but we all have our days. My dad used to say, *Some days you get the bear and other days the bear gets you.*"

"What does it mean again?"

"It just means that you have good days and bad days." I winked in Chloe's direction. "And some days will really suck. And sometimes when you think everything *won't* turn out, it does. Those are the best days."

"Thanks, Maggie."

"You're welcome, sweetheart. Don't look now, but here comes Walter." I waved to him.

Bones tugged at the leash as Walter's Spiderman flip-flops slapped madly against the sidewalk.

"Hi, Chloe!" Walter squealed as he gave her a big hug.

Chloe gurgled in his grip. "You're squishing me."

Walter laughed. "Come on, Harry's over there."

Walter hugged me tight, grunting as he squeezed. I moaned, "I think the bear got me," I joked.

Bones jumped up on Chloe from behind.

"Now I'm a sandwich." She moaned, and we all laughed.

Judy waved me over to where she sat on a bench. "I'll be over there."

Walter tugged at Chloe's hand. "Come on."

"I'm coming, I'm coming."

"Hey, Judy. I think spring has decided to stay." I shaded my eyes and noticed Judy's less than enthusiastic response.

She shaded her eyes. "Glad you guys called us. It's been a dreary day."

By the look on her face it wasn't the late break in spring getting her down. "Want to walk with Bones and me? He could use the exercise."

"Hey, Harry, watch Walter. We're going out to the point," Judy called.

"Got it, Mom," he replied.

"What's going on?" I asked. Judy didn't seem to be her perky self. Her curly short black hair caught in the wind. Her eyes grew dark. My gut wrenched as she put her sunglasses on and stared straight ahead.

"I think it's back," she muttered. "I found a lump."

"Oh, Judy," I said. "Son-of-a-bitch." I shook my head in disbelief.

Chills danced up my spine when I caressed my collarbone remembering my own battle. "Is there anything I can do?" Judy stopped in her tracks then faced me. Her shoulders quaked. I wrapped my arms around her. Wet tears soaked my shirt. "I'm so, so sorry. Have you seen the doctor?"

"Yeah, but I don't have a good feeling," she said, wiping at the corners of her eyes.

"Maybe it's nothing," I suggested, not knowing what her prognosis would be, but hoping like hell that she could fight it if it was malignant. Waiting for the results caused a pit of angst.

Judy pulled back, caught her breath, and tilted her face to the sun. "Okay, now that that's over, I can get on with it."

I rubbed her back and hooked my arm through hers as if we'd been friends for years. There was a familiar sense about her that made me wonder if we knew each other in a previous life. "Yes, you can," I said. "For starters, I can buy you an ice-cream bar at the snack stand."

"Can I have the one with dark chocolate and toffee bits?" she asked.

I winked at Judy. "You can have the moon if you wish."

"Great, I'd like some stardust, too. I hear that stuff can do wonders."

Her smiling dimples couldn't hide her weary eyes, rimmed with worry. Her sadness reminded me how quickly life can turn on you. It was like turning your back on the ocean.

Chloe ran at us, her arms flailing like a ragdoll. "Maggie, Maggie, you are not going to believe it," she hollered.

"Believe what?" I asked with caution.

"Harry just buried Walter in the sand. Only his face is sticking out. It's so cool. Come on!"

Judy and I glanced at each other. We picked up the pace. High-pitched yelps pierced my ears as we neared the scene. Walter's chubby face peeked out of the sand. Harry piled mounds of sand on his chest like breasts. I couldn't hold back the laughter. Judy unhooked her arm from mine and hurried across the beach. She shot Harry a look only a mother could cultivate.

"Get the boobs off." Walter squawked and stuck his tongue out at Harry. "He promised he wouldn't make me into a girl. Get them off."

Harry stood back, crossed his arms, and snapped a picture with Judy's phone. "Perfect."

"Harry," Judy said. "Get him out of there."

Harry cackled. Chloe did, too.

I covered my mouth trying not to encourage Harry's antics, but Walter did make a cute mermaid. "Wow, you work fast," I said to Harry as I watched Judy dig her little man out of the sand.

Harry grinned. "It's a gift."

"Good one," Chloe said, punching him in the arm.

Chloe's eyes twinkled as she gazed up at Harry, who was too enthralled in his brother's dismay to even notice a girl. My heart skipped a beat as I watched Chloe ogle over him in-between the giggles and the friendly punch to his bicep. Judy grabbed Walter's hand and yanked him up from the ground. Tiny bits of sand rained down all around him as he shook his body like a wet retriever. Judy winced as bits of sand pelted her shins. I couldn't help but smile. Chloe had found a way out of her funk. Harry and Walter unknowingly distracted Judy from her own worries. All of which, I found amusing to watch and happy to be part of.

My family was growing by leaps and bounds.

Judy's gaze caught my attention. She marveled at the three amigos running down the beach. With her hands on her hips, her face taut with concern, she watched them as if she were saying goodbye. I stood beside her. A sly grin crept slowly across her full lips. Wetness brimmed at the rims of her eyes. Compassion tugged at my heart. It wasn't fair. She didn't deserve another round of cancer. Her eyes met mine and my breath caught in my chest then shook my insides lose. All I could do was love her. Standing beside her, I wrapped my arm around her shoulders then held her close.

"I have to make it for them," she said. "They can't be left alone." Judy wiped at her eyes with the back of her hands. "I think it's worse this time."

Her broken words left me cold. A familiar shiver ran down my spine as she covered her quivering chin with her shaky hand. Her ominous stare frightened me. "I'll be with you. You tell me what you need." Her cheeks were stained with tears. No ice-cream treat would heal this wound. It ran far too deep. She slid her hand around my waist and squeezed.

We stood together as one, two women bound by circumstance and determination. We held on to each other knowing that strength was derived from the union of broken souls much like a tattered army limping along with hopes that the war would soon cease.

"You're going to be fine," I said, squinting into the sun. I shaded my eyes to see the kids better at the other end of the beach. They sat at a picnic table near the boulder of rock tossing pebbles into the lake. Lose strands of hair tickled my cheek as the wind sauntered by. The hint of summer kissed the back of my neck, the way John had done that special night.

Judy took a deep breath. Her shoulders rose and fell keeping in time with the gentle waves licking the shore. "You ready for some ice cream?"

She looked over to me, her expression fragile.

"What?" I asked.

"Maggie, don't wait too long," she whispered.

"For what?" I asked, leading her back toward the Snack Shack.

"For John."

This time, it was my turn for the heavy sigh. A wave rolled over in the pit of my stomach. "He's leaving, Judy. He going back to Montana to be with his dad. He's selling his house." Gravity tugged at the corners of my mouth. "He's got things he wants to do." I dug my toes into the sand deeper with each step. "So do I," I said, listening to Chloe's laugh in the distance. I put my flip-flops down on the sidewalk, brushed off my feet, then slid into them.

"You're brave to go to Chicago with Chloe and her mother," Judy said.

"Or stupid. This has disaster written all over it," I said, searching my pocket for money. Wrinkled green dollars felt cool in the palm of my hand.

"Yeah, you're right about that," Judy added with a giggle.

Chapter 14

Chloe and I rolled up to the Ritz at three sharp. The trek across Michigan proved interesting. Evidently, time skewed my memories of riding five hours with an eight-year-old. I didn't remember the incessant battery of questions, requests for snacks, and frequent time checks to see if we were there yet. Handing my keys to the valet dressed in red relieved me. I slung my purse across my body as my eyes focused on Chloe. My gut twisted with the unsure outcome of our journey. Her mouth dropped open as she peered up into the Chicago skyline. Stepping up onto the curb, I headed inside as another valet sporting a whistle greeted me. Chloe and Voodoo followed.

I glanced down as she tugged at my elbow.

"This is grand," Chloe said. "I don't think I've ever been any place this fancy before."

I smiled. Grand? By the sounds of it, she must have been watching Annie again. Thoughts of John and his dad's Montana ranch filled my mind. How was she going to adapt to that adjustment? The promise of wide-open land surrounded by majestic mountains and brilliant blue sky sounded like a dream. Would she like it there? Of course she would.

"Every day is a new adventure," I uttered under my breath, thinking about the responsibility I owned, questioning the position I'd put myself in, and worrying about the future. I hated how I carried the nagging unknown along like an invisible ball-and-chain. "We're meeting your mom later," I reminded Chloe. "She said she would call or send me a text."

Chloe beamed, her jack-o'-lantern smile changed again with the loss of another bottom tooth. Her cheery disposition reminding me this was about her, not me.

I remembered back to exasperation, tired nights, and long days with Bradley that trumped my own needs and dreams. Mom used to say, "It's not about you anymore." She was right, but now Bradley was off on his own, Beckett was on his own and I stood in a glamorous hotel lobby with an eight-year-old, who wasn't mine. Chloe had grown on me like a slow creeping fungus at first, but somehow she'd blossomed into an exotic creature that I adored. She'd barged into my life, made me question my very existence, my purpose, my next adventure.

"Look at the fountain, Maggie, and the skylight. The floor is so shiny," Chloe said.

Mom was right.

It wasn't about me.

"Mom," Chloe said, sliding across the immaculate floor and into her mom's arms.

"Hey, baby girl," Brook said back as she bent down to Chloe's level.

A thin smile lifted my heart with high hopes of a successful trip. Brook's hair swayed as she lifted Chloe up for a big hug. Brook's eyes met mine, her message different than last summer. This time she wasn't wearing Daisy Dukes and a T-shirt with an attitude. Her face seemed softer, glowing, genuinely pleased to see her daughter.

I made eye contact with the receptionist standing behind the counter. "Hello, I'm Maggie Abernathy. I have a reservation." With one eye on the clerk and one eye on Brook and Chloe, I dug out my credit card.

"She's a beautiful lady," he said with lustful eyes.

I waited for the familiar twinge of jealousy, but when it didn't come, I smiled. "Yup, you got that right. Amazing how beautiful a child can be," I said, admiring my spin on the situation.

The clerk's face soured.

"We have two queen beds, correct?" I asked as his fingers tapped over the keyboard. Leaning against the cool marble counter, I watched his eyes follow Brook. I read his nametag. Phillipo. He handed me the keys to our room.

"Is that your daughter?" he asked.

"Nope, that's *her* daughter," I replied, nodding in Brook's direction. Zipping up my bag, I headed over to fountain where Brook and Chloe sat chatting. Chloe's long hair fell into her face as she bent over to touch the water. With four-inch heels on, Brook towered over me when she stood to greet me. "Hey, there. Thought you were going to call."

"We had a break. Malfunctioning technology. So I thought I'd surprise you." Brook ruffled the top of Chloe's head.

Chloe took her hand out of the water and ogled at her mom. "You look beautiful."

Brook beamed. And Chloe was right. The spectacular skylight overhead flooded Brook with natural light. My eyes followed the contour of her cheekbones down to her dusty pink lips. "You look great," I said.

"So do you. Have you been working out?" she asked.

I laughed. "Not quite, but thanks." Brook sure didn't emulate the age of forty.

Chloe grabbed my hand. "Mom says we can go back to the shoot with her."

Chloe's puppy-dog eyes in combination with Brook's pleading expression got the better of me. "Sounds great. How about I make sure our luggage gets to the room?"

"We'll come with you." Chloe tugged at her mom's hand. "Come on, Mom. I can't wait to see my bed. Maggie said it's fit for a queen."

The elevator door opened. Chloe stood between us. The mirrored walls told an interesting story of a child, her exquisite model mother, and me, the lady next door. Brook caught my attention in the reflection and smiled a toothy grin. I responded with a grin trying to hide my wandering thoughts. I fiddled with the plastic keycard to our room.

"Before I forget," Brook said, "thanks."

Taken aback by her sincerity, I froze. "You're welcome."

Chloe slid her hand in mine. Her bright eyes stared through me and the story in the mirrored walls portrayed a twist in the plot, a child nestled between her biological mother and a friend who loved her as her own.

The elevator chimed.

"This is our floor," I said.

We followed the arrows to our room.

The bellhop stood outside the door with an empty cart. "Your bags are all settled, ma'am." He nodded and held the door open for us.

"Thank you." I handed him a tip then he left.

Brook sauntered to the window and peered out. She was rail thin in her dark denim skinny jeans. Chloe hopped up on one of the beds and did a little jump then plopped down and swished her arms and legs like she was making a snow angel.

"Wow-wee-wow." She giggled, took a deep breath, then sat up. "Can we go now? I want to see where you work!"

Brook turned, then ran her fingers through her long hair. "Sure, if it's okay with Maggie."

I unzipped my suitcase and found my makeup bag. "Let me use the bathroom and splash some water on my face."

Chloe unzipped her bag. She produced a box wrapped in blue paper then held it out to her mother. "Here, this is for you."

Brook sat next to her daughter on the bed. "Wow, I wasn't expecting a present." She rattled the box.

Chloe blew loose strands of hair away from her face.

Goosebumps covered my forearms. I closed the bathroom door and stared in the mirror. Fine lines from stress crept across my forehead. I splashed cold water on my cheeks. Doubt that I could ever have anything with John emerged. Girlie chatter behind the door only spurred the fact John's previous marriage would remain between us, along with Bradley and Beckett. I patted my face dry, applied some foundation, and freshened up my mascara. Running my fingers through my wavy hair, I gave myself a pep talk. When I opened the door, Brook was brushing Chloe's hair. She had a macaroni necklace dangling around her neck.

"Do you like it?" she asked.

"Exquisite," I answered, admiring the pattern of pink and orange pasta against her stark white blouse.

Chloe laughed. "You two are funny." She shook her head. "It's just macaroni. It's not like it's Tiffany."

Brook pursed her lips and batted her ultra-long lashes. "A girl after my own heart."

"Tiffany, huh. I didn't know about that until I was in my twenties," I said. "Not much of a jewelry hound."

Brook seemed dismayed.

"I guess I was sheltered," I added. "What can I say?"

Chloe's eyes dimmed. "Yeah, some of the girls have Tiffany necklaces at school."

"*Barnyard*?" I questioned.

"Yup, and she's always flaunting it like she's so great."

Chloe rolled her eyes at me.

"*Barnyard*?" Brook questioned.

"Yeah, she's that girl at school I slugged. She's a pain," Chloe said, stroking Voodoo's back. "She's the one who makes fun of me. She's mean."

Brook's gaze met mine. A flash of motherly worry flickered in her eyes. "Who could mean to you?" she asked, tucking Chloe's hair behind her ear.

I nodded at Brook and crossed my arms.

"She doesn't believe you're my mom. She says I'm ugly." Chloe took a deep breath. "She's stupid."

Brook's left eyebrow arched with concern. "Well, you're here now and we're going to have a blast." She kissed Chloe on the forehead.

I knew Chloe was thinking about career day at school. I also knew that visiting her superstar mom was not the same as having her visit school. "Let's not give old *Barnyard* the sense of satisfaction by sitting around here talking about her."

"She's pretty dumb," Chloe said, looking her mother in the eye. "Are you sure you can't make it to career day?"

Brook touched Chloe's cheek. "We've been over this before. I can't make it."

Chloe pouted. "Fine." She stood up and snapped to attention. "How do I look?"

I grinned as she inspected herself in the mirror.

"You look perfect," Brook said. "Shall we?" Then Brook checked her watch. "Oh, we better get going," she said, nudging Chloe out the door. I grabbed my bag and followed.

The wind caught Brook's mane as we hustled to catch a cab. She stepped from the curb, stuck her fingers between her teeth, and whistled. Chloe and I stood by each other's side, amazed at Brook's talent. A yellow cab stopped for us. Brook took Chloe's hand and helped her into the back seat.

"Where are we going?" Chloe asked.

"The Bean," Brook said.

"What's that?"

The cab swerved to the left as we passed Water Tower Place and a crowd on the sidewalk.

"Whoa, this is fun." Chloe held on to her mom's arm. "But what is this Bean thing all about?"

"You'll see when we get there," Brook said, digging into her oversized Louis Vuitton bag.

My eyes took in the passing scenery. Beckett and I had brought Bradley to Chicago when he was about ten. We were happily together, or so I thought. I couldn't help but grin about the day we spent at Disney Quest. Beckett had gotten sick after riding *Aladdin's Magic-Carpet Ride* in 3-D, while I rocked it out on the life-sized *Daffy Duck* pinball against some hefty ball player who did not take defeat well. Bradley had cheered with his fists in the air as I strutted around like Rocky Balboa when declared the winner. The victory celebration consisted of burgers and milkshakes at Ed Debevic's. I hoped Chloe would leave Chicago with some fond memories as well.

"Wow, check out all the shops. Can we go shopping?" she asked.

Brook glanced in my direction. "Not sure if I'll have time, but we'll try."

I smiled trying to hide my skepticism as usual. "The Bean," I said, pointing. The shiny metal sculpture shone in the sun. Beckett and I also visited without Bradley. Beckett attended an art conference while I roamed the city and explored the stores. We had a romantic dinner at the top of the Hancock building where he'd given me an anniversary ring. In hindsight, the loving token represented something different for him. He was trying hard to make things right, live an acceptable life with a wife, and be a father to his child. I inspected my plain hands with no jewelry. The ring was tucked away at home next to the gold wedding band I used to wear, a time capsule meaning nothing but a sliver of time spent together, documented by some metal and stones tucked away in my sock drawer-never to be worn again. A thin grin tugged at the seam of my lips. Beckett was gay. I accepted that. Life was funny and each time I thought about it my heart seemed a little lighter.

"Hey, Maggie," Brook shouted. "Come on. Get your head out of the clouds."

I slid across the vinyl taxi seat. The creepy driver with the gold teeth smiled. The heebie-jeebies crawled across my skin like maggots in a horror film. I jumped out of the cab, shaking off his leer. "Gross," I muttered, repositioning my purse across my body. Brook's stare unnerved me. Was she judging my choice of attire? "What?" I asked, stepping closer.

"You've got a good look going on," she said. "I like that bag."

"Thanks. I bought it in an airport. Who would have known? Not sure what kind it is," I said, knowing she was dressed from head to toe in designer clothing. I could never feel comfortable in shiny stilettos and skinny jeans.

"Those Frye boots?" she asked.

"Yeah, they're my favorite." I raised up the leg of my faded boot cut jeans to show her the brushed buckle on the side.

"I'll have to get some of those. Super cute." She winked at Chloe.

Chloe smiled then grabbed her hand. Blue sky and sunshine reflected off The Bean's shiny exterior giving us another splendid view of the great city. A makeshift fence surrounded the structure marking off the area where Brook's people were shooting. Pedestrians stood by ogling over the production.

Brook gestured for me to follow her and Chloe. "Over here," she shouted as she trotted through a discrete entryway to the shoot.

Two brawny bald guys stood at the opening. I wasn't sure if they were security or models with the flashy sunglasses. They didn't flinch as Brook moseyed past. My eyes scanned their bulging muscles.

The shorter of the two grabbed my arm. "Where you going?"

"I'm with Brook." I called out to her, "Hey, Brook."

Her hair bounced over her shoulder like she was in a shampoo commercial. "That's Maggie, she's with me. And this is my daughter, Chloe."

"Hi guys," Chloe said.

Bruiser let go of my arm.

"Sorry, thought you were one of those ladies that's been trying to make their way in here all day." He nodded to a group of middle-aged women huddled together in high heels lurking near the plastic fence.

I rolled my eyes. "Hardly," I mumbled, inspecting his rock-hard biceps.

Chloe yanked at my hand. "Come on, Maggie."

A man with a camera kissed Brook on the cheek. "Get yourself ready. We're back up and ready to roll."

Brook kissed the top of Chloe's head. "This is my girl, Chloe, and our friend, Maggie."

"Hi, girls, nice to meet you," the man with the camera said with a wink.

Chloe waved. I nodded hello. Brook thought of me as a friend. Who knew?

"I'm Fletcher Thompson. You can come with me. You from around here?"

"No. We live in Michigan," Chloe answered.

"My aunt lives in Ann Arbor," he told us.

"We live in Grosse Pointe," Chloe replied. "Are you taking the pictures today?"

"Yup." He snapped a few frames as Chloe spoke. "See those ladies over there in the chairs?" Fletcher pointed to a trio of models getting made up. Hairbrushes and makeup brushes flitted about as the women batted their long, black fake eyelashes that matched Brook's.

"Yeah," Chloe said, shading her eyes.

"Those are the models. Pretty special. Your mom's in the middle."

Chloe squinted. "Yup, that's her. You know Maggie took some pictures of my mom before. Last summer. At our park."

Fletcher lowered his glasses. "I saw those. They were really good."

Heat washed over me. "Thanks." Tongue-tied and embarrassed, I clammed up. His gaze connected with mine.

A flicker of attraction rustled my nerves. "I'm working on a new project," I added, not sure if taking photos of cows equated to anything in his world of half-naked models and jet setting.

"You've got talent. I'm sure whatever you're doing, you'll do great."

I glanced over to Brook then down to Chloe. Fletcher's stare focused on me. My palms sweated. "Thanks," I said. "Can we get closer to the models? See what they're doing over there?"

"Sure. Stay away from Jose or you just may end up in the shoot yourself."

"That would be cool." Chloe couldn't contain her enthusiasm. "Then I'd really have something to show *Barnyard*." She gawked at Fletcher and cocked her head to the side. "She's a mean girl at home. That's not really her name. That's just what I call her. She-is-not-nice." Chloe's finger waggled to and fro as she made her point.

Fletcher snickered and snapped more photos as she explained her situation. "I know the type." His eyes flickered as he talked. "Excuse me, I've got to get going, the light is perfect. Nice to meet you, Chloe. Maggie, it was a pleasure."

He leaned in closer. "Seriously, stay away from Jose, although I wouldn't mind seeing you in my viewfinder."

"I'd rather be on your side of the camera," I told him.

"That could be arranged, too."

My gut twisted at the attention and my cheeks smoldered with embarrassment.

Chloe held my hand. "Let's go see my mom."

"Sure."

"I think he likes you," Chloe said.

"I think he likes all women."

Chloe laughed. "Not sure what that means, but you're probably right."

Brook's hair was wound in a tight bun on top of her head. She had ultra-black lashes, a mile long, and ruby-red lips. The man with the makeup dusted her skin with powder. When the sun caught her cheekbones, it sparkled making her shine like an Egyptian queen.

"Look how pretty my mom looks," Chloe awed.

"Yeah," I said, taking note of strapless white dress. Heavy gold beads the size of golf balls adorned her neck. Her platform heels seemed even higher than the heels she had on with her jeans. She winked at Chloe.

Chapter 15

Chloe'd never been so quiet. We were both mesmerized by the action around us, the wardrobes, the hair, the makeup, Jose, the eccentric coordinator who flitted about chirping orders and coaching models. The scene was enchanting, something from *America's Next Top Model.*

The sun warmed the city and life buzzed like worker bees in a hive. We were on the cusp of summer, a time of rejuvenation and dreams, and it was turning out to be a great day.

I was completely absorbed by Brook's world.

"Hey, girls. No one sits around without working it," Jose said with a snap of his fingers. "Let's go."

Before I knew it, he had Chloe and me by the hand pulling us toward the makeup chairs.

"Wait, I'm just a spectator," I protested.

Jose stopped in his tracks. "Did you not hear me? If you're on the set, you work. Sit."

I did as I was told.

Chloe flipped her hair back. "I'm in! This is the best day of my life."

I balked at accepting the attention.

Jose ran his fingers through my messy strawberry-blond tresses. "Gorgeous."

I raised my eyebrows at him. "Just because I'm gorgeous doesn't mean I want to flaunt it," I jested.

"Hey, Victoria, can you make her up. Both of them."

A woman with long black hair tugged at my purse and jacket. "What do you have on under here?" she asked.

Chloe's laughter tickled my subconscious and reminded me that I should loosen up.

"White blouse," I answered afraid to move. Someone tugged at my hair from behind. My head jerked back. Victoria lifted the collar of my blouse and undid the next two buttons. I peered down into my barely-there cleavage.

"Wear this," she said, hooking a heavy silver braided choker around my neck. "Let her hair down."

My hair fell to my shoulders. Mysterious fingers fluffed my mane. Victoria came at me with some mascara and red lipstick like Brook's. She swished a soft brush across my cheeks.

"There. Wait," she ordered with a flip of her hair. She cuffed the sleeves of my blouse and stuck a matching silver braided band on my ring finger.

"Perfect." She beamed.

Speechless, I watched Chloe. The silent man in the fedora curled her hair. Brook stood behind her with a baby blue box, tied with a white ribbon. She'd changed back into her dark skinny jeans and white blouse. Her hair was tied at the nape of her neck, her lips ruby red. Blond strands stuck out giving her a chic messy look.

"This is for you," the quiet man whispered in Chloe's ear. He put the Tiffany box on her lap.

Emotion bubbled behind my eyes. Seeing this side of Brook astounded me. Chloe was right, this was the best day ever. And somehow, I knew we weren't done.

Chloe beamed. "OMG!" She untied the ribbon and flipped open the top.

Brook knelt in front of her. "I thought you needed some jewelry for the shoot, too."

Chloe fingered the silver engraved heart then caressed the pink enamel heart next to it. "It's perfect. I love it!"

"Let's take your jacket off so we can see it in the photos."

Brook undid the clasp and helped Chloe put the necklace on. "I knew you'd look fabulous in Tiffany."

Chloe wrapped her arms around her mom as she bounced out of the chair. Her eyes glanced my way. I'd seen the look before in her father's eyes and I gave a little clap trying to control the blubbering fit struggling to escape. Fletcher snapped frames then Jose jumped in rattling off orders. Victoria undid my thin belt and whipped a heavy leather braided belt around my waist. The color matched my Frye boots perfectly. "Where can I get one of these?" I asked.

Fletcher put his camera down for a split second. "It's yours. Keep the jewelry, too. It suits you. Brook, show them what to do, then it's a wrap." Fletcher hustled to the other side of The Bean.

Brook showed Chloe how to strut her stuff underneath The Bean then we huddled together staring up at our reflections. With our arms around each other's waists, Chloe in the middle, we sashayed out into the world. Fletcher snapped away. Brook picked Chloe up and I leaned into them. Fletcher snapped a close-up. Swallowed by the moment, I was free.

"That's a wrap," Fletcher said.

"Wait," I said, "I know this is a lot to ask, but can we get a group photo with Jose, Victoria, fedora man, and the brutes by the gate?"

Fletcher rubbed his bristly head. "Sure."

Jose called everyone over. Chloe nuzzled close to her mom. Jose wrapped his arm around my shoulder. The security guard that grabbed my arm earlier pressed his lips on my cheek. I laughed and Fletcher shot some more frames.

"That's a wrap." Jose words mimicked a songbird's call and with a snap of his fingers everyone began to scatter.

"Thanks for making this the best day ever!" Chloe yelled at the top of her lungs. She squeezed her mom tight.

I smiled at Brook and she smiled back. Fletcher came over and handed Jose the camera. "Here, take our photo."

He wrapped his arm around my shoulder. "Smile, beautiful."

As soon as my gaze met his stare Jose shot one frame. *Click.*

"I told you before, everyone works," Jose said as he studied us through the camera viewfinder.

Fletcher squeezed my shoulder. "And just so you know, no one has ever stopped me after a wrap and ordered more."

I grinned as he arched his eyebrow at me. "Sorry, but that's how I roll. Didn't mean to step on any toes."

"No worries," he replied with a grin.

"Great, then you won't mind if I request a set of proofs."

Fletcher snickered. "We'll get you a set of proofs. Anything else?"

"Thank you for letting Chloe and me be part of your day. It was truly spectacular," I said, giving him a peck on the cheek. The unexpected glee made me giddy.

Victoria handed me my purse and my jacket. "Here ya' go, sweetie. And just so ya' know, no one has gotten to this guy before," she said with a smirk.

He scowled at her then caught my stare. "Let me know how your cow project goes. Maybe I can help." Fletcher strolled away barking orders at Jose.

Jose handed me a card. "Here, Fletcher doesn't just do this for anyone. Don't lose this," he said. "It's been a blast. One of the best shoots ever with that serious mug."

Slipping into my jacket, I slung my purse over my shoulder, then headed over to where Brook stood with Chloe showing her racks of clothing and accessories.

"Ready?" Brook asked.

"I can't believe I have a real Tiffany necklace." Chloe beamed.

"I know. It's beautiful. I fingered my new belt. Fletcher's gift seemed all too generous."

Brook smiled.

I tucked Fletcher Thompson's card in my purse just as my phone buzzed. I checked the text. It was John wanting to know how the day went.

I tapped out a quick message. *So far so good. Having tons of fun.*

He replied almost immediately. *I knew I could count on you!*

"Who's texting you?" Chloe asked, squinting at the screen of my phone.

"Your dad. He says hi and hopes you are having a good time."

Chloe put her hand on her hip. "Take my picture. Send it to him."

"Please," Brook reminded her.

"Please, Maggie. Will you take my picture?" Chloe tilted her head and shaded her eyes with her hand.

I poked at the photo button and snapped a picture. "What do you want to tell him?"

"Tell him hello. Can I type something myself?"

I handed her the phone. "Here, have at it."

Brook helped her spell a few words as she sounded out her message.

Before tapping send, I read the message that said, *maybe we should rethink the Montana thing. Chicago is really fun!*

I giggled. "He's gonna like that."

"What?" Brook asked, looking perplexed.

"I don't want to move to Montana," Chloe said. "Dad says we're moving. I'm tired of moving."

Brook stroked Chloe's hair. "Can't one of you talk some sense into him?" She rubbed her chin.

"What?" Chloe and I said at the same time.

Chloe shifted her weight. "Now that you and Mom can get along, maybe you can double-team him."

We both raised an eyebrow at her.

"What? You don't remember last summer. Mom, Bones peed on your leg. Maggie, my mom wasn't exactly nice to you. Is any of it coming back?" Chloe gestured with her hands and raised her eyebrows as she spoke.

Brook covered her mouth and tugged at Chloe's hand as she walked. "Yeah, yeah, yeah," she muttered with a smirk.

I hadn't thought about Bones or my mom. I hadn't even called her to tell her I was here. I got out my phone again. There was another message from John. *Tell Chloe no.*

I replied. *I don't think so, buddy. That's all you, but she is right. This is a fabulous place. Besides, when you go to Montana, you won't meet any neighbors like me.* I clicked send then scrolled down my list of contacts until I found my mom's number. She answered after the third ring. "Hi, Mom. I'm here."

"Figured. How are things?"

"We're having a fun time. How is Bones?"

"Just a second, I'm on the floor. I have to put the phone down."

"Mom, what are you doing on the floor? Mom? Mom?" I said louder. Brook shot me a look before stepping to the curb to hail a cab. "Mom—"

"Hold your horses, young lady. I told you I was on the floor. I'm not as young as I used to be." Mom sounded irritated.

"What are you looking for?"

"Nothing."

"Mom, are you all right?"

"Yeah. Bones is fine. He's a good dog. He's keeping me company, but he misses you guys. He's kind of mopey. Guess, I'm not as much fun."

"You're loads of fun, Mom. We'll be home tomorrow, hopefully before dinner."

"Fine."

"You okay?" I asked, pressing the phone to my ear.

"Yes, Marjorie Jean." Mom's unusual snap worried me.

"Don't get me started, Glad," I said.

"Fine, I won't get you started, but I will have a surprise for you when you get home," she replied.

"Better not be another dog." Mom's cackle pierced my ear.

"Bye, Maggie."

"Bye, Mom."

"Come on, Maggie," Chloe urged.

Brook opened the cab door. I slid across the vinyl seat. Chloe and her mom followed. I noticed the time on the dash next to Habib's badge. My stomach growled. Brook probably didn't have that problem.

"I bet you guys are hungry," Brook said, scrolling through her phone. "I have an idea. How about burgers and milkshakes? There is a great place, Ed Debevic's on Wells Street. Chloe will love it."

"Funny, I was just thinking about that place earlier. Last time I was there, Bradley was about ten. He thought it was a hoot. Our server wore airplane goggles and sassed at us the whole time. It was great."

"You mean the servers are rude?" Chloe asked. "Aren't they supposed to be nice?"

"It's part of the show," I said.

"On purpose?" Chloe's right eyebrow shot up.

"No kidding, they dress up and are sassy."

"How old do you have to be to work there?" she asked.

I laughed as Brook ruffled her daughter's hair.

Chloe straightened the lapel on her jacket and sneered. "What do you want, lady? You talking to me?"

"You just might have a shot," I said. "Keep practicing, on second thought, maybe not."

Brook instructed the cabby where we were headed. Chloe fingered her heart necklace then kissed the silver surface.

Chapter 16

My mom stared at me over the rim of her new pair of purple-and-red-striped reading glasses. She hadn't stopped smirking at me since she poured herself a cup of coffee.

"What?" I asked.

"Nothing, honey," she muttered. "So tell me about Chicago."

"We had a good time. I think Brook and I have buried the hatchet. Chloe had a great time. We met lots of fun people and got to be part of Brook's shoot." I winked at her. "There will be photos." I couldn't help but smile. "Actually, the whole experience was fabulous. Very exciting to be an insider."

"I haven't seen you this happy in a while. Glad it worked out. I have a surprise," she blurted out.

"Yeah, what's that? It better not be puppy, hamster, or even fish. I see that Bones chewed up my slippers when I was gone." Rinsing out my cup in the sink, I wiggled my toes beneath his pudgy belly.

"That's just his way of telling you he misses you," the deep voice answered.

I dropped my cup in the sink at the sound of Bradley's voice. "Shit, I think I cracked it. Who cares? Get over here," I demanded. "Oh my God, I can't believe you're home." I wrapped my arms around his middle and drew him close. He was a whole head taller than me and he'd filled out since I'd last seen him. The whiskers on his chin tickled my cheek when he kissed me. I squeezed him tight. "I can't believe you're here."

"Nana bought me a ticket."

Mom beamed. "Thought you might like this much more than another puppy, although I think, Bones would prefer a new friend."

Bones barked and jumped up.

"Down," I commanded. He sat. "Good dog."

Bradley bent down and scratched Bones' belly. "Cool dog. How come I never could have a dog?"

I rolled my eyes. "Let the guilt begin," I said. "We were never here enough. You know that. It wouldn't have been fair."

"Yeah, whatever," he mumbled.

I ruffled his hair like he was seven. "How long are you here?"

"The weekend. Got any plans?" Bradley asked.

"I do now. What do you want to do?"

"Hope you're not disappointed, but I'd kind of like to lay low. I've been super busy. Maybe see Dad, if he's around." Bradley poured himself a cup of coffee and leaned against the counter. I watched him sip from the mug. When had my baby gotten so big? When had my baby started drinking coffee and grown a beard? "I'm in. It's your world sweetheart." I meandered over to mom, inspecting her height. She seemed shorter today. I kissed her cheek. "Thanks for the surprise. This was the best one yet." I wrapped my arm around her and squeezed.

The front door slammed.

Chloe came bursting into the party. "Hey, there's a tall guy here somewhere—"

"Bradley," I interrupted, "this is Chloe. She lives next door. She's in third grade this year. That makes her eight and she hangs out with us a lot."

"Oh, hi. I just wanted to make sure he wasn't a robber or something."

Bradley chuckled.

"Sure," I mumbled. "So Chloe, Bradley is here for the weekend. Glad flew him in. Isn't that a great surprise?"

Chloe stepped closer to Bradley, placed her hands on her hips, and stared up at him. "Wow, you're big. How'd you get that way? Your mom is kind of shrimpy."

"Hey," I said with a nudge.

Bradley laughed. "She's kind of right. Nice to meet you." He shook her hand. "So, you're the one that lives next door, huh? I think my mom has mentioned you." A sly grin crossed his mouth.

"Yeah, but my dad wants to put the house up for sale and move to Montana. He's having some sort of crisis, I think. I don't want to move. I'm tired of moving. Maggie, that's your mom, took me to Chicago for two days to see my mom. We got to miss school. That was awesome. I'm glad you're here. Bradley, your mom misses you. She talks about you all the time. She told my mom and me all about the time you went to Chicago. She told me about the time you got lost at the fair and had trouble reading in school. Your mom helped me read better last summer. I've been wanting to meet you," she spewed without taking a breath. "Last time you were here I was in California. That didn't end so well. It's about time we met."

Bradley grinned and shot me an unnerving stare.

Chloe scooted over to where I stood. She wrapped her arms around my waist and squeezed. "I'm super glad she doesn't have cancer anymore."

"Me, too," Bradley said with a wink.

"Me, three," Glad added.

"Don't forget me," a voice said from the hallway.

My heart skipped a beat. "Hi, John. Come on in. This is my boy, Bradley." I liked how John smiled at Bradley and shook his hand. I liked Bradley's smile even more and manly stature. My boy wasn't a boy anymore.

"I saw Chloe bolt. Thought I should investigate," John said.

Glad snickered. Her eyes sparkled as she scanned the cast of characters. Chloe tugged at the hem of my T-shirt, then beckoned me with a silent finger. I leaned down so she could whisper in my ear.

"Maggie, we should have special dinner with everyone here."

"What a great idea," I whispered back.

Chloe moved closer to my mom. "Special dinner, Glad. What should Maggie make us?" Her eyes darted over to Bradley. "Your mom is a good cook."

Glad set her coffee mug on the counter.

Bradley smiled. "Yeah, we were always the hang out house when I was growing up. Guess nothing's changed."

"Had to keep my eye on you somehow," I said, smiling at my mom.

John stood quietly in the doorway of the kitchen. His arms crossed. His face relaxed, something I hadn't seen in some time.

"You coming to dinner, too?" I asked. He winked. My spine tingled at the glint in his eye. I reminded myself, he was really going to move. "Since Bradley is the guest, let's have him chose dinner."

Bradley chuckled as he rubbed his chin. "I say we should have diner dinner."

Chloe squealed with excitement.

I grimaced at the shrieking.

"I love diner dinner!" she said, flitting over to her dad. "It's all the things that you love. Hot dogs, burgers, French fries, milkshakes."

John's gaze wandered in my direction. "I take it you've had this before."

"Yeah. Maggie made it for me before. Glad helped. Or Glad made it and Maggie helped. I don't actually remember, but I do remember I loved it."

John laughed, his jaw line softer. His muscles filled out the sleeves of his black T-shirt, sexier. I focused my attention back on Bradley. "So what kind of diner dinner do you want?"

"There's more than one kind," Chloe blurted. Her Tiffany hearts on her necklace jangled.

Her dad shushed her and wrapped his arms around her shoulders pulling her backward into his lean body.

Bradley hemmed and hawed. "I think chicken tenders, fries, and double-chocolate peanut butter milkshakes with whipped cream."

My stomach flipped. "Evidently, some things haven't changed." I opened the drawer behind me, grabbed a paper, a pen, and started the shopping list. "I can't believe you're here."

Bones barked and chased his tail in the center of the floor.

Chloe smacked her lips. "I can't wait. What time?"

"How about seven? That gives me time to go to the store and get things ready." I ripped off the shopping list and shoved it in my pocket. "Can someone walk that dog?" I asked, searching for my purse.

"I want to go to the store with you," Chloe said.

"Fine, if it's okay with your dad," I called from the entryway.

"I'll walk the dog," Bradley said.

"I'll go with Bradley," Mom added.

"Chloe, will you get the leash?" I asked with a smile.

She trotted into the kitchen. There was a heavy thud. The sound brought back memories of clunking heads, stitches, and John checking my head.

"I'm okay," she announced.

"Slow down," John scolded.

Chloe scooted past me, went outside, and got into the car.

John was on her heels. He caught my elbow on the porch. "You sure this is okay?"

"She can go to the store with me," I said. John's expression dimmed. "What?" I asked. His warm hand on my elbow was just as inviting as the night he kissed me then led me to the bedroom.

"I don't want to intrude," he replied.

My eyebrow shot up. It was a little late for that. I lowered my voice. "John, it's okay." I wanted to remind him that I thought of him as family. I thought of Chloe as family, for crying-out-loud, I took the girl to Chicago to see her mother while he worked, more like manipulated. "The more the merrier, generally speaking," I added with a wink of my eye.

His expression mimicked my snarky attitude.

"It's fine, really." This time I reached out to him and patted his forearm. "Glad will be disappointed if you don't stay." I leaned in closer to him. "I think she has a crush on you."

He leaned forward. We stood nose-to-nose. "More than her daughter?" he questioned.

His deep green eyes stared through me, I couldn't look away.

Chloe called from the car.

"I have to go," I said. "So are you coming to dinner or not?"

"I'll be here." John's hand caught my elbow as I turned to go. His eyes focused on mine. "I know this isn't the time or the place, but we need to set aside some time to talk."

"Sure," I replied, trotting down the front stairs, running away like the chicken I was. I didn't want to say goodbye. I didn't want him to leave. There was comfort in knowing he was next door. He and Chloe had unexpectedly turned my life upside down after Beckett had broken my heart. I wasn't up to another letdown and somehow John's void would leave a hole unlikely to mend.

Chapter 17

When Chloe and I returned from the market, Bones was sacked out on his bed by my desk. Bradley was in the kitchen removing dishes from the cupboard for dinner. I counted the number of guests twice.

"I think we are five tonight," I said, counting the six milkshake glasses.

"Um, no, there will be six," Bradley corrected me.

He lowered his gaze and checked his phone. "Um, I hope you're not mad, but dad is coming to dinner, too."

Chloe carried in brown paper grocery bags and my mom milled around in the refrigerator trying to help. I moved closer to Bradley.

"What did you just say?" I asked. "It sounded like you said dad was joining us for dinner." My voice was low and barely audible. My reaction saddened Bradley's expression. I swallowed trying to wash away my pride. I'd unintentionally inflicted hurt upon my boy, the flesh and blood that meant the world to me.

"I'm sorry, Mom. I thought it would be okay. You always seem to be okay when we talk about dad." He checked his phone again.

"Is that him?"

Bradley nodded.

"I'm sorry, honey, I haven't seen your dad in months. I didn't mean to be a downer."

Bradley hugged me as Mom strolled by. She stopped to pat Bradley's cheek.

"Get over it. It's one dinner. And you're right, Marjorie Jean, this is about Bradley, not you," she lectured.

Bradley and I stared at each other in dismay.

"Geez," I said under my breath.

"Beckett is harmless," she added.

"I—"

She scowled at me.

Bradley whispered in my ear. "I wouldn't mess with Nana, Mom. We could all go down."

Irritation prickled my nerves and brewed beneath my giggle. Mom didn't have any right to tell me how to behave in my own house, but she was my mom, and that's what she did. I took a deep breath. Bradley patted my back.

"It'll be okay, Mom. I'll protect you. How mad are you?" he asked.

I gave him a bear hug. "I'm not mad at you. I never could be. I'll be fine." I huffed with a soft whine.

Mom's leer questioned my sincerity.

"What? It'll be fine," I said, trying to sound reassuring knowing that Beckett would be sitting at the same table as John. The thought caused my stomach to do somersaults.

"What's this all about?" Chloe asked, dropping the last two bags of groceries on the floor.

"Nothing," I said in sync with my mom.

"At least we agree on that," Mom said.

"Yes, Glad, we do."

"Don't get sassy, young lady," she warned.

Bradley held my shoulders. His caring eyes steadied my nerves. "Thanks, Mom. I knew I could count on you. Now, if you ladies will excuse me."

"Mom, do you want to peel the potatoes?" I asked, pretending everything was *normal*. I knew it was the right thing to do, but damn it. I wanted Bradley all to myself. Didn't I have the right to be a little selfish? I wanted to immerse him in my world and that didn't include Beckett anymore. I handed Mom the bag of spuds.

"You'll be fine," she reassured me. "It's the right thing to do."

"I know." I took the chicken out of the package and cut the breast fillets into strips just the way Bradley liked them. Mom and I worked quietly on the island.

"So when are you going to tell Bradley that you and John are an item?" she asked quietly.

Stunned, I peered into her eyes. "What?"

Mom leaned forward. "Oh come on, it doesn't take a rocket scientist to see that you two are a thing. Does Chloe know?" she whispered, looking around.

"Shush. What has gotten into you?"

"You have, what's the big deal?"

I stacked the slender chicken strips to the side of the cutting board and reached into the bag for another hunk of cold poultry. "There is nothing going on, and we're not discussing this right now," I said under my breath.

"Fine, have it your way. What kind of bird does Bones want for a sister?" she asked through a mischievous grin.

I stopped slicing chicken, tightened my grip on the handle of the knife, and closed my eyes for a brief second. "You are incorrigible."

"Parrots are nice. They will talk to you. My friend Hester had one that said shit before every sentence. Pretty amazing." Mom beamed with pride.

"What do you want to know?"

"Why are you so stubborn about letting the man in? He seems to like you and he's got a cute rear end."

I started laughing. "Oh my God, are you on some new medication that I don't know about?"

"On no, we are not making this about me, Missy," Mom jested.

Mom and I bantered as she peeled and sliced, and I sliced and breaded. "There is nothing going on, and in case you haven't heard, he's putting his house up for sale, selling his practice, and moving to Montana to work with his dad."

"That does sound like a quandary, but I won't believe it until I see it."

Chloe ran in from outside, her hands filled with peonies, a pink satin ribbon tied around the neatly snipped stems.

"Um, where did you get those flowers?" I asked.

"He gave them to me," she said, motioning to the French doors leading to the patio. "Can we eat outside tonight?"

"Sure," I answered.

"I figured I'd better bring a peace offering," Beckett said with a wave. "I think I'm the party crasher tonight."

Chloe handed me the bouquet. The scent washed over me, reminding me how much I loved pink peonies. "They are beautiful." I opened the cupboard and found my favorite Roseville vase on the top shelf, filled it with water, cut off the ribbon, and immersed the stems. "Here, Chloe, can you put these on the kitchen table?" I trusted her to take the flower arrangement.

"Whoa, this is heavy," she said, teetering back and forth.

Beckett took the vase from her. "I'll give you a hand."

"Thanks, Beckett. Is it okay if I call you that, or do you want me to call you Mr. Littleton or Mr. Maggie?" Chloe rambled on with a furrowed brow. "Maggie, what's your last name again?"

"Abernathy," I reminded her as if she didn't know.

"You always did want to keep your name," Beckett said.

For a split second, I thought things might have turned out differently if we'd stayed together and kept his name. Beckett wasn't the only one who wanted out of our marriage, and I needed to remember that, but sometimes the guilt singed my soul like a branding iron. "Bradley's in the den," I said.

Beckett nodded, his brown eyes sincere. His sense of peace gnawed at me. I should have admired his dignity, but instead it irked me. *Damn him.*

Mom wiped her hands off. "You handled that nicely. Now let's see if you can sustain your hospitality."

"You're funny." I sneered at her then let out an evil laugh.

"I'll get the oil going. We're going to need two pots."

"Oil is in the bag," I said.

The clock said a few minutes after six. The mound of chicken strips and fries looked like enough to feed an army. I cleaned off the island while Mom found two large pots in the lower cupboards. We did make a good team.

"Chloe," I called. I waited. No Chloe. "Bradley, can you come set the table?"

Bradley meandered in with Beckett at his side. They discussed Boston and the sights Beckett would have to see when he visited next. When had he visited before? Feeling left out of the loop gnawed at me even more. I hadn't gone to Boston, yet. The urge to stare consumed me.

Mom brushed past me. "Now, now," she whispered. "Hold steady, dear girl.

I arched my eyebrow in her direction as I wiped my hands on the kitchen towel.

Chloe sauntered into the kitchen with Bones. "I hate to be the bearer of bad news, but Bones ate your shoe."

Chloe held up my black patent-leather ballet flat. I took the shoe that dangled from her finger. "Nice." I got down on Bones' level. "Sit," I commanded. "This is very bad. Bad dog. No more chewing." I poked my finger in his face. He tilted his head. Drool dripped from his chops. His eyes kind of resembled Beckett's. I glanced over to Beckett. Yup, he had dog eyes, big, brown, and carefree, not a worry in the world even with a waggling finger of judgment. "Go lie down," I said.

Chloe tugged at my elbow then pointed to the clock. "It's past his dinnertime. Can you really blame him?"

"That doesn't give him the right to chew up my stuff," I reminded her. Chloe shrugged. "Why don't you feed the beast then help Bradley set the table so we can get cooking?" My suggestion made her raise an eyebrow. "Leave the milkshake glasses in here."

"Okay," she said. "Can I put the whipped cream on top when you get to that part?"

"Bradley, is it okay if she puts the whipped cream on?"

"Mom, I'm not seven any more. She can put the whipped cream on the milkshakes." As Bradley picked up the stack of plates, the light hit his sideburns, redder than his strawberry blond hair.

"Hey, I'm eight," Chloe declared.

Beckett took the silverware and Chloe tagged behind with a handful of napkins and the ketchup bottle.

"Let's start frying," Mom said, checking the temperature of the oil with a single french fry.

The creak of the screen door echoed through the foyer and into the kitchen. Bones lifted his head from his feeding bowl long enough to let out a little woof. I purposely didn't make eye contact with my mom who stood beside me frying up mounds of golden fries. She had a magic touch for diner food.

"He's here," she said.

"Stop it."

"Hey, Bones," John said, bending down to pat his rump that swayed from his wagging tail. "What's my job?"

"How do you feel about making milkshakes?" Glad said.

"It's easy. Throw in some ice cream a couple blobs of peanut butter sauce, some milk, and blend away."

I pointed to the counter where everything was neatly organized.

John shrugged. "Sounds easy enough."

"That ice cream is nice and soft, easy to scoop. Have at it," Glad said.

He winked in my direction. A spatter of grease hit my finger. Mom's grin and girlish stare eased the burn.

Chloe ran past. "Hi, Dad. Be right back." Her voice faded into the air after the front door slammed.

John helped Mom carry the food to the table while I grabbed extra napkins, barbeque sauce, salt and pepper, and a can of whipped cream just in case someone needed an extra squirt.

Strategically seated between John and my mom at the dinner table, I hoped no one besides Mom had an inkling about my true feelings for John. Every time I saw the man, it felt like we'd known each other for years. I wondered if there was a divine plan in which all paths would lead me home because the more we were together the more he felt like home.

Chloe stopped everyone before the first bite. "Wait!"

John shot Chloe a look.

"Don't look so worried, Dad. I have a little speech." She cleared her throat. "And it's appropriate." She produced a small box from beneath her cushion that was tied with a rumpled white ribbon. "First of all, I think it is so cool that I get to meet Bradley. I was wondering if you *really* existed. I thought maybe your mom was just making you up. That's beside the point. Anyway." She held out the box in my direction. "This is for you, Maggie. Thank you for taking me to Chicago to see my mom and thanks for not kicking me out of your house when I'm a pest."

The box passed through John's hands then into mine. It rattled as I untied the bow. I knew what was inside, and I smiled. Tears welled at the back of my throat. "It's perfect. Thanks, Chloe." I put on my macaroni necklace with pride. Unlike her mom's, Chloe had dyed my macaroni different shades of blue.

"I tried to make it the color of water. I know how much you love the lake," she said.

I winked at her. She got up. The table tipped and John almost lost his milkshake. Chloe hugged me from behind.

I kissed her hands that were clasped around my neck. The macaroni necklace that Bradley had made me years ago was tucked inside my jewelry box. The pieces splintered over time. The colors faded from wear, but there was something special about dyed macaroni. "This will never go out of style," I told her. Her breath was hot in my ear as she snorted through her giggles. "Maybe we should eat," I said as she gave me one last squeeze.

Beckett's gaze dimmed. All I ever wanted was a child when we were married and he gave me that. Bradley sat next to his dad, different in so many ways, but solemn like his father. Beckett sent a silent message in my direction. He wanted so much more for me and although it took him years to admit his own identity, he had helped me find mine along the way.

Chapter 18

Everyone had gone. Bradley and his dad had ventured off to the jazz café on the hill. I fingered the blue macaroni necklace that Chloe gave me as I swung on the porch swing reading my book. The bag of papers from school had been pushed aside for another time. Bones rested his head on my lap, his eyebrows twitching to the beat of his dreams.

"You can't ignore me forever," John said, coming up the stairs.

"I don't think I've been ignoring you," I said.

Bones lifted his head and inspected my visitor then settled back down with a heavy sigh.

John came closer. He leaned against the stone pillar at the edge of the stairs and crossed his arms.

"What are we going to do?" he asked.

"About what?" I asked, knowing what was on his mind.

He lowered his gaze and his eyes turned dark.

"Fine." I sighed. "I'm not sure what you want from me. You said you were planning on selling your house and moving to Montana, that's not exactly around the block." My heart sank. "Around the block would be better. Way better," I mumbled. "Now you're the one making this difficult."

"It's what I have to do," he said, shifting his weight.

"Then it's a done deal. You're going. I'm staying. Chloe's going and we will say we'll call, but that won't happen because of circumstance. It's like a one-night stand—" My voice broke off. "But way worse," I added, dog-earing the page where I'd left off reading.

"Don't compare us to a one-night stand. This is different."

"Not sure how. We slept together, and now it's over."

"That's the thing, Maggie, I'm not sure I want this to be over."

"We can't always get what we want," I said. "I didn't want cancer and I got that. I didn't want Beckett to be gay and I got that. I didn't want Bradley to move to Boston, but I got that. I didn't want to like Brook, but Chicago changed all that. I didn't want to get close to Chloe and now she's leaving and so are you. It's a world of disappointment, I'm afraid to say. Sometimes I look around and it seems surreal. I'm standing still, stuck in time and the people I care about are fleeing at warp speed," I said. "What do you want from me?"

"I want you to be my friend."

My chest wavered with a gulp of fresh air. "A friend?" John's eyes flickered at my harsh tone. An ugly wedge divided us. "I don't know if I can just be your friend." The words hurt. My heart knocked against my chest walls. Too stubborn to cry, I glared at him. I was too old for this stuff. I scooted over to the corner of the swing when he stepped closer. Bones stirred and leaped down from my lap with a heavy sigh. He had heard enough, too. John took the book out of my hands then pulled me up so we were standing nose-to-nose, the intensity in his eyes like fury.

"Damn it, Maggie." He sighed. "Don't you think I don't know about being on the short end of the stick? I didn't want Brook to leave me for some jet-set career. I didn't want to be a single parent. My job brought me here. It's not where I wanted to be either. The only saving grace was meeting you and that has turned out to be utterly exasperating. And it doesn't matter how hard I try to stay away, I can't."

"What do you want from me?" I asked, staring into his green eyes that darkened with the night horizon.

"There's not one part of you that wants to know what *we* could be?"

John's warm lips grazed mine. The lump in my throat ached. I couldn't see past the three years I'd left in my career. Abernathy's never quit. Abernathy's are self-sufficient, strong, but his kiss melted me to the core.

"I just don't see how a long-distance relationship could ever work." I didn't have the heart to tell him I'd rather be alone than take on such an endeavor. Judy's words rang in my head. I could hear my mother scold me. Judy and Mom would tell me to drop everything and run naked through the fields with this guy, but the thought of John not being close made me ache from head-to-toe. I didn't want to ache.

John leaned back. "I think you're being pigheaded."

"I think you're being unreasonable."

"Jesus, Maggie," he said.

His hands freed mine. And I was alone again even though he stood before me asking for something I craved, but didn't have the guts to go after. "Sorry, John," I whispered, feeling the pools of wetness form at the corners of my eyes.

John wiped my tears away with my thumbs as he held my face. "I know it seems complicated."

I nodded in agreement, ignoring the plea in his eyes. Amazed at the dense darkness that surrounded us, I reminded myself life wasn't about me. A door shut beyond the hedges between our houses. I wiped my eyes and turned my back to John at the sound of Chloe's voice.

John cleared his throat and caught her as she bounded up the stairs. "Let's give Maggie a break," he said. "It's late and you need to get in bed. Besides, I have to work tomorrow."

I forced a thin smile after reaching for my book. "Your dad's right, you both need your rest."

Chloe pouted. "But tonight was so much fun."

"We can do it again some other time," he told her.

Doubt shrouded me. "Night, you two." I picked at my thumbnail, thinking that morning would come soon enough even if I didn't want it to. "Ugh," I muttered.

John shooed Chloe away then touched my elbow. "This doesn't change how I feel and it shouldn't change how you feel either." He lowered his gaze. "Night, Maggie. Have a good day tomorrow with Bradley."

"Thanks," I said, not letting my eyes wander from his face. I opened the screen door and closed it slowly behind me. I turned to see him one more time, but he'd gone. All that was left were deflated dreams, and the sound of John and Chloe's voices drifting by in the night air like strangers.

I locked the door behind me and answered the ringing phone. Judy's voice quivered as she said my name.

"Hi, Judy," I said, trying to get a grip on my own strife.

"Hi, Maggie. I don't mean to bother you on a Saturday night, but do you have a minute?"

I bit my thumbnail off as I listened to her voice tremble. I'd never known anyone like her. She was upbeat, never seemed to get rattled about anything, and could handle two boys like nobody's business. "Sure," I answered.

"Can I come in?" she asked.

"Um, where are you?" I said, peeking out the front window.

"I'm driving around the block. I pulled up before, but you were with John and I didn't want to interrupt. Are you sure it's okay?" she asked a second time.

Unlocking the front door, I answered her. "Um, yeah. You can park in the drive. No one is coming or going," I said matter-of-fact. "That's for sure." I thought about the conversation with John. "I'll see you in a minute."

I stood in the doorway. The lights from her Suburban flashed across the front yard as she drove up. A rabbit darted into the perfectly trimmed hedges. Judy opened the back door of her truck. I smiled at her petit frame against the huge vehicle. She carried a brown paper grocery bag, her face lined with worry as she walked up to my house.

"What's going on?" I invited her inside.

"I didn't know where else to go. Hope you don't mind. I brought some wine. You sure you don't have any plans?" she asked, inspecting my quiet house.

"Just you. Everyone has gone for the evening and Bradley is out with his dad listening to jazz." I closed the door behind her, followed her into the kitchen, then shuffled past her to get two glasses from the cupboard. "We had a family dinner tonight. It was so nice of my mom to fly Bradley in. Chloe and John joined us." I popped the top off the wine. "Beckett was even here, weird."

Judy's face remained stoic. "Sounds fun." she said, pouring the wine.

"Where are the boys?" I asked. They were always together, three peas in a pod, a momma duck with two ducklings in tow at any given time.

"They're with Pink," she answered, taking a long drink.

"Who is Pink?" I asked, never hearing about a friend by that name.

She swallowed and answered with a smirk, "Bill."

"How'd your husband get that nickname?"

"Let's just say he blushes easily. And he'd cringe if you knew that."

I grinned. "Love it." The earthy smell of red wine wafted up my nostrils, relieving the weight John left upon my shoulders. I slid out a stool and sat beside my friend. "So, it's not like you to be driving around the neighborhood with a bottle of wine in your backseat this time of night. What gives?"

Tears formed at the corners of her eyes, and I dreaded what she was about to say.

"What if I have to go through chemo? I don't know if I can do it again." Judy drained her glass then refilled it.

I touched her forearm. "Oh, Judy, you came through this before, you can do it again. What did the doctor say?" I watched as she drank half her glass of wine in one gulp.

"I get the results on Monday."

"We can do this," I reassured her. "What does Pink think?"

She snickered. "I haven't told him yet. I have to get a grip, know the exact prognosis before I drop the bomb. Last time was so rough on him and the boys."

"Do you want me to go with you?" I took a swig of wine trying to mask the lump in my throat.

"I'm so afraid," she answered, gulping for air.

"I'm going with you. What time shall I pick you up?" I asked.

"My appointment is Monday at noon."

I poured myself some more wine. "I'll see you at eleven-thirty. The boys will be at school. Pink will be at work and you and I will go see the doctor." I patted her hand.

"I should have brought two bottles of wine," Judy said, tipping the first one to the side. "This one's almost gone, bummer."

I sipped and studied Judy's profile as her eyes inspected the bottle.

"They're going to tell me I have to have this lump out. It all starts there."

"I know. This really sucks," I muttered, wishing I could take away her angst.

She puffed out her chest. "I'm already flat as a pancake, how much more could they take. The girls in my book club thought I was crazy for not wanting implants after the double mastectomy. What was I going do with those?"

"Tip over?" I joked.

Judy shot me a look then cracked a mischievous smile. We both laughed. "So those things aren't implants?"

She laughed even harder. "No, my petit mounds of prosthetics." She pushed out her chest again.

"Yeah, big boobs wouldn't look good on you."

"I like my tomboyish figure," she said.

"Me, too," I added, holding up my glass to her. "You're perfect just the way you are, and I bet Pink thinks so, too."

"Thanks, Maggie. You're a good friend."

Judy reached over and hugged me. "I love you, Judy. We'll get through this."

"I just hate waiting. I want to know and I want to know now."

Her black curly hair brushed my cheek. The strands were coarse and prickly, so unlike her. "Monday will come soon enough." I closed my eyes and prayed. I couldn't lose her, too.

"Mom," Bradley yelled from the front door. "I'm home."

Judy leaned back and shifted her weight on the stool. I brushed her hair away from her face and caressed her cheek.

"Where are you?" he called.

"In here," I answered, turning to see him as he entered the kitchen. "Did you have a good time?"

"Yeah, and I met some of Dad's friends. Crack-ups."

I smiled. So Beckett had friends. I wondered if they were new friends, how much had he transformed his social circle, and then dropped the thought. I was happy to see him move on. "I'm glad. This is my friend Judy. Judy, this is my one and only son, Bradley."

Bradley shook Judy's hand. Her expression only something I could read, the expression of a woman praying she'd see her sons grow into adults.

"Nice to meet you," Bradley said.

"I've heard a lot about you. Your mom is very proud of your accomplishments."

Bradley smiled. "Thanks."

"I better get going. Pink and the boys will wonder where I am." Judy covered her mouth to yawn.

Bradley put his hands in his pockets. "You don't have to leave on my account."

"Really, I should go. Harry will give Pink a run for his money if I'm not there to help."

Bradley snickered when I glanced in his direction. "Yeah, I remember those days."

"I bet you do. I'll see you Monday," she reminded me.

"I'll walk you out."

"It was nice meeting you," Bradley said. "Have a good night."

"Bye," she replied with a little wave.

Judy and I walked out on the front porch to say our goodbyes. Her eyes darker than night. Her pointer finger shot up as her eyes gleamed with thought. I crossed my arms listening to the stillness that surrounded us.

"Hey, you never told me what you and John were discussing."

"Nothing," I said.

"It didn't look like nothing." She fingered her keys.

With pursed lips, I hesitated. "He wants a long-distance relationship. It's complicated."

"And?" she prompted.

"And I don't know if I want complicated. It sounds exhausting. Montana is a long way away. It's not like I can hop in my car for the weekend."

"Maybe not, but then again, there are probably lots of woman who'd give their eye teeth to meet a man like him, but who am I to judge?" Judy pursed lips and stared at me.

I closed my eyes and let out a groan.

She poked me in the arm. "See you Monday," Judy said. "And just so you know I overheard a mom at the library the other day talking about her child's hot pediatrician.

I opened my eyes with the spur in my side.

"She was gossiping about *your doctor* and all she had were good things to say about him. I want you to know I stayed an extra ten minutes to hear the whole conversation." Judy inspected me from head-to-toe. "You're pretty hot, too, if you'd give yourself a chance."

My ears prickled at her compliment. "Great, would you like to date me? You live a lot closer than Montana."

"Maybe so, but I won't be wearing chaps and a cowboy hat, although Pink would love that. Something to think about."

It was the first smile I'd seen cross her face all evening. I laughed. "See you Monday." Judy strolled down the porch stairs to her oversized Suburban. She climbed in with a little hop and a whole lot of kick ass.

Chapter 19

Mom stood with her back against the counter sipping coffee from her favorite mug.

"How come I never get to come to your house?" I asked, refilling my coffee cup. The scent of hazelnuts woke me up, making me crave chocolate for breakfast.

She cleared her throat. "Well, for starters, you sleep too late on the weekends. I might as well get out and come here. Besides, when we talk about you, you're on your own turf and I think you find comfort in that."

"Nice," I retorted. Her eyes flickered with conquest as she peered over the rim of her ruby red reading glasses. I forced a grin. "Clever."

"That's why I'm the mom," she said.

"Ah, but you forget, I am a mom, too," I reminded her, sipping at my coffee.

"Yes, but your conquest is different."

I waggled my finger at her before reaching into the donut box for another nutty dunker. "Ah, but that's the difference between you and me. I don't view Bradley as a conquest." I bit the donut in half. Like a chipmunk with overzealous ambition, I chewed and chewed and chewed, savoring my breakfast treat. "Yum." I moaned in my mother's direction, tiny crumbs dropped from my mouth.

Mom handed me a rumpled napkin. "Bradley's not my son. You chose your battles. And I'm choosing you. So tell me about this whole John and Montana thing."

I rolled my eyes and swallowed. "Mom, he wants a long-distance relationship. It's not like Montana is next-door or even within driving distance. Don't you think I've thought about this? I don't want him to move, but he feels like this is something he has to do. He's unhappy here."

"So are you. Why don't you just pack up and go, too?"

"Who says I am unhappy?" I ate the other half of my nutty dunker.

"Oh come on, Maggie, your job is a chore for starters. Education has shape-shifted into a monster and it's eating you alive."

"I'll agree with you there, but I started this career and I'm going to finish it. Three years. Just three more years."

"There's no doubt in my mind that you can make it. You have the determination of a bloodhound. The only thing that can stop you when you get going is probably that hunky neighbor of yours. So try your hand at a long distance thing. He's not packing up and leaving tomorrow. By the time he sells and gets organized you'll have another year together under your belt."

"What are you talking about? It's not going to take him a year to get organized. And why is this so important to you?"

"Because I see something that you don't."

"And just what is that?"

"You, happy."

Deflated, I let out a sigh. Was I really that unhappy? I thought about the conversation that Judy overheard at the library. I thought about John and me on the porch. I thought about John in chaps and a cowboy hat. I thought about John and me, rolling around in my bed without a care in the world. I let out another heavy breath of air and put my head down on the counter. "I have to finish my career."

"Fine finish your career, then get on with it. I hear Montana is a lovely place. Every time I see a picture of the wide open Montana blue sky, it makes me want to jump on a horse and ride the open plains."

"Oh, geez."

"Morning," Bradley said. "What's going on in here? Who's going to Montana? Now there's a place I'd like to run away to."

"Thought you loved Boston," I said. "And no one is going to Montana." Mom slid the donut box across the counter in Bradley's direction. "Want a donut?" I asked. "I'll share."

Bradley grabbed a nutty dunker and made it disappear in two bites.

"Your mom's being stubborn. She has the chance of a lifetime."

Bradley sat next to me and nudged the donut box back in front of me. *Good boy*. I smiled and carefully picked my next bite. I nibbled at the end as tiny bits of peanuts dropped in front of me. Mom stared at me through narrow slits.

"So what's the opportunity?" he asked. "Nana, can you pour me a cup of coffee, black?"

"There is no opportunity?" I said, not wanting to discuss my love life with my son, not wanting him to give Beckett the skinny on my personal life, after all he did try to set me up with that designer, Paul Mitchell last summer, but not for the right reasons. He thought I needed to be with someone. I held Mom's gaze.

"What's with the attitude?" she said, refilling her coffee cup. "We're all adults. Bradley can handle this."

Bradley reached for the last donut. "Do I want to know what you two are discussing?"

His questioning eyes stared through me.

"Don't you think your mom deserves to be happy even if it means doing something out of her comfort zone?" Mom asked.

"Still not certain what you two are debating here, but sure, if you have an opportunity take it. You never know when the next one will come along. Montana sounds pretty cool." Bradley finished his donut. "Anyone going to make bacon and pancakes?"

"See, Mom, it's all about the food," I said, patting Bradley on the shoulder.

"I thought I saw bacon in the fridge," he added.

I snickered, thinking bacon and pancakes sounded like a great idea.

"I still say John is great guy. Give it a chance," Mom mumbled, not quite under her breath.

Bradley shot me a look. His eyes brightened with question. "The guy next door with the kid? Really?"

"Her name is Chloe." I tightened the belt on my robe. "Yes, the guy next door." I waited for my son's two cents. Uncomfortable with the silence, I got up, then found the pancake mix and a mixing bowl.

"You sure you want to date someone with a kid?" he asked.

"Silly me, and here I am worrying about distance." The shift in perspective reminded me just how crazy the whole idea was, but it wasn't about Chloe. It was about John and me. Chloe just happened to be in the middle like a rose between two thorns. A blob of batter dripped out of the bowl as I stirred with vigor, gritting my teeth. I liked how things were going with Chloe. Openly dating her father would throw a curveball in her direction, most likely to leave her with a walk to first base where she'd be stranded. "Jesus," I said under my breath.

"How much do you like him?" Bradley asked.

I stopped stirring and threw a handful of raspberries into the mix as I glanced in his direction. "Can we please change the subject?"

"Go ahead," Bradley said. "But it sounds like you have some thinking to do. What do you have to lose?" he asked, scooting his stool back.

The griddle banged against the cupboard door. Mom took the pan from my hand and started the bacon. "Yeah, what do you have to lose?"

"Seriously?" I said. "You two have me packed already, don't you?" I asked, watching the silent interaction between them. "You've already discussed this?"

Bradley shrugged. "Don't get mad at Nana. I was the one that asked her about it after dinner last night. It's kind of obvious."

"It is not," I insisted, avoiding eye contact with Bradley.

"We're not blind, honey. It's pretty obvious," Mom said. "And there's nothing wrong with you wanting to move on."

Her voice was sweet and tender. My guard slipped away, my defenses vulnerable. Oh, how I loathed when she did that to me. Mom came closer, our eyes locked in one of those stares that suggests silent conversation with wicked banter. Mom winked. She was really just trying to help. My mind forwarded to a far off dream. *Shit*, they really did have me packed and ready to go.

I pointed at Bradley. "You should not pick sides. It's not good for your inheritance, young man. I swear when they cremate me you'll have to put me on your mantle and I will haunt you forever." I smirked. It was our private joke. "In a good way of course," I added.

He laughed. "Yeah, right. In a good way."

Mom flipped each piece of bacon. "Bradley's no fool. Now will you just get on with it and get out of your own way," she snapped as she swatted me on the backside.

"Nice," I uttered while cleaning up the griddle for pancakes.

The doorbell rang.

I prepared myself for the invasion of Chloe as Bradley sauntered to the front door. Her voice drifted down the hallway from the foyer and into the kitchen. She said something about mail. Bradley invited her inside.

"Hey, Maggie. Hi, Glad."

Mom gave her a quick squeeze, then Chloe held up three

envelopes. "These are yours. They ended up in our mailbox yesterday by mistake. Silly mailman."

I handed Mom the spatula and took my mail from her. Inspecting the return label, I'd forgotten all about my book submission with the trip to Chicago, John, and the arrival of Bradley. I hadn't been in my library in days. I hadn't touched my cow project. I neglected to check my emails. I read the rejection letter. *Figures.*

"What's the matter?" Bradley asked, coming closer.

"Nothing. Just a rejection."

"*Jection* for what?" Chloe pulled out a stool and inspected the empty donut box. She nibbled at the left over peanut bits. "You guys making breakfast?"

"Yes," I said, buttering up the pan. "Who is watching you today?" I asked, ignoring her first question.

"Some girl dad got from a friend," Chloe answered.

"Didn't you eat breakfast?"

"Does cereal count?"

"Yes."

"She wouldn't let me have anything else. She said she doesn't do dishes," Chloe answered with a wrinkled chin worse than Bones'.

"Does she know where you are?" Bradley sipped his coffee and stared at her. "Chloe?"

"Kind of. I told her I was going to return your mail and that I'd be right back. Dad told me to let you guys have some time together." She looked over to Bradley. "You should stay longer so you and me can hang out, too."

Bradley cracked a smile. "I don't mind. It's all good. We're just hanging out."

"That's what I said," Chloe added. "Great minds think alike. That's what my dad says."

Mom chuckled.

There was a knock at the door.

"I'll go," I said, taking the mail with me. "Let's go, Chloe."

Chloe got up and skulked behind me. "You're really not going to send me back there. She's boring. B-O-R-I-N-G."

"That's not the point."

A tall blond stood at my front door. She appeared to be nice enough.

"Hi there, I'm Maggie. Are you looking for Chloe?"

She chuckled as she shoved her phone in her pocket. When she looked up, the grin left her face. "Hi, I'm Marlow. I'm watching Chloe today." She peered past me with authority.

Chloe stood like a Muppet beside me. She drooped from head-to-toe.

"You know what your dad said. You're supposed to stay home today. He gave us strict instructions. You have chores and homework."

"Oh, boy," I said.

"I'm hungry." Chloe stuck out her bottom lip. "Can I please just have a pancake? Will you make me pancakes if I come home? I promise I'll do whatever I'm supposed to do, but I just want some more breakfast."

Marlow shifted her weight as I opened the screen door to see her better. She couldn't have been more than twenty. Her skinny physique told me she wasn't about food. Her long blond hair was curled perfectly, but her skin was pale as alabaster china. Chloe shot me a look. Trying to stay out of trouble myself, I stood silent between the two. Marlow's huff could have cleared a room. She inspected me and not in a friendly way.

"Come on, Chloe, we don't have time for this," she said.

Her prickly voice irritated me. I wondered what she did have time for.

"I don't cook. I'm only here as a favor to my mom. Your dad is supposed to be a catch," Marlow explained.

I pursed my lips trying to keep calm. Chloe scooted in front of me and stood with her hands on hips ready for battle.

"Well," I said, "what do we say that Chloe stays for breakfast and then she'll be home? And in the meantime, you can do whatever it is that she's interrupting." Marlow glanced over her shoulder. Her impatience grew so I joined her on the porch to see what the issue was. A red Subaru was parked in John's driveway. Chloe held the screen door open behind me.

"Who are you anyway?" Marlow asked.

I didn't care for her abrupt tone. "Chloe, can you go ask Glad how much longer until breakfast?"

Chloe nodded, her eyes unsettled.

I assumed she sensed my irritation. "Let's just say," I continued, "I'm someone who cares. We can do this the easy way or the hard way. You choose, Marlow. Like you, I don't have time for this," I said, not wavering. "Chloe can stay for breakfast. When she is done, I'll make sure she comes home." I paused, peering over to the red car in John's driveway. "She will do her chores and her work." I waited for Marlow to respond. She twirled the ends of her hair and glanced toward John's house. "I take it you're not from the babysitting agency." She crinkled up her forehead. "Nice," I muttered, wondering who set this arrangement up.

"Um, no. Like I said before, in case you didn't hear me, I'm doing this as a favor for my mom. She thinks that kid's dad is hot. I don't see what the big deal is."

Crossing my arms over my chest, I took a deep breath. "When you take responsibility like babysitting, regardless of the circumstances, it is a big deal," I lectured in a soft voice, trying to convince myself John had no clue about the girl's mother. First, Judy hears a conversation at the library about John, and now this? "I'm going to go eat my breakfast with my family and Chloe. When she is done, I'll bring her home and maybe that red car will be gone and the person slouching in the front seat trying to be invisible will be gone, too. Chloe will do her work, chores, whatever, sit around, give you a hard time and when her dad gets home, you will get paid and go home to resume your social life."

Marlow rolled her eyes at me.

I arched my eyebrow. *Shit.* And I was trying so hard to be good. I took a deep breath.

Chloe yelled from the foyer, "Glad says breakfast is ready now."

"It's time for me to go. Are we straight?" I asked, stepping back reaching for the door.

Marlow rolled her eyes again. "Yeah," she said in disgust.

The smell of bacon and pancakes tickled my nose just as Chloe popped out from behind my library doors.

"Thanks, Maggie. I knew I could count on you," she said, hugging my waist.

"Yeah, well, this could bode badly for both of us," I whispered.

Chapter 20

Bradley finished off his first stack of pancakes just as Glad put a fresh batch on the table. "So, Mom, what was that rejection letter all about?"

"Just a cockamamie idea I had. I submitted my cow photos thinking they would be published in a children's picture book." I soaked up the rest of the syrup with my last bite of pancake and shoveled it in my mouth. "Evidently, I see more merit in my work than the publishing house."

"Your cow photographs? I like them," Chloe said.

"Me, too," Mom added.

Bradley scratched his head. "So try another publisher. I heard it could take years to get something published."

"You guys are just being nice," I said, reaching for another pancake. "Great pancakes today."

"De-lish!" Chloe said, elongating each syllable. "I'll help with the dishes."

I raised my eyebrows with surprise.

Bradley chuckled.

"Interesting," I muttered. "What do you have up your sleeve now?"

Chloe scrunched up her nose. "I'm not sure what you mean about having something up my sleeve, but I just thought I should help after you saved me from Marlow. She's not very nice."

"You're right about that, little girl." I wasn't sure what irked me more. The fact that Marlow didn't want to watch Chloe or the fact that her scheming mother was deviously checking John out. Mom sat down across from me, her eyes inspecting my every breath, move, reaction, her smirk said, *I told you so.*

Chloe flipped her hair back. Her Tiffany necklace swung across her chest. I'd forgotten about Brook's photographer, Fletcher Thompson. Maybe he'd have a lead for my cow photos. It wouldn't hurt to contact him. He was overly flirty though and that made me uneasy. I hemmed and hawed silently as Chloe watched Bradley eat, her battery of questions amused all of us especially when she asked Bradley what it was like to live with me. Bradley took her in stride like a true champion. Finally, with a sigh, she ate her last bite of bacon and leaned back in her chair.

"You really should stay longer." Chloe eyed Bradley. "I'm just getting to know you. You have a cool mom. You should have heard her with my babysitter. Man, she should be a lawyer or something, but I bet you know that already."

Bradley smiled and finished the food on his plate. "Yeah, I know." He raised his eyebrows at Chloe and gave her a thumbs-up. "She can be tough. Let's just say I didn't get away with much."

I smiled, leaned back, and took a deep breath. "Well, I'd say that was another successful meal thanks to Nana." I liked having Mom around even if we got under each other's skin at times. I could always count on her to be there. I could always count on her to keep the moment lively.

I kept my word with Marlow. As soon as breakfast was over, I escorted Chloe back to her house. Looking forward to a quiet afternoon with Bradley I waited for Chloe to go inside. She tugged at the side door, but it was locked. The red Subaru was gone and the front door shut. "Does your dad still have a spare key in the garage?" I asked.

Chloe sped over and punched the code into the small white box on the outside of the garage. She scooted under the door as soon as it was high enough for her to slip under, her dexterity that of a cat burglar. She scooted back out before the door was halfway open. I held the side door to the house open while she maneuvered the lock. I waited in the kitchen as she ran through the house calling for Marlow, but there was no answer.

Chloe sauntered back in. "She's not here," she said, scratching her head. "I wonder when she'll be back."

I sighed. "Yeah, I don't think she's coming back."

"That wasn't very nice of her to go without leaving a note." Chloe opened the refrigerator door. "Can I have a juice box?"

I shrugged. "I guess so. Now what? You can't stay here by yourself. Your dad is not going to be happy about this."

Chloe slurped the juice from a plastic pouch. "Oh well," she said, taking a breath. "Now what?"

"What chores do you have?" I searched the counter for some kind of note from John to the babysitter.

"I'm supposed to clean my room up and do my homework."

"Let's go," I said. "I'll help you do your room then you're going to get your homework, all of it, and come back over to my house."

"You should charge my dad."

"Yeah, I should," I replied with raised eyebrow. I called Bradley to tell him I'd be back after I helped straighten Chloe's room then followed Chloe upstairs. Her room was actually organized. "Wow, you're way neater than Bradley." I casually inspected her things, the nooks and crannies, the bubble gum wrapper left on her desk next to an open book. I smiled, glad to see that she'd been reading. John's presence hung in the air. He kept her safe and gave her the things she needed. Being immersed in their lives consumed me with peaceful awe. I wondered if Chloe felt this way when she came to my house. Photos of her, her mother, and her father decorated the bookshelves.

How did I fit into all of it? Was I *meant* to fit in?

I thought about the kids at school with stepparents, the kids I'd known with so-called uncles and live-in boyfriends and girlfriends, the kids who thought they were really brother and sister because their parents had moved in together. It was all so confusing to me, mystifying how people could morph into families without hesitation.

Chloe made her bed. Not great, but she did it. She picked up her clothes and put them down the laundry chute in the bathroom. "Is this your bathroom?" I asked, examining all the hair ties and wadded up purple pajamas in the corner.

"Yup."

"Wow, you're lucky to have your own bathroom. Maybe you could do something about that pile of dirty clothes. It might win you some brownie points with your dad." I pointed to the mound of jammies in the corner. She shoved the pile down the chute then picked up around the sink. Her effort pleased me.

"I have to do a couple more things in my room," she said, switching off the bathroom light.

I sat on Chloe's bed while she sat on the floor sorting through a pile of papers. She slid out a plastic storage bin from under her bed, the outside covered in an array of stickers. She carefully made a neat stack after scrutinizing each paper. "Is that schoolwork?"

"Yeah, I'm saving the good ones to remind myself that I'm not always dumb. Plus, I figure it makes me look good when mom visits. If she visits."

"You're not dumb. I wish you wouldn't say things like that," I said, even though I knew the feeling and suspected we all felt inadequate from time-to-time.

"Fine." Chloe didn't appear to be convinced. "Let's just say these remind me of the good days. Look, a B-plus on my math test."

Her eyes sparkled at the accomplishment. "Very nice. Where'd you get all those stickers?" I fingered the one that said Sleeping Bear Dunes, remembering family vacations in the baby-blue Ford station wagon.

"These are some of the places I've been with my mom and my dad when they were together. Some of the places I don't remember because I was a baby, but dad gave them to me anyway. He said I should know where I've gone in this world even if I don't remember."

"You've been to Paris? I see the Eiffel Tower here."

"No. Mom's been there with Dad. He always says that's where I came from. Not sure what he means, but I sure would like to go and see what it's all about."

Chloe's hair fell forward as she kneeled over the box to pack her stuff inside. I knew she'd figure out how she came from Paris later on in life. She was bold like a Parisian, not afraid of herself, full of life.

Chloe pointed to a big round sticker with a horse and a mountain. The word "Montana" was scrawled across the bright blue sky. "That's my grandpa's state. I guess I went to Montana, but Mom didn't like it. I can't imagine not liking horses."

Chloe peered up at me with sad eyes. I knelt down beside her then handed her the rest of her papers to put in the box.

"I don't want to go. I don't want to leave you, Maggie."

I brushed the hair out of her face with my fingers and tucked it behind her ears. Her cheeks baby soft and rosy. *I don't want you to leave me either.* "I know how you feel."

"Dad says we're going to see Grandpa together when school gets out."

"Sounds like fun."

Chloe's green eyes sparkled as sun streamed through her bedroom window. She had her daddy's eyes. A river of sadness washed over me.

Chloe snapped the lid back on the storage container and gave it a shove, hiding it back under the bed. She got up and grabbed a hair tie off her nightstand. I watched her pull her hair back and twist the orange sparkling elastic tie around a messy ponytail. Her Tiffany necklace dangled around her neck.

"You know what would be super cool?" she asked with a toothy grin.

"What?" I said, getting up off the floor with a grimace.

She reached out to help me. "Wouldn't it be super cool if you came to Montana with us?"

Her hand was warm on my forearm, her touch gentle and caring, her thought a whim like that of an eight-year-old child who believes in magic.

I smiled and ruffled her ponytail. "Just like a horse's," I said. "When you ride this will bounce and sway, and you'll feel free. You'll be a real cowgirl."

Chloe laughed. The corners of her eyes crinkled. "I wish you could come with us."

Me, too. I touched the tip of her nose with my pointer finger as I kept my secret wishes hidden beneath my stoic façade.

"How's my room look?" she asked, putting her hands on her hips.

I nodded. "Pretty good. How about you get your homework and let's go." I followed Chloe into the hallway. She went into a room that appeared to be an office. John's diplomas and certificates hung neatly on the neutral colored walls. There were some boxes stacked in the corner. Freshly packed or lingering leftovers from their move in almost a year ago littered the floor. Chloe opened a closet door and rummaged to the back. I watched curiously as she pulled out her book bag. Voodoo's string dangled from the half-open zipper. "Is that where you keep your backpack?"

"I didn't want Marlow to find it. I really wasn't planning on doing my homework," she admitted.

"Figured that."

"I knew she wouldn't look in here. This is Dad's room although she was pretty nosey."

I leaned closer to see his bachelor's degree from Michigan State University. I wondered how a Montana boy ended up there, but then again there was lots I didn't know about John except he had roped, tied, and harnessed me with his green eyes, vivacious daughter, and clever banter.

Black-and-white photos caught my eye. A strange presence urged me to pick them up. A boy in an over-sized cowboy hat sat in front of a burly man on a tall horse, his grin all too familiar. Goosebumps covered my arms. I carefully scanned the next few photos trying not to leave any evidence they'd been touched. Chloe stood beside me studying the images, too.

"Aren't those cool? That's my dad and my grandpa." She took the pictures out of my hands.

I let her. I staked no claim.

"Don't worry, my dad lets me look at these. Check this one out." She dug to the middle of the pile.

I leaned down to get a better look. A boy in a white T-shirt was looking into the camera as if caught off guard. The pitchfork was twice his size, and his face smudged with what I wanted to believe was dirt even though he was mucking out a horse stall.

"Yuck, that's horse poop." Chloe cringed. "Stinky."

"Really?" As I eagerly waited to see the stack of photos of John in his youth, my insides begged for more. I was being drawn into the period of time that shaped the man reining in my heart. Chloe's fingers searched the pile as if she had their order memorized.

She produced a picture of John sitting on his mother's lap on a boulder in front of a house. Her smile was kind, her hair windblown, her arms wrapped around her boy with pride. "She's pretty."

"That's my grandma. I never knew her. Daddy says she was the best woman in the world."

"I bet she was," I said. A shiver ran up my spine.

"Here you can look at the rest of them."

I took the stack, flipped to one more picture of John and his dad riding side-by-side. John looked to be a teenager, a skinnier version of his dad with less bristle, but just as much brawn. I straightened the pile of photos on the shelf then followed Chloe out of the room.

"We should get going. I don't want to spend all day dinking around with this stuff. I want to play." She nudged me out of the John's office. "Dad said he'd take me for a ride on his Harley if I did what I was told." She stopped in her tracks. A flash of worry crossed her brow. "But if there's no babysitter here when he gets here, I wonder if he'll hold that against me?"

"I'll vouch for you," I said. "It wasn't your fault."

"This time," she muttered.

Chloe hopped down the stairs, her backpack bumping each step. Voodoo's head popped out. The black stitched eye that my mom sewed on last summer winked at me. Her voice whispered to me even though she was back home with Bradley, yucking it up, no doubt discussing me with my grown son, her message loud and clear.

Chapter 21

Studying my cow photographs, I picked up the rejection letter and mulled it over one more time. Too afraid to check my email, I shut the laptop and sat down in my chair. Pretty soon I wouldn't have a thumbnail left. Fletcher Thompson said I could contact him. Did he really mean it? Would he even remember me from Brook's shoot in Chicago? I flipped up the top of my Mac to access my email willing to give it a shot. What did I have to lose?

"Hey, Mom," Bradley called from the kitchen. "I'm going to order a pizza. Want anything special?"

"No, order what you want. Get enough for all of us." When I looked up, he was standing in the doorway, munching on cookies and watching me. "Sorry, I forgot about lunch, I'm a little sidetracked."

"I can see that," he said, joining me at my desk.

"Where's my girl, Chloe?" I asked, rearranging the pictures.

"She's in the backyard with Nana. They're playing with Bones. That dog is so cool."

I glanced back at the computer screen. It was two o'clock. "I should check to see if her homework is done."

"You sure do spend a lot of time with her," Bradley said, picking up the *Fourth of July* cows. "These are really neat."

"Thanks.

"Why do you do it?"

"Because I love photography and hand coloring photographs is fun, keeps my mind intact, a distraction from worry and things that depress me."

Bradley sat down in the leather chair near the window. He propped his feet up on the ottoman and sighed. "I meant, why do you spend so much time with Chloe?" He brushed cookie crumbs from his belly.

"Does that bother you?" I leaned back in my chair and took off my glasses.

"No. I just wondered. I mean, I'm finally out of your hair and you can be free, do whatever you want after spending all day almost every day with kids. I don't know. I thought you might be tired of children."

I leaned back then saved my message to Fletcher Thompson before closing the top to my computer, again. "I really like Chloe. A lot." *I more than liked her.* "And for the record, I'm not tired of children, just all the other stuff. You know what I mean."

"You're not doing it because of John, are you?"

Bradley's stare met mine.

"Nope," I said.

"And you're not lying to me?"

"Nope. She came barreling into my life and has grown on me like nobody's business." I smiled at him. "But no one could take your place." His eyes twinkled after hearing my words. "Ever."

"Thanks, Mom. I just want you to be happy. It's your turn." He put his hands behind his head and leaned back.

"Thanks, honey."

"You really like John, don't you?" Bradley asked, taking a deep breath and sinking deeper into the chair with closed eyes.

Holding my breath and resting my elbows on the desk, I leaned against clasped hands. I didn't respond. The curves of John's face were etched in my mind, his kiss, and how natural it seemed to be around him. Bradley opened his eyes then checked his phone.

"If you don't want to talk about it, it's okay."

Words didn't come right away, only a heavy sigh. "Maybe I do," I whispered. Bradley's expression brightened. "It's all too complicated," I added.

"So work it out or at least try. What do you have to lose?"

He stared through me. A laundry list of consequences and dismay reeled freely through my brain.

"Don't look at me like that. That's what you'd tell me," he said as he sat up, stretched, and checked his phone once more.

"What time is your flight in the morning?" I asked, changing the subject.

"Ten. I'll call for a taxi today."

"No need. I'm not going to work tomorrow. I can drop you off." I fiddled with the pile of bills on the edge of my desk. Highway robbery, we were all being held hostage nowadays. "You doing okay with money?" I asked, making eye contact. Bradley was never one to ask for help even when he should.

"Yup, I'm making enough to pay the bills and save a little."

"I like to hear that, but if you ever need a hand, I'm here and I'm sure your dad would help you out."

Bradley grinned. "He and I already had this conversation. You guys are funny. I want to do it on my own."

"But, if you need something, please ask. I'd be happy to help my baby out."

His cheeks brightened and his silly toothy grin reminded me off his younger years. He was still my baby, even if he stood taller, lived on the East Coast, and was an adult.

"I know." Bradley scooted up and out of the chair. "And Chloe's right. I do have a pretty cool mom."

"I'm your number one fan and always will be, even if you did move far away," I reminded him.

"Come visit. Dad's coming in June," he said. "I'd like the company. You can see where I work and meet some of my friends. Last summer you were out of commission, but there's no excuse now."

"That would be lovely," I replied, thinking back to a summer of radiation and the fight to beat cancer. The little black tats would always be there to remind me. "I'm in. I'll start looking for a flight soon and let you know what I find."

"I'm going to get the pizza." Bradley shook the car keys in his pocket and kissed me on the forehead.

My stomach rumbled glad that he was taking care of me today. "Excellent. I'm starving." I stood up and stretched, ready to go see what Chloe, my mom, and Bones were up to. "Thanks for getting the pizza, Bradley."

"No worries. Sorry about the cookie crumbs on the floor. Guess some things never change."

Bradley wrapped his arms around me then gave a squeeze. His bristly cheeks rubbed my face and it tickled. I breathed him in and remembered a time when I was the one who nuzzled him close. His arms swallowed me whole as I leaned against his warm body. "No worries. Bones will get them."

"I love you, Momma," he whispered.

I swallowed away emotion. "I love you too, Pooh Bear." I hadn't called him that in years. I held him tight. "I love you to the moon and back."

He chuckled. "Me too, Mom."

I stood on the front porch as he backed the car out of the driveway. It seemed eons ago that he was the little boy who used to sit in my sedan for hours and pretend he was driving. If he wasn't going to the store, he was trekking across country in his dreams and all without leaving the driveway, funny how things had changed. Time was a magician in its own right.

A crash from the kitchen made me jump. I hustled to see what was going on. Visions of blood or someone passed out panicked me. Contemplating the worst came easily for me. Bones stood next to my mother who sat on the floor in a pile of broken dishes. Rushing over, I caught my breath. "Sit still, let me get the sharp pieces up before you move. Are you okay? What happened?" Blood trickled down her left hand. Her eyes focused on my face, her brow creased.

"I was getting the dishes out for lunch. I guess I can't reach as high as I used to."

She held out her hand. I grabbed a dishtowel from the counter above her head. Chloe ran in from outside. "Stay there, I don't want you to get hurt," I told her. "Hand me the trashcan from under that counter." I pointed to the cupboard then focused on Mom. "Does anything hurt? Do you think you can get up?"

"My butt hurts. I fell smack dab on my butt."

I wiped the blood from her hand to see the cut. It didn't seem too bad. "Chloe, can you go in the bathroom and get me a warm wet wash cloth?"

Chloe trotted off without saying a word.

I picked up the two plates that didn't break and set them on the counter. Then I collected the large chunks of everyday china and pitched them into the trashcan. "Just stay put for a second." I tossed the bloodstained dishtowel on the counter as Chloe handed me a fresh warm cloth. Bending down, I knelt in front of Mom. Her dazed eyes thanked me. "Let me see that hand again." I wiped the cut clean. "I think a regular bandage will do fine. No stitches for you."

Bones gave a little woof.

I stared at him. "What did you do?" I scolded him as he tipped his head with sorrow.

"He didn't do anything. It was all me. Getting a little clumsy in my years," Mom said. "He was just making sure I was okay. Good dog," she praised, patting his head.

I stood, grabbed Mom's hands, and helped her up. She groaned as she got on her feet. "Are you sure you're okay?"

I asked, not wanting anything to be wrong with her. With Bradley home, it just reminded me of how we were all getting older.

"I'm fine," she muttered. "I can't believe I did that. I'm sorry about the dishes," she said, her eyes rimmed with disappointment.

"We can replace the dishes any old day, but we can't replace you." I patted her hand.

"That's for sure." Chloe held her arms out toward my mom wanting a hug.

I unhooked my arm from Mom's. "Can you help her to a chair at the table?" I asked Chloe.

Chloe nodded, her eyes serious with concern. Her usual free spirited self stepped aside in the moment. She held my mom by the elbow and escorted her slowly to the table. Mom rubbed her tailbone. I swept up the last chards as Bradley returned.

"What happened?" he asked, stopping abruptly.

Mom smiled sheepishly. "I did," she said in disgust.

Bradley put the pizza on the counter. "You okay, Nana?"

"Yeah, yeah, yeah," she sputtered.

I looked over to her. "We all have our days. I'm just glad you're not hurt."

Bones sat at Chloe's feet, his tail wagging.

I retrieved a stack of paper plates from the pantry. "Nothing fancy, but I think these will do the job," I said, closing the closet door.

Bradley set some napkins next to the pizza. Chloe leaned over as he opened the box. She closed her eyes and took a deep breath. Bradley snickered.

I handed him a plate. "Looks good."

"Smells divine," Chloe added.

"Where did you hear that?" I asked, handing her a plate, next.

"On television. I think it sounds better coming from the lady in high heels." She eyed the pizza. "This is a hard choice. The piece with the bubble or the piece with extra pepperoni?"

I served Mom pizza. Appearing deflated, she leaned back in her chair. "Thanks, Marjorie Jean."

I raised an eyebrow in her direction. She didn't seem to have lost the edge to her middle naming routine. "Sure thing, Glad," I responded. "You okay?" She rolled her eyes at me. I went to the cupboard and got her some pain reliever. "Take this. It might help."

"What a klutz."

Chloe patted her arm. "I know how you feel. Look at all the klutzy stuff I do. Remember when I split Maggie's head open?"

Bradley's interest piqued as he sat on the opposite side of the table. "Really?" he asked.

"Really," Chloe interjected. "It was ugly, blood, guts, stitches."

"There were no guts," I said under my breath. "Just some stitches and a mongo headache."

Chloe shrugged. "It sounds better when I say there were guts."

Mom smirked, and I knew she'd be okay. Her ego was bruised more than her body.

"That was something," Mom said.

"Check this out." I brushed my hair back away from my face so Bradley could see. "Got the battle scar to prove it." He inspected my left temple.

"Looks like a *doozy*, Mom."

Chloe laughed. "You use the craziest words sometimes. I love it. Glad say something funny because you have crazy words, too."

Mom bit off a hunk of pizza. Her eyes focused on Chloe. "Kill two birds with one stone."

"That's what I'm talking about. How does that even happen?" Chloe shook her head. "What's that mean?" she asked, cocking her head like Bones who inched closer to her searching for a nibble of pizza.

"You know get two things done at one time," Mom explained.

"Who would be in that much of a hurry?" Chloe said. "Not me." She chewed, and chewed, and chewed, then smacked her lips together. "This pizza is yummy."

Bradley smiled. "Glad you like it. So your babysitter really left while you were over here eating breakfast?" he asked.

Chloe sighed. "Yeah, she was a weirdo. She said something about her mom wanting her to babysit so she could meet my dad. Who does that?"

Mom's bright glance laced with discerning intent sent shivers down my spine. Her message unveiled, letting me know not to drag my feet where John was concerned.

Bradley leaned back. "Sounds desperate to me."

Chloe tilted her head. I grinned, keeping my mouth zipped. I winked in his direction. Mom smiled, too. I gobbled up my pizza and got up for seconds. "Anybody want more?" As I turned to serve up the requests for more slices, John appeared in the kitchen doorway.

"Daddy!" Chloe's squeal startled Bradley.

John bent down and kissed her on the cheek then rumpled her hair. "Hi, kiddo. The house was abandoned so I figured you were here," he said, glancing my way.

"It wasn't my fault this time. Really. Ask Maggie."

I arched my eyebrow. "She's right. Marlow had her own agenda, and it didn't include watching Chloe," I said. "Have some pizza."

"I would love a piece. It's been a long day and I'm starving."

Bradley's eyes followed John as he entered the room

then he glanced over to me. His approving smile eased my nerves as I thought about mingling families.

"You can tell me about Marlow later," John said to Chloe.

John glanced in my direction. I shrugged and bit off the end of a fresh slice of pizza. "What can I say? There's more to the story, but we can chat later."

"Can I still go for a ride on the Harley? I did my chores and Maggie made me do my homework."

John's eyes connected with mine. "She's right. I witnessed it with my own eyes. You'll just have to see if it's up to your expectations." I fiddled with my napkin.

"I did my best, Dad, really."

Bones barked and nudged Chloe's thigh with his nose.

She dropped him a bit of crust. "There you go, boy." Then she picked off a hunk of cheese. "Watch this," she said, staring into Bones' pathetic eyes. "Sit, down," she said. "Roll over," she commanded.

Bones rolled over then stayed put, lying beside her. We all watched as Chloe dropped the cheese just above his nose. With one bite, he snatched the morsel from midair and licked his chops. Mom gave a little clap then rubbed her tailbone.

"Cool," Bradley said.

"You two are a couple of tricksters," I said, watching John get situated on a stool at the counter, next to the pizza boxes.

"Well, can I, Dad?"

"Let me check out your room and check over your homework, then we can go," he answered.

"Where you going?" Bradley asked.

"I don't know. Maybe to get ice cream." Chloe flashed a toothy smile. "I have my own helmet and everything."

"Really?" Bradley questioned.

John swallowed and dabbed his mouth with a napkin. "Yup, I have a Softail Classic, sunset orange. You should come over and check it out."

"I'd look good riding that," Bradley said, puffing out his chest. "Mom would kill me if I got a motorcycle. First, I couldn't have a dog as kid, then she nixed the whole motorcycle thing." He pretended to pout. "Deprived, is all I can say."

"I feel so bad for you." I glanced over to Mom who was a quiet bystander during all the conversation. "You okay?"

A flash of concern crossed John's face.

"She had a little fall getting some dishes out of the cupboard. She landed on her tailbone."

"I can check you out," John offered, but I'm not sure there's much I can do. Only an x-ray will show if it's broken and even then there's not much to do for that."

"I'll be fine. My ego hurts more than my rear end."

"Maybe you should get it checked out," he suggested.

"We'll see. Maggie gave me some pain reliever. I'm sure it's nothing," Mom said.

Chloe shoved the rest of her pizza in her mouth. With bloated cheeks, she started to talk. John put his hand up as she mumbled. "Swallow first and next time don't put so much in your mouth," he said, standing up with an empty plate.

I pointed to the trashcan imagining John in leather chaps, riding a horse. "It's in there." I pointed to the cupboard next to where he stood.

Chloe hopped up then pushed her chair in. "Thanks for the pizza, Bradley. It hit the spot," she said, chuckling. "That's something Glad would say. Just cracks me up." She skipped over and threw her plate away.

John raised his eyebrow at her manners.

"Thanks again for rescuing me from Marlow," Chloe said as she twirled her finger next to her right temple. "She was a little crazy. If you ask me."

"Hope your room meets the standards," I said.

"Me, too," Bradley said. "You are so lucky."

Chloe gave my mom a peck on the cheek. "Hope you feel

better. Remember, *some days the bear gets you* or something like that," she said. "Is that right, Maggie?"

"Pretty much," I said.

Mom smiled and patted Chloe's arm. "You are so right."

"Come on, Dad, let's ride!" Chloe howled, pretending to rev the engine with her two hands placed firmly on the make-believe handlebars.

Bradley grabbed another piece of pizza from the box after throwing his plate away. "Maybe my mom can go for a ride when you get back," he suggested with a grin.

"What do you think, Chloe?" John raised a mischievous eyebrow.

Chloe grinned in agreement. "She would like it."

I shot Bradley a look, thanking him for offering up the crazy idea.

Chloe scratched her chin as she sized me up.

Bradley's sinister grin amused me.

"You're welcome. Any time, Mom."

Chapter 22

Tapping the send button, I hadn't bargained for such a speedy reply. Fletcher Thompson's response made me uneasy. I blinked as I read it. "Are you kidding me?" I mumbled to myself. I shouldn't have accepted the jewelry from the shoot with Brook, but I had no idea it would spur such a crazy invitation. I closed the email and sat back in my chair. He requested to see my work and attached an invitation to Los Angeles. Intriguing as it was, I questioned his motivation to befriend me.

Bradley's flight departed on time and now it was time to get Judy to the doctor. I closed the laptop, picked up my purse, and left the house. With Bradley gone, my house seemed empty. While here, his presence comforted me, made the old days seem not so long ago. Vivid memories flooded my mind and kissed me with sweet surprise as thoughts of Judy's appointment crept into my mind. My heart pinched in my chest for her, for me. It could be me.

Adjusting the rearview mirror, I told myself not to look back. School would be over soon enough and Sundays would have new meaning, at least for a while. Judy waited on her porch and smiled as if nothing was wrong. Her dark curly hair reflected the welcome sunshine, her bounce the sign of a woman willing to persevere.

I met her gaze and smiled back as she opened the door to get in. "Hey there," I said, gripping the wheel trying to calm the waves in my stomach.

"Let's go," Judy muttered, buckling her seatbelt. "Thanks for going with me today."

"No worries. I wouldn't think of being anywhere else." I glanced over at her. Her jaw twitched as she clenched her lips and stared out the window. "What are you expecting today?" I asked, muting the radio.

"I've had the mammogram. The doctor has seen it. I'm not sure what they'll tell me."

I took a deep breath. "Well, whatever happens, I'm here."

Judy wiggled in her seat and tucked her purse into her lap. Her white knuckles gripped the leather straps. I prayed.

"Turn here," Judy said, pointing to the entranceway to the cancer center.

I glanced over to her. The pit in my stomach ached.

"I forgot, you know the way," she whispered.

"It's okay." I hadn't been here since my radiation ended. I wasn't due to see Dr. Withers, my radiation oncologist, until June for a check-up. I swallowed and gave Judy a little smile trying to lighten the moment. I thought about the cane that they'd found that first day of radiation with my dad's name on it that now hung in my house. His spirit got me through the fight and I pondered who Judy's guardian angel was and how they were connected. I knew it was time to take down the pink ribbon on my front door and pass it along to her.

Judy signed in. I sat away from the other patients. My breath caught in my throat. My stomach flip-flopped when a hunched over woman scooted by. Her walker clanked with each step and the black scarf tied around her head reminded me of Harriet Tubman. Her tired eyes focused on the path to the elevator as her husband held her elbow. I dug in my purse pretending to search for something. I scolded myself for not being stronger as worry scraped at the bottom my belly. Judy sat beside me.

"You look about as comfortable as I feel," she said.

"It's that obvious," I whispered, connecting with her stare. "I'm sorry."

"Don't be sorry. I never thought I'd be back here for this."

Zipping up my purse, I tucked it down beside me, and took a deep breath. I said another prayer. "I don't want you to be here. You need to be at home baking cookies for the boys while they're at school. You need to be out shopping or cleaning the oven."

Judy patted my hand. "Soon we'll know. Will you come in with me?"

"I will if you want me to," I answered.

"I don't think I can do this alone. It's too nerve-wracking."

Her dark eyes beckoned for support. I patted the back of her hand as I forced my own fears to the dark part of my mind.

A thin smile crossed her lips. The door to the office opened and the nurse in the pink scrubs called her name. We both stood, I gave Judy's hand a squeeze and followed her into examination room number two. She sat on the end of the table. The nurse in pink with the bubbly attitude handed her a gown and told her to change.

"Let me know when you're ready. I'll step outside," I said as the nurse took Judy's blood pressure. I leaned against the wall just next to the examination room. Judy was right. This was *nerve-wracking*. Memories flooded back. It could easily be me sitting on the exam table. It'd been over a year since Doctor Walters transparent smile alarmed me as she entered my examination room, took the novel out of my hands, and told me, my mammogram was abnormal. Bam! In that spilt-second, my world turned upside down. The sooner we got out of here the better. Judy's voice interrupted my flashback. A woman with a white coat followed me into the room.

"Hi, Judy," she said.

"Hi, Doctor," she said, fidgeting with her gown. The paper on the table crinkled. "This is my friend, Maggie. She's my moral support today."

"Nice to meet you," the doctor said, lifting her gaze from Judy's file. "I'm Dr. Nelson."

"Nice to meet you," I responded, thinking *not really.* The thought of cleaning the bathroom, calling the plumber, testing another child seemed joyful in comparison. I stared at the back of Dr. Nelson's head as she stepped closer to Judy.

"Well, I reviewed the films and it appears—"

My breath caught in my chest as I saw Judy stiffen, her eyes like glass, her jaw rigid with fear. Dr. Nelson rubbed her hand.

"It appears that the lump you have is a cyst."

"What's that?" Judy asked, crossing her ankles sitting up straighter.

"We can drain it today. We think it's a benign cyst that's filled with fluid. Of course we'll run the fluid through some tests just to make sure, but I think we can end this today."

Judy's shoulders quaked. Dr. Nelson put her arm around her patient, my friend, Harry and Walter's mom, and held her tight. "It's okay."

I thanked the heavens. Judy wiped at the corners of her eyes. My eyes brimmed with tears as she relaxed and looked to the sky with laced fingers.

"Seriously, a cyst? I've been so worried." Judy inhaled deeply then slowly released the cleansing breath, her petite chest rising and falling with ease.

"Yup, a pesky cyst," Dr. Nelson replied, arranging some sterile silver instruments on the counter.

I caught Judy's attention.

"*Oy vey*, are you kidding me?"

"I'm not kidding," Dr. Nelson assured her. "Maybe Maggie would like to wait in the waiting room for this part. I'll get Ann and we'll get this over with."

I smiled at the dismissal. "See you in a while, crocodile." I winked at Judy, blew her an air kiss, then wound my way back through the office trying to find the exit. I thanked God with each step wondering what we could do to celebrate for the time being even if we had to wait for additional test results.

With a sigh of relief, I opened the door to the waiting room. Surprised to see Jenny McBride reading a magazine, I stopped in my tracks pondering how I could escape the area without actually making contact. She glanced up, her red-rimmed eyes locked with mine. I walked over to where she sat. "Hi, Jenny." A shadow drifted through her stare. Her eyes weren't the crystal blue I'd known when we worked together or the day she announced she was hired in as principal.

"Hi," she replied.

Her bottom lip quivered as she greeted me. I sat down in the chair next to her.

"I'm here with my friend," I said, before clearing my throat, deadening any misgivings I felt toward her. They'd chosen her over me when it came time to name the new principal and the way things were going, it probably was a blessing in disguise.

Jenny closed her magazine and set it back on the glass coffee table. "That's nice that you came with your friend."

I nodded. "She needed the support."

Jenny's pursed lips held secrets, her gaunt cheeks harsh and sharp like her business tact.

Uncomfortable with the scene, I leaned back in the chair and closed my eyes. I counted to ten by twos then opened them slowly. Jenny and I were the only women in the waiting room. What was I supposed to say? She blew her nose and tucked the tissue into the pocket of her sweater.

"I know you don't like me," she mumbled.

My conscience jerked me to attention. My eyes met her stare as I turned toward her. *Three more years*, I told myself. *This is not the time to make enemies*. I swallowed. "I don't dislike you," I said.

"You made it very clear that you thought you were the right one for the job," she said, taking a deep breath.

"I was disappointed. I'm sorry if anything I said was misinterpreted."

She snickered. "That's just it. You're so politically correct, people look up to you, you have a gift, and you don't even see it half the time."

Jenny's words cut me. "Look, I'm just trying to make it from day-to-day just like everyone else." Where the hell was Judy? We had some celebrating to do? This was not what I bargained for. Uneasiness rushed through my veins.

"Funny, I don't know how many days I have left. My prognosis isn't optimistic. At least you have a family. And friends."

Startled by the hitch in my breathing, I gripped the armrests on my chair. What did she want from me? Was I supposed to feel guilty for what I had? "I'm sorry you're sick, Jenny. I've been there, fought my own battle, or should I say battles, especially over the last few years." Keeping my personal life private was priority. I took a deep breath. "I'm sorry if there was something that I said or did that hurt you. This office isn't foreign to me nor the scars I carry from the surgeries or my past," I said, holding steady.

"Maggie, I can do lots of things, but I don't know if I can do this."

"I know." The door opened and Judy emerged. "If there is anything, I can do to help, let me know." Jenny and I started out together, held each other's hand at one point in our careers, but the inertia of promotion divided us, changed the feelings we once shared. Jenny's stare cut me. "My number is still the same." The corner of my mouth curled thinking back to a time when we chatted openly as friends until ugly ambition tarnished our bond.

"Thanks," she said.

Judy meandered over to where we sat. She gave me a little smile.

"You all set?" I asked.

"Yup, good to go," she replied with a nod.

"Good. Judy, this is my friend Jenny. Jenny, this is my friend Judy."

"Nice to meet you," Judy said with a nod.

"Same here," Jenny said. "So we're all in the same boat, huh?"

Judy grimaced. "I wish I could say no, but that seems to be the case."

"Cancer should not divide the sisterhood." I patted Jenny's hand. "Nor anything else," I added, not sure the rift would ever mend. "Call me."

"The phone works both ways," she responded, straight-faced.

I nodded, knowing that her hard exterior was a façade for her fear-driven attitude. It wasn't Jenny's fault that I'd closed myself off. At the time, it was the only way I knew how to put one foot in front of the other to move forward. "I wish you all the best, Jenny. Let me know if there's anything I can do." A thin grin crossed her lips as her eyes flitted back and forth between Judy and me. I hooked my arm with Judy's. "Well, we should get going," I said.

"Yeah, I'm kind of sore." Judy faced Jenny. "It was nice meeting you," she said. "Good luck with everything. Stay tough." Judy unclenched her fist and handed Jenny the miniature silver angel she'd clung to.

Jenny's questioning expression softened as Judy handed her the trinket. I knew that "the old Jenny" loomed somewhere deep beneath the melancholy stare. There was no doubt in my mind that she'd fight, but I wondered what was in store for her. Sadness washed over me as Judy and I meandered to the elevator.

"Somebody from work?" Judy asked as the stainless steel doors opened, our reflections disappearing.

"Yeah, long story," I said, "but can I just say that I don't want anything to come between us, ever?" Our reflections reunited as the doors closed and we rode down to the main floor. Her kindness consumed me. "On a different note, we need to celebrate your good news."

Judy's wide grin made her cheeks bulge. "Let's have a cocktail at lunch."

"You got it. I'm starved." My belly grumbled as if I hadn't eaten in days.

"You're on." Judy let out a breath of relief. "That was so scary," she said, shaking her curls free.

"Yeah, I know what you mean."

"I hope the test results prove Dr. Nelson correct."

"Me, too," I said. "Me, too."

Chapter 23

Sun streamed through the windshield as I drove up the driveway. I parked the car, sighed, and pushed my sunglasses to the top of my head. The day drained me. First Judy, then Jenny, who knew, and I was beginning to feel the cocktail I'd had with lunch. The sofa called my name. My waist called for the yoga pants.

A box from the florist waited on the porch for me. My heart fluttered at the unexpected delivery. Pretty sure Sam Elliot didn't know I existed. Who sent me flowers? The contents tickled my senses as I peeked under the lid, and the scent of fresh blooms washed over me.

I scooted the box out of the way to open the door as Bones barked inside. "I'm going as fast as I can," I called to him, juggling my purse and keys eager to inspect the contents further and solve the mystery.

"Down," I commanded.

Bones sat at my feet trying to control his excitement.

"You have to go out," I said, leading him to the back door. The quiet house was growing on me even though it seemed more like home when filled with people and chaos. Bones wiggled as I unlocked the French doors to the patio. He butted his way through the door with his snout and bolted into the backyard.

I went back to the front porch to get the flowers, brought them to the kitchen, then lifted the majestic arrangement from the packing. Somebody had gone overboard. Scads of petals covered the card. Carefully, I plucked the mysterious message from puddles of orange, yellow, and purple hues. It was from Fletcher Thompson.

My assistant is sending you the photos from Chicago. I'm glad that Brook brought you along. I look forward to seeing your work. Attach the photos to an email and we'll see what we can do. These flowers reminded me of you. I'm serious about Los Angeles.

Marveled with the invitation I knew, I wouldn't go. I booted up my computer and opened my email. This was insane. Things like this didn't happen to me. The thought of spending time with Fletcher Thompson bristled my instincts. I flipped up the top of my computer, then downloaded photographs of my holiday cows. I wrote Fletcher a note.

Thanks for the lovely flowers. Although Los Angeles sounds intriguing, I cannot take any more time off from work. Attached are the photos of my work. These were intended as illustrations for a children's picture book. Your generosity is much appreciated. Sincerely, Maggie Abernathy.

Pressing the send button, I didn't worry one iota about the outcome. The idea was a whim and John's interest consumed me.

In the kitchen, I picked up the heavy vase with two hands, sniffed the flowers, and carried them to the coffee table in the living room. I plopped down on the cushy sofa and put my feet up. Heavy eyelids squashed the sense of productivity and treading upstairs for yoga pants. Nestling into the cushy sofa, I dozed off.

Far off rumbling shook me from my sleep. Disoriented, I blinked my eyes wondering how long I'd been out. My sleepy eyes beckoned for more shut-eye. I sat up, steadied myself, then rubbed the sleep from my face. Not sure if today was a dream or reality, I thought back, trying to discern what really occurred. Did I really meet Jenny in Judy's doctor's office? Did flowers arrive with an outrageous invitation, and did Fletcher really request to see my work?

One thing was for sure. Judy's prognosis was positive, and I was relieved for her. I said a prayer and crossed my fingers. My phone buzzed. I read the text.

Hi, Mom. I'm back in Boston. Almost home. Talk to you soon. XO Bradley.

I moved my fingers to see the photo he'd attached of the Boston skyline. Bradley filled my heart. I wondered how it was possible. There were days that he engrossed me, physically, and emotionally. We shared tired days, days filled with angst and joy. Now the days we shared were much different. Our long distance connection consisted of thoughts for his wellbeing, thoughts for health and happiness, and for God to keep him safe. The hectic day-to-day life we shared in his youth was filed in the back of mind. Without him, there was no one to sidetrack me from the future, except me.

Standing up, I stretched, and thought some exercise would do me good. The sound of John's bike unmistakable. I sauntered to the front window to see, but the street was empty and the sound had dissipated. The excitement of him tickled my skin. The doorbell rang, and I shuffled to see who was there. Peeking through the peephole, I grinned. John stood with a motorcycle helmet in hand. When I opened the door, the laugh lines around his eyes danced as he smiled at me.

"Wanna see if this helmet fits. You heard Bradley. He thinks it would be a good idea if you went for a ride."

The thin smile grew as I took the heavy, black helmet from John. I inspected it for a skull and crossbones decal, but found nothing. It should've had a decal, something that quietly stated, *badass.*

"I don't know," I said, trying to picture myself on the back of John's orange Harley.

"How about a ride? Chloe's at her friend's house for another hour and the weather is beautiful. We can drive by the lake?"

Enticed by the invitation, I nodded. The lake's mystical power called to me. I loved the water. "I've never been on a bike before. I'm not sure I know what to do," I said.

"You don't have to do anything but sit tight and hold on. I'll do the rest. "It'll be fun."

Narrowing my gaze, I crossed my arms. "Really?"

"Really," he replied. "Those biking classes really paid off."

I envisioned myself standing in the middle of the road. The only person impeding the path was, me. Bradley's image flashed before me. He was a toddler, and I was holding him on my hip, singing and laughing, and then he was sixteen and we were celebrating his driver's license, then he was twenty-one and holding a bottle of beer at a barbeque and then he faded into the distance, grown, smiling, nervous yet happy to be starting a new chapter in a place far from the place he'd grown up and I was left behind to find my way. The *fork in the road* more evident than ever. Dear Bradley was my beacon, our roles reversed.

The corner of my mouth lifted and I went back inside the foyer to check myself in the mirror. Putting on the black shell, I buckled the strap beneath my chin, my wavy strawberry blond hair ready for the wind.

"Looks great." John smiled at me as I joined him on the porch. "We better go before we run out of time." I tugged the door shut.

"That's more like it," John said, trotting down the front stairs ahead of me.

"This thing is heavy." I reached up to adjust my helmet. It felt crooked, my neck scrunched from the weight pressing down. I thought about who might see us riding together and this time I didn't care. John straddled the bright-orange Harley and gestured for me to join him on the sleek motorcycle. I swung my leg over and caught my foot on the seat. My hands landed on his thick sturdy shoulders as I caught myself. I settled into the leather seat and he smiled back at me.

"Hold on," he said.

Holding onto his waist, I thought about our night together, his skin against mine, his breath in my ear, our bodies intertwined. He revved the engine and kicked up the stand. I tightened my grip with the jerk forward. He glanced back at me and gave a little wink, his green eyes sparkling in the early evening light.

We rolled out of the driveway and hung a left. The motor purred. I loosened my grip as I became more comfortable. John maneuvered the bike along the tree-lined streets of our quaint town of Grosse Pointe. The lake appeared on the horizon as we passed Grand Boulevard. Sunlight danced on the rippled water sending bright flashes of hope and dreams into the atmosphere. The sun at my back nudged me closer, prodded me to reach out, and grab the water's offering.

John slowed the bike and veered into the park where so much had happened, a place that seemed so different to me from Bradley's younger's days. I pictured John strolling down the beach with Chloe, that horseshoe tattoo on his left shoulder, their voices dancing in the breeze, and their hands linked together. The sun had lit up Chloe's freckled face as she stared up to her dad while I stood secretly contemplating what it would be like to be with him. And now I knew.

The man at the gate checked John's identification. After parking the Harley, I undid the strap and wiggled out of the helmet. John watched my every move with a sly grin.

"You don't mind if we stop here, do you?"

I shook my head. "Nope."

"I thought you might like to sit by the shore, take a load off for a few minutes."

My pulse raced. John and I rarely spent time alone like this. This was different territory than the front porch, the backyard or the kitchen where we knew Chloe lurked. We hadn't been alone together since that night when everything seemed so right. My skin prickled. Brushing my hair away from my face, I lifted my chin to the sun.

"You act like you don't know me," John said. "You seem so nervous."

He *was* making me nervous, my pulse unsteady. Damn him. I smiled. "I do know you, most the time," I said.

His brow furrowed. His laugh lines at the corners of his eyes creased when he flashed his rugged smile.

"Most of the time?" he said. "What does that mean?"

He slowed his pace as we neared the rocks at the shoreline. I followed as he stepped up and across one jagged rock onto a large flat boulder wide enough for both of us. He reached out to help me balance and I grabbed his hand. My legs dangled near the wet surface when I sat down. Lapping water threatened to slurp my toes like wet dog kisses.

"I didn't even know this spot existed," I said, scanning the horizon for freighters.

"Chloe found this place. We come down here when she's feeling blue."

"What would we do without Chloe?" I said, smiling.

John sighed.

I mulled over his sullen expression, his tender eyes displaying true feelings, feelings I could relate to when it came to Bradley. He rubbed his chin. His chest rose and fell with the swaying lake beneath our dangling feet.

"I don't know. Life certainly wouldn't be the same. That's for sure," he said, taking the black Ray Ban sunglasses from his collar.

"Yeah, it certainly would be different," I mumbled. "I'd probably be living next door to a beauty queen and her perfect husband with three amazing kids."

John chuckled.

I glanced at him. He tossed a pebble into the lake. *Plunk.* "I think I prefer you guys." I shaded my eyes. The corner of my lip curled to the perfect blue sky.

"So you don't think you know me, huh?"

"Only sometimes." The black-and-white pictures of the ranch that Chloe shared were fresh in my mind. "Chloe showed me some photos of you and your family," I said with smiling eyes. "I liked looking at them with her."

"She told me."

The breeze picked up. It rustled the loose sleeves of my tunic blouse. A shiver tickled the nape of my neck making my shoulders twitched. John scooted closer and put his arm around me.

"All you have to do is ask, Maggie."

I settled into the curve of his body. It felt like home. "What if it doesn't work out? I don't know if I can survive another broken heart. It's bad enough that we—" I paused, thinking about our night together.

"We what?" he asked.

"Um, slept together," I answered.

"That was more than just sleeping together," John said, kissing the side of my head. "You're a mystery to me, Maggie Abernathy. Most the time you act like nothing has happened between us."

I sighed. "I can't help it. Tell me about your mom and your dad."

"Well, you know my dad still lives on the ranch where I grew up. Winston Ludlow McIntyre," he muttered in a low grumbling voice. "He's got a great name. His parents knew what they were doing." John threw another stone into the water.

I snickered. "He sounds like a movie star. I bet he's burly."

"Yeah, wouldn't want to meet him in an alley." John chuckled at his own words. "He's got a few horses, but he likes his cattle."

"What about your mom?"

"I think following my dad's dream proved challenging, but farming and wrangling ran in her blood. She was as hearty as the land."

My spine stiffened.

"She got sick one summer, said she wasn't feeling good, but the doctors couldn't find anything and then she just left us one night in her sleep. The woman was as healthy as a horse, stubborn as a mule. She and my dad belonged together. You could just tell."

"Sounds like it." I snuggled closer to John.

"Yeah, he got tired of city life. Had some money, moved to the country, met Mom, and settled down. Not sure why it was so important for me to get out of ranching if it was good enough for him. Maybe he thought I needed to experience the world to truly appreciate my roots."

I contemplated Brook's need to live in the city. "So Brook brought you to the hustle and bustle of city life? You wanted Brook to have what she wanted?" I asked, treading lightly.

"I never thought of it like that. I was on a fishing excursion with my buddy, Mac, in Mexico, and she was there on a shoot. We met in a bar. Somehow we stayed in contact and I met her in Paris on a break, my first and only time in Paris."

"I see," I said, remembering Chloe's sticker collection. "Chloe told me she was your Paris Girl."

"She's right. I married Brook because she was pregnant."

I stared at John's profile as he squinted into the distance. He was just trying to right thing.

"I wanted to move back to Montana and practice medicine there, but Brook wouldn't have it. She needed the city, any city. Coming to Detroit was never in the picture. Some days, I have no clue what went down to land me here." He took a deep breath. "Actually, I do know, a job offer."

"Well you won't have to be here much longer," I reminded him. "You're putting the house up soon. Please don't sell to a cat owner. Bones hates cats."

John laughed then sobered quickly.

"I'm going to miss you," I said, putting my hand on his chest.

"You don't have to, Maggie. We can make it work," he said.

"How? My work isn't like yours. And I don't have family in Montana."

"Is that what's holding you here Maggie?"

His glare rustled my nerves. "I made a commitment, John. I want to finish my career. I'll have thirty years in three years and I'll be able to collect my full pension. I just want to finish what I started."

John tucked me closer. "I'm not so sure that's the whole reason. Maggie, I couldn't bear knowing you were living with a broken heart," he said. I chastised myself for being impulsive with my thoughts. "I thought. . ." He paused and let out a sigh. "I just thought maybe . . ."

I stared into his eyes. I wasn't the only one struggling, teetering between reality and fantasy. "I know, and I appreciate the thought. And you're right, what we shared was something more. I feel it, too."

John kissed the side of my head again. "We'd better go. I should get Chloe," he said, pushing his sunglasses to the top of his head.

John reached for me. I took his hands as I lifted myself upright. He drew me close. My chin rested on his chest as my gaze met his. "You're something else, John McIntyre."

He smiled.

He wrapped his arms around my waist and I rested my hands on his thick shoulders. I tilted my head back, my lips met his, and the world seemed right, even if life seemed to make being together impossible. I leaned back and he released me. Was I capable of risking a life-altering change that would turn my world upside-down? I opened my eyes. John swept away the tear at the corner of my eye.

"We can finish this conversation later."

I nuzzled my cheek into the palm of his hand wondering if I was making the biggest mistake of my life.

Chapter 24

I lit the fire, then arranged my book and hot tea on the coffee table before sinking into the sofa. Although Mondays were usually pretty rough, this Monday brought a different type of work. I never thought I'd run into Jenny McBride. We hadn't spoken in a long time. A familiar hurt resurfaced as I thought about our early friendship. When I found out they passed me by, I confided in her, I'd no clue she applied, too. I sipped at my tea thinking about her red-rimmed eyes as she sat alone waiting to see the doctor at the cancer center. Maybe I was wrong to take her tactics as a blow. Maybe we could salvage something from the past, probably not, but I knew animosity didn't breed loyalty and that was something I prided myself on.

Setting my teacup down, I diverted my thoughts to something more productive, reading. Picking up the book, I inspected the cover. A young woman crouched near the ground luring me into her world. I hadn't read this author before, but Judy assured me I would get sucked into the prose and magic.

"Sarah Addison Allen," I whispered. "What do you have in store for me?"

Bones trotted by, sniffed around the table, and hopped up at the other end of the sofa. He put his head on the armrest then snorted in disgust.

"What? You had your walk, now it's my turn." I gave him the stink-eye. He puffed out his chest and let out a monumental sigh of disagreement. "Sorry, Charlie," I said.

I fingered the cover of my newest novel thinking about John. He was asking me to do something I didn't know if I had the guts to do. Chloe was doing fine here, couldn't he just stay for her, for me? He was following his heart. I was trying to follow mine and although our attraction mutual, maybe it just wasn't meant to be. The firelight bounced off the bright hues of Fletcher's flowers arrangement.

I mimicked Bones' sigh and opened to the first page of my current read. Not before long, I found myself immersed into a world other than my own. Night set in as I got lost in the pages. Bones nuzzled into my body with his wrinkly head on my thigh, my robe wet with drool. I checked the time, finished the chapter, then got up to head for bed. Bones yawned then stretched, his hind quarters in the air.

"Come on, boy. You're going out."

His tags jangled as he followed me out of the living room. There was a knock at the door. I peeked out at John, flipped on the foyer light, and opened the door slowly. "Hi, is everything okay?"

"You have a minute? I was hoping you were up."

"Sure, meet me round back. I was just about to let Bones out." I shut the door and headed to the kitchen. Bones sauntered ahead. His waggling bottom made me smile, along with John's unexpected appearance. Bones ran out into the yard making the motion sensitive light go on. I heard the click of the latch when the gate shut. Standing on the patio in my pink fluffy robe, I peeked into the dusky evening, inspecting Chloe's bedroom window. A dim glow lit up her room.

"Hey there," John said. "Sorry to bug you."

"No worries."

Bones darted past and back into the kitchen.

"Why don't you come in?" I said. "Is Chloe okay?"

John rubbed his chin then closed the door behind us after we headed inside. There was a crash from the living room.

"Oh, no," I mumbled, rolling my eyes at the sight. Bones stood on the coffee table licking tea from a puddle. I scuffled to the kitchen, grabbed some towels then went back to clean up the mess. "Bones," I uttered, putting the teacup back on the saucer that now had a crack down the center. "Get down," I scolded.

Bones backed up. His rear end nudged Fletcher's flower arrangement toward the edge of the table. John lurched and caught the vase before it tipped. The card fell on the floor.

I grabbed Bones by the collar and yanked him down to the floor then I sopped up the rest of the mess. "Crazy dog," I said with a waggling finger. "Look what you did."

John placed the flowers back on the table then picked the card up from the floor. He lowered his gaze. Realizing he'd seen Fletcher's message, my insides collapsed.

"Is this the same Fletcher Thompson that works with Brook?" he asked.

"Yes."

John came closer, his eyes glazed with doubtful anger. "What is this?"

"It's nothing. Fletcher was just trying to help me get this cow thing off the ground," I said.

The fire crackled and John's temple twitched rapidly. "Los Angeles doesn't sound like nothing." His eyes flickered with distrust.

"I told you it's nothing."

John paced back and forth across the room.

I crossed my arms over my chest, angry with his accusation of something that was never going to happen. "He was just being nice," I said through clenched teeth.

"That's what Brook said right before she slept with him."

Every muscle in my body constricted. This was a side of John I'd never seen before, a different kind of upset that went beyond usual irritation.

The card flitted to the table after john dropped it.

"You are reading too much into this," I said.

John's eyes flickered. "That's what Brook said when he showered her with freebies, shoot after shoot."

I swallowed and thought about the jewelry I'd tucked away from the shoot in Chicago. "I'm not Brook," I said, shifting my weight and narrowing my gaze.

John's jaw clicked as he gritted his teeth.

"Why did you come over, John?" I asked.

He came closer. "I came over because . . ." John's chest rose and fell. He rubbed his head then lowered his gaze.

"What?"

"I haven't stopped thinking about you since I parked my Harley in the garage, how we talked like human beings." His voice broke.

"What?" I said as emotion built at the back of my throat like a hard knot unwilling to budge.

He stepped closer, my insides not giving way.

"I came over here because all I could think about was kissing you goodnight because that's what you deserve, but now . . ." He paused and glared at the flowers. "But now, I don't know."

I wanted to grab him and shake him for being so pig-headed, but I froze, shocked by his jerk reaction over some flowers. I swallowed. "You think I slept with him in Chicago, don't you?" I asked. "How could you?"

John stiffened.

I stared into the green eyes that questioned me. "Yeah, that's what I had time for while I was busy watching your daughter so her mother could do her job." The lump at the back of my throat throbbed. I couldn't cry in front of him, give him the satisfaction or whatever it was he was searching for. "I think you know where the front door is," I said, avoiding his gaze.

John stalked past me.

I touched his arm. "And today was so perfect." My voice quivered. I ached for a kiss goodnight, a white flag, an apology. Why couldn't he just let it go? I wasn't Brook. I wasn't anything like Brook.

John caressed my cheek, his warm touch not in sync with his tone or cold eyes.

"I'm not her," I whispered. "I shouldn't have to try and convince you. Goodnight, John," I said. "Besides, I don't have the energy for that."

After John left, I shut and bolted the door then stomped into the kitchen, shut off the lights, and whistled at Bones to follow. He trotted to the front door and sat with his nose pressed against the wood. "What is it, boy?"

He stared up at me with pathetic eyes. There was a secret in his soft groan. I knelt beside him and listened. I thought I heard the porch swing so I tiptoed into my office and peeked out the front window. It was John swaying in the breeze, staring into the darkness.

Damn him. I tiptoed back to the hallway, shut off the light in the foyer, and made my way upstairs. Not hearing Bones' nails against the hard wood, I checked to see if he was on my heels, but he wasn't. He sat at the bottom of the stairs with his nose pressed up against the door as if he was the one in the doghouse. "You both can stay down there," I uttered in disgust.

I undid my robe and threw it on the end of my bed. Climbing under the covers, I sprawled out on my back and stared into the darkness, pissed off that I didn't have a chance in hell of going to sleep. Why were men so stupid? I didn't deserve this. Shit, it was like a nosedive on a smooth flight. I kicked my feet, loosening the sheets around me. A wave of heat started in my toes and worked its way up leaving me even more exasperated. I kicked off the covers freeing myself from the weight. While time ticked away on the clock, I counted the minutes until the alarm would ring.

The doorbell rang.

Bones barked.

"Now what?" I grumbled and wiped the sweat from my forehead. Stupid hot flashes. I stomped down the hallway and downstairs.

Bones sat at the front door wagging his tail.

"You are just as stupid as he is." I unlocked the door and opened it with a swift jerk. "What?" I hissed.

John held a droopy bouquet of purple lilacs in one hand and a small flashlight in the other hand.

I narrowed my gaze. "Seriously?"

"Can you open the screen door?" he asked.

I unlatched the screen door.

He handed me the flowers.

I waited.

"Thanks for opening the door."

I stood silent.

"I know you're not Brook."

Bones sat between us licking my toes, a rose between two thorns. The night air felt refreshing as it kissed my hot skin. I locked gazes with John, but said nothing. *Yeah, stand there and feel uncomfortable.*

John swallowed. His Adam's apple twitched. "Sorry."

I searched his eyes. The scent of lilacs washed over me. No one had ever brought me flowers at midnight.

"You know, I could have been sleeping," I said.

"You were not. I know you too well. Now maybe you can get some shut-eye," John said, touching my cheek.

I raised an eyebrow at him.

John stuffed his hands in his pockets. "I'm really sorry."

"Apology accepted," I said, pondering if my quick acceptance would work against me. "You still owe me a goodnight kiss," I whispered, "but not tonight, or else I really won't be able to fall asleep."

The corner of John's mouth lifted.

Crickets serenaded me as I focused on him. "Night." I shut the front door and bolted it. I heard John trot down the porch stairs.

Bones' nose twitched as I sniffed the purple bouquet.

"He can go home and think about that." I took a deep breath as I headed for the kitchen to get a vase.

There was another knock on the front door. I placed the lilacs in water and returned to the front door. Bones wagged his tail. I peeked out through the peephole. I should've been more irritated, but wasn't. "Now what? Seriously, I have to get some sleep. And you need to be at home in the house with your daughter."

John reached for the screen door. "You didn't lock it." He stepped inside. "You look a little worse for wear," he said with a smirk.

"Gee, I wonder why?" I replied.

"*Touché.*"

He held my stare as he stepped closer.

"I really should remember to lock all the doors," I said.

John cradled my face in his warm hands. "I thought this was too important."

John's lips grazed mine, seeking acceptance. I hesitated. "What could be so important at this time of night?"

"This," he whispered into my breath.

John kissed me again. *Perfect.* I opened my eyes with a sigh. A strange calmness washed over me. He pressed his lips to my forehead.

"There, now we can all get some sleep," he said.

"This isn't over," I mumbled, knowing he was right.

"I know."

I smirked at the inflection in John's voice.

"Now," he said, "lock all the doors this time."

Chapter 25

Chloe slumped on the porch swing next to me as I swayed to the beat of the words in the novel I was reading. I was nearly three-quarters the way through and anxious to see how it ended.

"Why the long face?" I asked, thinking about another rejection letter that I kept to myself.

"The career fair is this week. I got nobody," she said.

I slid the bookmark in my book and set it down next to me. "So sorry to hear that."

"I really thought my mom would surprise me."

The porch swing bounced as Chloe kicked her feet in disgust. She yanked at the purple string, and Voodoo landed in my lap.

"So who is the babysitter today?" I asked, knowing that John was still at work.

"Her name is Patty. She's actually kind of nice."

I raised an eyebrow to the acceptance. "This is new."

"What? I don't hate *all* the babysitters." Chloe rubbed Voodoo's ears. "This career day is going to suck."

"Hey, hey," I cautioned.

She rolled her eyes. "You just don't get it. *Barnyard Hilary* is all up in my grill cause her dad's brother is a movie producer and he's coming. How can you top that?"

I raised an eyebrow. *Or pretending to be one,* I thought to myself as I patted Voodoo's raggedy head.

"Wish you'd quit doing that," Chloe muttered.

"What?" I asked, inspecting the front lawn that needed to be mowed.

"That thing with your eyebrow. It's like you don't believe me or something."

I gave the swing a gentle push, and Chloe settled down. "It's not that I don't believe you, but really, you don't have to *one up* her."

"What does that mean? One up her?" she asked.

I liked how the bridge of her nose wrinkled when she spoke. "You know, do better than her?" I watched Chloe think as I explained what I meant.

"It's not that I want to, *one up her,* I just want someone to be there besides my dad. He's always around."

"Oh," I said, stopping the swing. "Does Patty know you're over here?"

"Yeah, she told me not to stay too long. She's making me dinner soon." Chloe chewed at her thumbnail.

"Hmm. Dinner?"

"Yeah, dinner. We're having pancakes and bacon. She knows how to make that."

"Sounds tasty." I dreamed of long summer days, my favorite kind of time when being lazy was acceptable and the days were filled with sun to light my way.

"I guess," Chloe said.

"Now what?" I pried, watching her face droop like Bones' when he doesn't get to go for a walk.

"We don't have too much school left."

Chloe picked at Voodoo's hand-sewn eye. It made me wonder where my mother was hiding out. She said her back was feeling much better since her tumble in the kitchen. I hadn't seen or heard from her in a few days. Suspicion grew. "You want more school?"

Chloe moaned and leaned back against the swing. Her feet dangled just above the porch floor. Her toes skimmed the stained wood boards when she stretched her legs. She was getting taller.

"No, it just means it's almost time to go to Montana. I want to stay here and swim in the lake with Walter and Harry. And my friend, Autumn. She's new at school."

John still hadn't put up the "For Sale" sign in his front yard. I wondered why he was dragging his feet. "That's nice that you have a new friend."

"She's super nice. She's nice to everybody, not just some kids."

I smiled. Being in third grade was tough work. "Glad to hear there are some good eggs out there."

Chloe peered at me with a wrinkled brow. "Yeah, she's a good egg. Funny, too."

"Do you want me to come to your career day?" I asked.

"No offense, but no. Besides, I think it should be someone from my family."

"None taken, I was just trying to help."

Chloe smirked. "You're like that."

"Like what?" I asked, catching a glint in her green eyes.

"You'd help your worst enemy," she replied.

"Not so sure about that," I said, thinking about Jenny McBride, not that she was an enemy, but we certainly didn't see eye-to-eye. But Chloe was right, I'd help her if she needed it.

"I am. You were nice to my mom when she wasn't being nice to you. That takes some gumption as Dad would say."

Or stupidity. "Junie B. has gumption."

"That girl sure does. More than I'll ever have," Chloe mumbled.

"You have plenty," I said.

Chloe peered over her shoulder when we heard the side door to her house shut. "I think I should go. Maybe dinner is ready."

Stopping the sway of the swing, I firmly planted my foot against the porch flooring, Chloe stood up and Voodoo dropped to the ground. Chloe tugged at the purple leash and Voodoo bumped along behind her.

I picked up my phone and sent John a text. *Not that it's any of my business, but is anyone going to career day with Chloe?*

Before I could open my book, my phone buzzed. It was a reply from John. *Got it covered.* As soon as I put the phone down, it buzzed again. John's name flashed across the screen. I opened the text. *Why is Chloe at your house? Where is the babysitter?*

Tapping out a reply, I grinned. *She's just visiting. The sitter is making her pancakes for dinner. I think it's all good.* I sent my message.

The phone buzzed again. *Thanks for keeping an eye out. Gotta go, screamer in Room Three.*

I smiled, relieved that the screamer was at his end of the line. My eyes grew wide with amazement as a brand-new baby-blue convertible Volkswagen Bug pulled into my driveway. The top was down and my mom waved at me from the driver's seat. I stood, walked to the stairs, then jogged down the steps. Mom had a silk scarf tied around her head. She turned off the engine then hollered to me. "What do ya' think?"

Shocked, I covered my mouth and narrowed my eyes. "Are you serious?" I asked. "Who does this, really, belong to?" I asked, touching the shiny new finish.

"Me, it's all mine." Mom beamed as she ogled over her new car.

"Really?" Bones tongue waggled as I leaned over to scratch his head.

"Really," she sang.

"I love it. I really love it" I peeked inside at the yellow Gerber Daisy to the right of the steering wheel. "You are so cool."

"Well, it's about time. I've been trying to convince you of that for years," she joked.

"What made you do it?"

"Well I've had that sedan for ten years. Thought it was time for a change. Change is good. Don't you think?" she asked, peering over the top of her cat-rimmed sunglasses.

"Is this about you or me?" I asked.

"It's about all of us."

"What did you do with the sedan?" I asked, leaning against the door with folded arms.

"It's sitting in the garage. I'll drive it when the weather is crappy," she replied. "Not worth a trade-in or even selling to a teenager."

Bones barked.

"Come on, throw Bones in the back, and let's go for a ride."

"Hang on." I hurried inside, grabbed a blanket from the chest, and my purse. I slammed the door behind me.

Mom fiddled with the dash while I covered the back seat with the blanket for Bones.

"Good thinking," Mom said.

"Yeah, I've been trying to convince you for years that I have a brain," I said.

"Ha. Ha." Mom moved the side-view mirror. "Let's go."

Bones sat by the passenger side of the car wagging his tail with anticipation. He jumped in the seat like it was old hat. He nudged the blanket with his nose to make a nest just right for his bottom and sat down.

"Let's go get ice cream," I said.

Mom adjusted her sunglasses on the bridge of her nose. "Are you buying? I just spent a wad on this toy."

"Sure," I said, thinking about her *making a change* comment. "What made you do it? I had a feeling you were up to something."

Mom started the engine. She peered in my direction. "It dawned on me that I wasn't getting any younger. And when I fell and broke all those dishes, I thought Glad, what have you always wanted, now just might be the time to get it and here she is."

Mom put the car in reverse.

"How come you didn't ask me to come with you?" I fastened my seatbelt.

Mom put her foot on the brake. "No offense, sweet pea, but I thought you might want to talk me out of it. It's not practical."

"Am I really that much of a stick in the mud?" I asked as the car rolled backward toward the street.

"Not always." Mom checked the road both ways. "But this was something I just had to do. I've always wanted another Beetle. Your father and I had one when we first got married. And even though this one's new, every time I see one, it reminds me of him and all the good times we had in that car," she said. "I sure do miss that man."

Too emotional, I swallowed. "Yeah, me too," I whispered, glancing back at Bones who had drool hanging from his top lip.

"Rides like a dream," Mom hollered over the rush of air that washed over us.

Bright sun highlighted the creases in her face making it all too clear that time stops for no one. I wondered what it was like to be married to one person for fifty years. I'd never know.

I lifted my nose to the sun and closed my eyes. The heavenly aroma of spring in Michigan grew stronger and sweeter with the lilac blooms and tulip blossoms. When I opened my eyes, the lake twinkled before me. The past few days of weather had been perfect. Speckles of heaven danced across the water's surface like fairy lights. Mom slowed and stopped at the corner. A solemn grin crossed her lips as she smiled at me.

"This was always your happy place, but happy places can change, my dear."

The corner of her mouth curled upward. She put on her blinker and we cruised Lakeshore. She pointed to the glove box. "Open it."

I clicked the latch and a silk scarf spilled out.

"It's for you," she said, glancing over.

I fingered the smooth orange and blue paisley design that reminded me of my favorite dress when I was in fifth grade. I adjusted the mirror and tied it around my head like a fat headband, the tail ends caressed my neck as they fluttered in the wind. I adjusted the scarf as I inspected myself in the side mirror. *Perfect. Just like the movies.* "I love it."

"I knew you would, but do you love it more than my last gift?" She cackled with pride.

I raised an eyebrow and peered back at Bones who was biting at the wind that blew in his face. "I'm not sure," I said. "My life would be pretty dull without that beast."

Bones leaned forward and stuck his face between the seats. He nibbled at my elbow. I patted his thick head.

Mom smiled and let out a gleeful, "Woo-hoo!"

Chapter 26

When Mom and I got back from our drive, Chloe was sitting on the front porch reading a book.

Mom beeped the horn. "Yoo-hoo, over here," she called as her new convertible rolled up the driveway.

Bones barked, and Chloe's jaw dropped. She ran to greet us.

"Holy, moly, Gladiola. Wow-wee, hot stuff." Chloe's eyes bugged out of her head. "How'd you get Maggie to put that thing on her head?" she asked. "Fancy."

"See, Mom, she thinks I'm a stick in the mud."

"You're not a stick in the mud, but sometimes you're pretty serious. It's good to let loose once in a while," Mom advised with a scornful look, her eyes dancing with her own agenda.

I glanced at myself in the mirror. Maybe she was right. I'd have to try and let go a little more often. Mistakes happen. Lessons are learned, but all roads led home.

"Can I try on your cat glasses, Glad?" Chloe asked.

"Sure, darlin'," she said, taking them off. "Do you think the black frame is too much?"

Chloe put the sunglasses on then craned her neck to see herself in the mirror on the door next to Mom. "No, they're perfect."

I opened the door and got out.

Bones waited for me to tilt the seat forward before hopping out and running to Chloe, who tickled his belly as he rolled in the grass.

"Mom, do you want to stay for dinner?"

"I was counting on it. I don't care what we have."

"Where's your sitter?" I asked Chloe.

"She's doing dishes. She told me I wouldn't have to help if I read a book. So I chose that."

"Good girl," I said, strolling up to the house. "When's your dad getting home?"

"Not sure, he said something about a surprise for me and career day. I sure hope it's my mom so I can show that *Hilary Barnyard* a thing or two."

"I wouldn't get my heart set on that," I advised.

Mom crinkled her nose. "*Hilary Barnyard*?"

"You know, Glad, that mean girl I punched. I call her *Barnyard* on account…she stinks. She doesn't really stink, but she's as bad as the smell of cow poop."

"Oh, I see," Mom said. "I do recall this conversation."

"I sure hope my dad doesn't think that he can trick me into taking him to career day," she moaned. "He keeps talking about it. Not that he's boring or anything, he just an ordinary doctor."

"Oh, I see," my mom repeated.

I narrowed my eyes in her direction. She knew something I didn't. She was holding out.

"What do you know?" I asked, sauntering up the stairs behind her so Chloe couldn't hear.

She put her hand up. "I know nothing."

"Not buying it, sister. What do you know?" I prodded.

"Nothing," she responded without acknowledging my poke.

I peered over my shoulder and called to Chloe, "Hey, can you please get the leash and run Bones around the block?"

"Sure, let me tell Patty where I'm going," she answered.

Mom eyes filled with excitement, her laugh lines prominent.

"Have it your way. I don't want to know," I grumbled.

"I don't think I can keep it a secret anymore. John is flying his dad in for career day. Bet none of those kids have a rancher in the family," Mom rambled. "I can't wait to meet him."

"How did you get privy to such information?" I asked, holding the door open for her.

"I called John. Chloe was all bent out of shape over this whole thing and I thought for sure there would be someone who would come for her. It just took a little convincing."

"So now you and John are in cahoots. What else did you discuss?" I asked, following her to the kitchen hoping like hell they didn't talk about me, but my instincts told me otherwise.

"Nothing." She turned on her heel and cut me off short. "Nothing."

I set my sunglasses on the counter then headed for the fridge. Assessing the contents, I shut the door. "Again, what else did you two talk about?" I asked, meeting Mom's stare.

She cracked a thin devious smile. "Let's just say that I'm easy to talk to." She shrugged. "What can I say?"

I inspected my hair for split ends as I debated on how much to trim off.

Chloe's voice echoed through the house, and Mom and I headed for the porch.

"This is not over," I told her.

"Maybe it is." She batted her eyes and fluffed her hair.

"You are so annoying."

"That's funny, earlier I was super cool," she reminded me.

"People can be lots of things, Glad." I leaned against the counter reluctant to tell her how lucky I was to have her in my life.

"I know. That's my point."

"Maybe we should check out what's going on out there."

The screen door creaked as I opened it. Bones was running in circles around Chloe's feet. There was a tall rugged man approaching her. She ran to him and leaped.

Her legs wrapped around his middle as he caught her midair. John stood behind them with a sheepish grin on his face.

"Grandpa," Chloe crooned. "What are you doing here? You hate the city," she rambled. "Look, Maggie, it's my grandpa."

Mom gave a little clap and giggled. She shot John a look of glee. "I'm so happy it worked out. And to think I had a hand in the whole thing."

I glanced sideways at her as she swatted me. "You have a hand in most things. When don't you get your way?"

She smirked.

"I wish I had your secret powers," I said, flexing my muscles in jest.

"You do, my dear, you just don't know it yet."

I shook my head at her mumbo-jumbo. "You are something else."

John motioned for us to join them. I headed down the stairs trying not to stare. John's dad sure was tall, broad, and handsome. He had a glint in his green eyes like John and Chloe.

"I like your cowboy hat." Chloe ran her finger around the edge then down his jaw line and across his cheek. "Your cheeks tickle." She giggled as she inspected the lines at the corners of his eyes.

"Long time, no see, short stuff," he growled, setting Chloe down.

"Grandpa, this is Bones." Chloe rubbed his hindquarters. "He belongs to Maggie. That's Maggie."

I stepped forward when Chloe pointed to me as if I were in a lineup. "Hi there, nice to meet you. This is my mom, Glad."

"Welcome," Mom said, shaking his hand.

"Hi there." Chloe's grandfather nodded.

I watched the interaction between my mom and John's dad. His grin morphed into a stern welcome. He glanced back to me. The shimmer in his eyes serious.

Trying to cover my uneasiness, I smiled. John stepped forward sensing the edge. What could I have possibly done? I hadn't even met the man. He was much bigger than life. The only cowboy in Grosse Pointe was the one on the cover of a paperback novel at our local Barnes and Noble. And none of those images came close to mirroring Chloe's grandfather.

Chloe picked herself up off the ground then dusted off the seat of her pants. She squinted and shaded her eyes with a tilt of her head. "Grandpa, you are way taller than I remember. I can barely see you from down here."

"That's if you even remember," John chimed in. "It's been a while."

John's grin narrowed and his eyes held an untold story. Frozen in the moment, focused on my own silent investigation, I watched. Mom could converse with anybody. Me, I needed a little room for reaction before saying much.

Winston McIntyre reached out to his granddaughter. She fell into his arms and he scooped her up with one smooth motion like he'd been doing it all his life. "You are the spitting image of your daddy."

John shrugged. I knew he was thinking she wished she had some of her mother's beauty. I smiled at their exchange.

"So," Winston said, his voice deep like a Montana canyon, "your daddy tells me you have something special coming up at school. Do you have a rancher on the schedule?"

Chloe wrapped her arms around his neck. His cowboy hat fell to the ground as she nuzzled against him. John and I both reached for the hat at the same time. Our eyes met. He gave me a wink as we brought the hat up together. John brushed it off.

"Put the hat on, Dad," Chloe begged.

John put the Stetson on with a mighty grin. I couldn't figure out if he was a doctor, a motorcyclist, or a cowboy. He fit all three. Now that was the guy I saw on the cover of my Harlequin. My belly flopped around like I was thirteen and

Shaun Cassidy just entered the room. I hoped no one noticed my moment of swooning for the guy next door, but in my mind we were both still picking up that hat together staring each other down, trying to read the future.

Winston nodded with approval. "Looks good, son. Pretty soon you'll be able to wear your own everyday all day."

John's eyes met his dad's. It was the same expression he wore in the black-and-white photo of him riding with his dad that Chloe showed me. His pride, his enjoyment right there in the open. This wasn't some black-and-white photo. This was his life, a dream that called him home. And I couldn't be the one standing in his way.

"So tell me about this career day," Winston said. "What do you have in store for me?"

John stepped closer, his forearm grazed mine. While I was lost in the moment of casual skin-on-skin contact, he was lost in the moment being shared by Chloe and his dad, Winston Ludlow McIntyre. I didn't move, I relished the innocence between us until he glanced over in my direction, his eyes bright, his intention clear with another story, a story that included me.

"It's a day that you come to school," Chloe said. "I have to make a poster with facts about your job. Ranching is a job, isn't it?"

"Oh yes, darlin', it's a job and a hard one if you're doing it right," Winston answered.

"Good, I thought so. Anyway, the kids come through the gym and I introduce you to them and they ask questions. Wait, did you bring any pictures with you?" Chloe asked, slowing her speech.

"Hm. Afraid not, but I bet your dad has some pictures of the place."

"We can try and get some photos online, I have lots of cow photos, not exactly from his ranch, but we can pretend," I suggested.

Winston shot me a look. "You don't look much like a cow lover."

I grinned. "Just a hobby."

"She has tons of pictures, Grandpa. Cows everywhere. Maggie *is* a cow lady."

"If you say so, darlin'. When is this all gonna go down?"

"In two days," Chloe answered.

"Perfect, my saddle and gear should be arriving tomorrow."

"What?" Chloe's voice cracked. "Will there be a horse and a cow?"

"Um, no, but there will be plenty for your friends to look at. I'm not a social kind of guy, but for you I could tell a story or two."

Chloe smiled, her adult teeth, more prominent with each passing day, her hair bounced off her shoulders like Brook's as she fawned over her grandfather.

Chapter 27

Stopping in front of the mirror, I leaned closer to examine my skin, then left the house anxious to see Chloe's project. I stood on the front stoop of her house and rang the bell.

Chloe answered the door. "Come on in," she said. "This is nice having you visit. Seems like I'm always at your house."

"You are," I said with a wry smile.

"Well, anyway, come on in."

Chloe led me into the dining room. The table was covered with western riding gear and a tri-fold poster. My heart skipped a beat. This was a bigger story than I thought.

"Wow, this is something." I caressed the embossed saddle, its rich, worn leather soft with history.

Chloe knelt in a chair and rested her belly on the table, her eyes glued to the photos of her dad when he was a youngster working with his dad.

I smiled. "So are you ready for tomorrow?"

"I think so. I got some butterflies in my stomach though."

"I think that's pretty normal," I picked up her report and read the first few sentences. "Did your dad help you write this report?"

"A little. Mostly Grandpa. His whole name is Winston Ludlow McIntyre." She beamed with pride.

It was sweet the way she articulated her grandfather's name, but I liked the way it rolled off John's tongue better. Strong and proud. "It's pretty amazing that he flew all the way here for your career day."

Chloe scrunched up her nose. "He's got other business with Dad. He's not just here for that."

"Oh," I said, letting my fingers flit across the saddle wondering about Winston's life, his wife, and life in Montana. "Well, I'm glad he's here for you," I said. "I like how the leather smells."

"Me, too," John said, joining us at the table. "Hi, Maggie."

"Hey," I said, smiling. "Chloe was just sharing her project. The pictures are fabulous."

"I like the saddle," Chloe said with a glint of adventure in her eyes. "I can see myself riding a horse and roping doggies, as Grandpa says. Still not sure why they call the cows, doggies, though."

John smirked. "Did you tell Maggie what your granddad brought you?"

Chloe leaned across the table resting her chin on her fists. "Oh yeah, my grandpa's not the only one with a cool hat." She popped out of the chair and skipped off.

"You're really going to go, aren't you?" I stared into John's green eyes.

"Yeah, it's something I have to do."

I sighed, but couldn't blame him even if it made my heart ache. "I know." There were things I had to do, too.

"My offer still stands." He held my hand. "I know you can't see yourself there and I know you have to do what's right for you, but please consider it."

John was killing me. I couldn't believe he was the same guy I met almost a year ago in my backyard who chastised me for his daughter's behavior. "When does the sign go up?" My mind pondered his invitation to join him and I couldn't believe I was turning him down.

"June fifteenth. Chloe's last day of school," he answered.

"It'll be here before you know it." I fiddled with the horn on the saddle. "I can't believe this school year is almost over. It's been a rough one and next year will be even tougher with the additional requirements not to mention another pay cut."

"Another cut?" John asked.

"Yeah, it's the sign of the times, I guess. Things will be tight, but let's not talk about that."

John's stare softened. "You deserve so much more. It's a shame, the kids will be the biggest losers."

"I know." My heart beat faster. John understood the ramifications.

Chloe trotted back into the room wearing a cowboy hat. Her long dishwater-blond locks flowed out from beneath the brim. "Do you like?"

"I like." I winked at her. "Glad will like it, too."

John smiled.

"Can I have a snack? My work is all done." Chloe announced the accomplishment as she pranced around her poster with Vanna White gestures and a gleaming toothy smile.

"Sure," he said. "Clean up whatever you get out."

Chloe tipped her hat then skedaddled.

"You're doing a great job with her," I said.

John rubbed his chin. "I gotta tell you, ever since we moved here and she's met you, it's been much easier."

Chills ran down my spine. We were connected in more ways than just Chloe. "I'm not sure about that. We've had our rough patches," I reminded him.

John chuckled. "Yeah, she wouldn't have made it this long without you. She's really bonded with you."

My mind flashed back to the evening when I first met John. His gruff scowl and prickly demeanor put me on edge. How things had changed! I chuckled. "Chloe's one tough cookie."

"And so are you," he added.

John crossed his arms over his chest and leaned back in the chair. I raised an eyebrow in his direction.

"You have no idea how powerful you are, Maggie Abernathy."

"Not sure what you mean. I'm just the lady next door with a crazy dog and open cupboards."

John leaned forward. He cupped his hands over mine, his warmth familiar and telling.

"You're so much more than just the neighbor lady." His smoldering voice lured me closer.

"You're not going to let this go, are you?"

"Not while I'm still here," he whispered.

The sound of Chloe's flip-flops grew louder.

I pulled my hands away and sat back in my chair. Something inside urged me to hide my feelings. John's gaze held my attention. I felt my face warm with embarrassment at the glint in his eye.

"Hey, Dad." Chloe sucked in a deep breath of air and played with her silver Tiffany necklace. "Are you coming to career day?"

"Afraid not, you're only allowed one customer, and it's up to your granddad to hold down the fort now that he's signed on."

Chloe scrunched up her nose. "Okay."

Winston towered in the doorway behind Chloe. She peered up at him. He snickered at her and rubbed the top of her head. "I think I can manage. It's been a long time since I've been in a school. And your daddy's school was nothing like the fancy one you go to. The country ain't nothing like the city."

"Ain't isn't a word," Chloe informed him. "My dad doesn't let me say ain't."

"Well he's a pretty smart man. You should listen to him," Winston told her. "You too, Maggie Abernathy."

Winston's gaze roused my senses as he spoke to me. My cheeks smoldered like midnight coals, his voice smooth as velvet. John laughed. Chloe looked from me to her father then to her granddad. Intimidated by his presence, I sat frozen. What was I supposed to say to that? What did he know? What had he heard? *Shit, he was from the same planet that beamed my mother to this world.*

Chloe trotted off.

My sweaty palms stuck to the table as I pried myself up from the dining room chair. "Well, I really should be going."

"Don't leave on my account," Winston said.

I forced a smile and tucked my hair behind my ears. "Really, I've got some school work to finish."

Winston crossed his arms atop his chest just like John. He squinted in my direction, deep thought reflected in his eyes.

My insides squirmed.

"I'll see you out," John said.

"I'm sure I'll see you later," I said to Winston. "You did a great job on the project. The students will love it. They'll love hearing your stories."

He gave me a nod as I exited the room. He unnerved me more than his son.

John held the door for me as I left. "Don't mind him. He's just a meddling parent. He doesn't mean any harm."

"What did you tell him?" I asked as John followed me out.

"Not much, just that you're important."

"Important?"

"Yeah, you know, that you feel like family."

A thin smile crossed my lips. "Yeah, you do, too," I mumbled.

John strolled beside me as I meandered back to my house.

"Does Chloe know how you feel about me?" I asked, holding his stare.

He glanced down. "I haven't said anything. I don't think so. Why?"

"I just don't want her to get hurt." I didn't want anyone to get hurt, most of all, me. John's arm brushed up against me, and our eyes locked.

"You can't live life trying to prevent every bruise, cut or heartache. It doesn't work that way. Getting thrown from the horse can make you a better rider."

I knew he was right, but I stifled my expression.

"You never know, you just might find happiness at the end of a rainbow or in the mountains of Montana. I'm trying to be patient," John said, leading me home.

I stood against the pillar at the top of the steps, avoiding eye contact. My insides ached. "I know," I whispered.

John patted the seat next to him on the swing, and I joined him. He scooted closer then put his arm around me. His shoulder made the perfect headrest.

"I really should finish that school work," I said.

"When my mom died, my dad shut out the world. Don't shut out the world."

Raw emotion stung the back of my throat. "I don't want to shut out the world," I said.

John sighed.

"I just don't know what to do. What's right? What's wrong? I don't know." Closing my eyes, I imagined myself under the blue Montana sky.

"Maybe it's not about knowing what to do. Maybe it's about following your heart," John whispered.

Chapter 28

Anxious to hear about Chloe's career fair, I rushed home. Her presence had been scarce with Winston around. All day, I found myself stopping in the middle of things just wondering what was going on at John's house. I couldn't finish a task without distraction. John's words wafted through my head and tugged at my heart. Pulling into the driveway, I peered over to Chloe's house. Loud eruptions of laughter came from their backyard as I stepped out of the car.

Bones jumped on me the second I was inside the house. I scowled at him as he knocked me backward.

"Get down," I growled at him then he nudged the screen door open with his stubby nose. "Hey, hey, hey," I said. "Stay."

He stopped momentarily then gave the door a final thrust and out he went.

I dropped my bag in the foyer and slung my purse into the messy front closet. "Crap," I said under my breath. Scurrying out the front door, I chased after my little runaway.

"Bones," I called, my voice growing louder. "Bones, where'd you go?" I rounded the side of the house. The back gate was closed.

Chloe's laughter cut the air like a knife.

Winston came around the corner with Bones under his arm. Chloe followed behind.

"Sorry about that," I said.

"No need to be sorry. It seems that this guy likes my granddaughter."

Chloe smiled up at her granddad.

"That he does," I said. "Here, let me get the gate."

Chloe led the way to my backyard. Bones' tongue waggled as he panted. His stumpy legs dangled against Winston's muscular build. He wiggled free as his paws hit solid ground.

"Get me." Chloe egged Bones on. She darted back and forth across the yard.

I picked up a faded tennis ball and lobbed it past both of them.

Bones bolted, snatched it up, and Chloe tumbled into the grass after tripping over him.

"That's quite some arm," Winston said, tucking his fingers into his front pockets.

His presence seemed less intimidating today. I stared at him. His stature, majestic, rugged, and strong, like a human mountain. Feeling more at ease, I crossed my arms and focused on Chloe and Bones' tug-of-war game.

"Chloe can't stop talking about you," Winston said.

"Kids are like that." I smiled. "Watch the flowers," I called as Chloe and Bones wrestled near the planters.

"Sure thing," Chloe shouted back. She stole the ball from Bones and threw it under the Dogwood tree. Chloe cackled as Bones' ran under the low branches to their hiding place. Bones grabbed the ball and plopped down.

Chloe knelt in front of the tree. "Come on out, boy." She crouched lower. "Come on. I'll rub your belly."

Bones slunk out after hearing Chloe's enticing request, then he rolled over on his back in front of her.

"How did it go today?" I asked.

"I think I did okay," Winston replied.

Chloe's gaze met mine for a brief moment. "You were better than okay! You were the most awesome person there. Everyone wanted to be a rancher after talking to you except *Barnyard* and her stupid BFF," Chloe said. "Oh and those geeky boys that want to design video games. That doesn't sound like much fun to me."

"Me neither," I concurred. "Would you like to sit?" I invited Winston to the patio.

He sat in the chaise lounge next to me. His long legs hung off the end of the chair, his pointed cowboy boots like jagged peaks grazing the sky. The doors behind us jiggled.

I glanced over my shoulder. "Hi, Mom."

Chloe stood and ran toward Glad.

"This was the best day ever," Chloe said, hugging Mom. "Except for that part when Jillie Sander's grandma started flirting with grandpa."

I smiled.

Winston greeted my mom.

"Stay put." She scooted a chair over and sat next to me.

"Yeah, she was something else," he responded, shaking his head. "The women around here are something."

I glanced Mom's way, wondering if we were included in that demographic.

Winston's lip curled when he caught my jeer.

"Are they now?" she jested.

Winston chuckled. "No wonder my boy is having such a hard time making up his mind."

There it was, a ray of hope, a shred of insight that he and Chloe just might not move. I held my breath. I glanced over to my mother who read my face with impeccable timing.

"So, John's not sure he's ready to move to Montana? He's thinking about sticking it out here in the Midwest?"

I studied Chloe's profile as she rubbed Bones' belly in the shaggy grass that needed to be mowed. My yard went from waking up to overgrown in a matter of days.

Winston cleared his throat.

I focused on Chloe not wanting to seem overly eager with Winston's nugget of insight.

"I don't think it's for me to say, but there's something here that's caught his attention. Sure wish he'd get on the stick and come home. You know, I used to be a city boy, but the mountains called to me. They'd whisper to me in the midnight hours and that's all I dreamed of."

I gazed into Winston's face. His mind was in Montana, but his body was in Michigan. I desperately wanted to ask about his wife, but couldn't bring myself to because it seemed like prying.

"It must be beautiful there," Mom commented.

"It's beautiful, all right, and can be mighty tough at times."

Melancholy washed over his expression. I pictured him riding with the herd through harsh weather.

"I imagine so," Mom said. "Especially raising a teenager on your own."

John's mom had passed when he was young. I waited for the story. I wanted the story. I needed the whole story.

Winston sighed. I expected resistance, but when I acknowledged his soft gaze, his jaw softened as well.

"Yeah, that was a tough time. John was in high school when we lost his mother . . ." His voice trailed off.

"I'm so sorry," I said.

They had something in common that I couldn't sympathize with, but could only surmise the devastation from losing a spouse. I wondered how that grief measured up to losing one in a divorce. A loss was a loss despite circumstance.

"It's okay, darlin', but I appreciate your kindness. I can see how my boy and Chloe are so fond of you."

Bones sauntered in-between our chairs. Chloe stood up, stretched, then did two cartwheels in our direction.

"Hey, Grandpa, what's for dinner?" she asked.

Winston ran his hand through his white hair. "I'm afraid I'm not much of a chef, little darlin'." He checked his watch. "And your dad's not due home for an hour or so.

In true Glad fashion, she chimed in. "We have a grill right here. We could cook something up and have it ready by the time John gets home. Maggie and I could use some grub, too."

Winston laughed. "I can grill a mean steak."

"Then steak it is," Mom said. "I'll go to the market and we'll get started."

Chloe sat on her grandfather's lap, admiring his cowboy stature. Bones licked her toes, and I wondered how Mom was able to mastermind an impromptu dinner probably more for my sake than any other reason. I smiled, then reached over to pat her knee.

"Grandpa, are you really going to make steak?"

"Sure am," he replied.

Winston's eyes connected with my mother's then he glanced over to me. "Couldn't let these two go hungry now, could we? Seems like they've done a lot for you. It's the least I can do to repay their generosity."

Chloe giggled.

"Plus you need to get some meat on your bones. You're looking a little scrawny, runt. You must get that from your momma," Winston said, trying to pinch her belly. "What do you say we go with Glad to the store, help her shop, and get out of Maggie's hair for a few minutes since she's been rustling kids all day. I imagine that's more difficult than roping the White Park Cattle we got back on the ranch."

"White Park Cattle?" They sounded mysterious.

"There isn't anything like them for miles. They have a lot of history."

Soft lines appeared at the corners of Winston's eyes.

I smiled at the analogy, his language, and the love for his animals.

Transfixed by her grandfather's voice, Chloe's eyes grew wide and bright as she took him in like a summer breeze.

Bones stared up at me then put his paws on the edge of the lounge chair. His tongue waggled and he gave a grunt as if to say he wanted steak, too.

I patted his beasty head then stood up.

"Can we get cake at the store? That will fatten me up," Chloe claimed.

Winston patted his slim belly. "Maybe it will fatten me up, too. All this grandpa stuff is making me hungry."

Chloe climbed down from her Grandpa's lap and gestured for Bones to follow her into the house. I followed. Mom and Winston discussed a shopping list, more like Mom listed what we needed and Winston listened, and nodded.

"Your grandpa is a nice man," I said. Two days ago I was unsure about his gruff exterior. He and John probably had more in common than I realized.

Chloe's slender fingers warmed my hand. She stared up into my face. Hints of her daddy's personality resonated in her green irises.

Chapter 29

I sat at my desk and made a list of things to do before the school year ended. My chest tightened. "God, I hate this time of year," I muttered to myself, running my hand through my hair. I leaned back and closed my eyes to escape just for a moment. Visions of green valleys washed across the mountains in my mind. Clear and beautiful. Buttercup flowers danced with the wind that whisked puffy white clouds overhead. I could almost smell Winston's country. His words stuck in my mind like pinesap on a pair of jeans after climbing a gnarly tree. He'd said when he slept that *Montana whispered in his ear*. Those were powerful words.

A knock at the door brought me back to reality, but visions of God's country littered my mind with beautiful imprints. It was Winston.

"Hi, there," I said, curious about his presence.

"Sorry, to interrupt, but your mom asked me to find you. She's in the kitchen and was wondering if you could help her."

I smiled. Mom's motives were clearly not a cry for help in the kitchen, more like a subtle hint of meddling that only a daughter could detect and hopefully deflect.

Winston inspected the top of my desk.

"You can come look if you want," I said, spreading out the photographs of my cows.

His cowboy boots treaded softly on the wooden floor, his face somehow gentler as his gaze scanned my work driven by a fascination with cows, who knew? Some of which had sprouted wings during their ordinary lives milling around the fields. I know I wanted wings.

"Thought you were a teacher?" His eyes met mine.

"This is what I do in my spare time. Keeps me sane." I counted at least thirty finished hand-colored photos. When did I have time? There were advantages to being a hermit. I thought about Fletcher then disregarded the interest. My brow furrowed as I tucked my hands in the back pockets of my jeans. There was nothing there, just some photographer, the guy that slept with Brook wedging that final spike of deceit between Brook and John. I wished I would've known, but then again, Chicago would've been a whole different ball of wax covered in tar and feathers, if I had. Sending the belt and jewelry back to Fletcher Thompson was at the top of my to-do list.

"You're very talented. I'm partial to cattle myself." Winston picked up a black-and-white matte photo of three cows munching hay as they stood by a rickety trough. "Guess we got something in common, little lady."

"Guess we do," I said, thinking we had more than that in common and by the glint in his eye he did, too. He sure was tall. He seemed comfortable hanging out with my mom and me, and that made my heart happy. I snickered, realizing that Chloe had somehow managed to bring another person into my life, another missing link. "Probably should go help my mom. You never know what she's up to. You can make yourself comfortable if you'd like."

"If it's okay with you, I just as soon come back into the kitchen." Winston rubbed his whiskery chin then let his green eyes connect with mine. "I have to admit, we don't get many ladies around the ranch."

Smiling, I nodded. I enjoyed being the hangout house when Bradley was younger and although the players had changed, warm fuzzy feelings filled me. "You're welcome anytime."

"Chloe was right."

"Right about what?" I rearranged the photos and logged off the computer.

"What a nice lady you are. Who else would let a fellow like me hang around?"

Winston was more than just some *fellow*. He was John's dad. His eyes flickered, and for a moment, I saw my own father standing there before me giving me a sly grin. "Well, we'll see about that. You have some cooking to do," I said. "It's not every day I have a cowboy show up on my doorstep willing to grill me a steak."

Winston chuckled. "Don't go holding your breath. It's just a slab of beef."

"Can I see your boots?" I asked, intrigued by the leather design creeping out beneath the hem of his Levis.

Taking in his funny expression, I grinned.

"I probably sound like one of Chloe's friend's at the career fair, but I have to see them," I said. He lifted his faded blue jean pant leg. "Fancy. Very nice."

"They're my traveling boots. My work boots are back home. They're not so fancy. Thought mud and manure might not bode well for Chloe since she was having troubles already."

Chloe trotted in. "What are you guys doing?" she asked. Her eyes glanced toward her granddad's boots. She bent down and stroked the leather. "Soft. Smells like the country." She smiled, her gaze twinkling with love. "Grandpa, Glad says it's about time to put the steaks on. I can't wait to sink my teeth into that. They look gigantic, big enough to feed a whole posse of wranglers."

He winked. "She's a fast learner."

She stood up and took his hand. "Come on, Glad is pretty hungry, too. She's nibbling on everything. We have to feed her."

I rolled my eyes. "I'm pretty sure no one is starving around here."

"She's hungry, Maggie. You don't want your momma to be hungry, do you?" Winston smirked.

"I guess not."

Bones ran in. His tail whipped across Winston's calf.

"See, he's hungry, too," Chloe said.

"He's always hungry," I grunted.

Chloe pinched my side. I rubbed my skin where she left a red mark. "What was that for? Geez."

"To remind you that you need to eat more, too. Put some meat on your bones. Not all of us can eat like a bird."

That wasn't my eight-year-old friend talking. "Eat like a bird?" I questioned.

Chloe crinkled the bridge of her nose in thought. Then the left side of her mouth curled up. "Yeah, I think that's what Glad said, eat like a bird. But I'm not sure what that means cause I'm pretty sure you wouldn't eat worms."

I uncrossed my arms. "Okay, I'm coming."

Mom stood at the counter tossing a salad. "Well, it's about time. This old lady is starving."

"You're not old," Chloe and I said in unison.

"Jinx, you owe me a Coke," we both said in unison, holding out our pinky fingers. Chloe hooked her pinky finger with mine and laughed.

"Here you go, Mr. McIntyre," Mom said, handing Winston a platter of steaks. "The grill is on and ready to go. I'll bring out the salad." Mom continued tossing the salad then winked at Chloe.

"I'll get the bread," Chloe said, scurrying over to my mom's side.

"What can I do?" I leaned against the counter wondering how I'd live in this big house alone once Chloe and John were gone.

"Nothing," my mom said. "Tonight we're taking care of you."

Winston strolled out to the patio.

As nice as that sounded, I feared her hidden agenda. "Why? Do I look tired?" Stepping closer to Mom, I picked up the wicker basket of napkins.

"No, you look lovely. I thought we could take care of you for a change," she said quietly.

Chloe smiled. "Yeah, it's probably a good idea. You take care of all those children at school then you come home and help me and I'm not even yours."

I raised an eyebrow to both of them. "Thank you." Resting my finger beneath Chloe's chin, I tilted her head back so I could see her better. Her hands wrapped around me and she squeezed tight. "You're squishing me."

"Sorry." Chloe looked me in the eye. "That's why you need to put some meat on your bones," she added. "Grandpa said I need more meat, too."

"You're a funny, kid," I said.

Mom's eyebrow curved toward the ceiling as she shrugged her shoulders with innocence. "Okay, Bert and Ernie, let's go get us some grub."

Chloe expression questioned me.

"Grub, that means food," I clarified.

"Sounds like something my grandpa would say," she said, wiggling free.

I handed her the breadbasket.

She smiled. "This is warm. And smells delicious. I can't wait to eat!"

"Like I said before. No one goes hungry around here."

Chloe skipped out to the patio humming an unfamiliar tune. Mom took the salad from the counter and led the way. Winston stood at the grill. Sizzling sounds popped. He closed the lid then faced us. I couldn't help but fixate on his stature. The gate creaked and I investigated to see who our visitor was. John came around the corner with a smile on his face.

"Daddy." Chloe ran to John and wrapped her arms around his waist. He picked her up with a grunt.

I set the napkins on the table. Mom put the salad down then subtly flashed me a look. She leaned over and whispered, "You sure you want to give that up?"

Mortified, I glanced to Winston who was engrossed in flipping steaks. "This is not the time, Glad," I said under my breath. "And I am not giving them up. They are the ones who are moving."

"It's all relative, my dear."

I cleared my throat then stepped away.

Winston focused on the grill. "Almost done. Then we'll let those boys rest a spell."

John put Chloe down next to the table. His eyes danced at the scene before him. A blind man could've felt his energy.

I met his gaze. "Glad you got home in time for dinner."

Mom handed Winston a clean platter. She helped hold it while he piled a mountain of beef upon the dish.

"Got the new guy to finish up so I could be here." John loosened his tie.

There was a new guy?

Winston brought the steaks over to the table. He helped seat my mother. Chloe pulled out a chair for me. Then she pulled out a chair for her dad. Mom plunged the tongs into the salad and scooped some onto my plate. I watched John interact with his dad. Their playful banter like young pups amused me. Chloe munched on her salad and gave Glad a thumbs-up.

"I saw that," I said as she snuck a bite of bread to Bones. "You're always good for a nibble."

Chloe smirked, her mouth full. "Can't help it," she said, "He's so darn cute."

"Don't talk with your mouth full," John reminded her.

"Sorry," she sputtered, trying to speak through closed lips.

John's carefree attitude infectious. That was not a man unsure of where he was going or when. Not wanting to break the spell, I ate quietly taking cautious bites as the men spoke.

Winston glanced my way. "You have the summer off?"

"Yes."

"She's got time?" Winston said.

"Time for what?" I asked with trepidation, thinking back to Mom and Chloe's generosity in the kitchen.

Mom smiled at me as she plopped a cherry tomato in her mouth.

Chloe shoveled food in her mouth like she hadn't eaten in days, her eyes glued to me. Ambushed? What now?

Chloe chugged her water. "Grandpa said you should come see the ranch this summer. That's where the real cows are. I think it's a great idea. Please, Maggie. I'll be there."

John lowered his gaze at her.

Winston shrugged.

Mom's smile, as usual, screamed instigator.

I'd interrogate her later. With a polite grin, I sipped my water pretending to wash down food. Interesting.

"He's got enough bedrooms for all of us. He even said that Walter and Harry could come with their mom."

I scanned the cast of characters with a questioning smile. John caught my stare. I looked from him to Chloe. His eyes filled with as much hope as his daughter's. His gaze held a quiet plea. "Wow, that's some offer."

"Pleeeaaaassse, Maggie. We'll have so much fun. There's a pond and a creek and everything. I can teach you how to fish."

"You know how to fish?" I asked, nibbling at my garlic bread.

"Yeah, Dad taught me how. We fish at the park. I can touch the worms now and everything."

John beamed with pride. "It's true."

Chloe leaned on the table.

Bones trotted over, stared at me, and plopped down. His wrinkly jowls just as pitiful as the eyes upon me.

Chapter 30

There we were, two peas in a pod. Mom and I, feet propped up on the coffee table, holding a hot cup of tea sipping simultaneously as the fire flickered. The question posed at dinner etched in my mind, the faces, the pressure.

"You're not going to say anything?" my mom asked.

Focused on the flames licking the firebox, I sat stoic. My eyes narrowed as I lifted the cup to my lips. Green tea tickled my bottom lip the way John had when he kissed me. I set my teacup down on the table beside me, crossed my arms, and leaned my head back to close my eyes.

"I can wait," Mom said.

Her cup clanked against her saucer. I felt the shift of her weight in the cushions. I could go, but what would be the purpose? It would be a golden ring on a carousel that I just couldn't reach because my arms were too short. It would be leading him on. What would be the purpose? I had things to finish here.

The droning thoughts smothered Mom's questions.

"You think too much," Mom whispered.

She'd had been telling me that since I was a child. "What does that even mean?" I mumbled.

"Good, for a moment I thought you were asleep."

She slurped her tea. I didn't look.

"You're the one with the degree actually a couple of them. It's pretty straightforward. It means what it sounds like it means."

I opened my eyes. She spoke her words into the fire as she knelt before the hearth poking at the embers with the brass poker. Her profile aglow, like she was a girl at a campfire stoking fortune from charred kindling. Her lip curled as she glanced in my direction, monkey business brewing behind her eyes. I wondered like hell why I hadn't inherited that gene. "You think I am boring, don't you?"

"No, darling, I think you're old enough to throw away the rule book and play."

She turned back toward the fire then pushed herself up from the ground after leaning the poker against the mantle. I got up to help her as she teetered.

"Careful," I said, holding her elbow. When had my mother started to teeter? "You okay?"

"Yeah, I just can't get up like I used to," she answered.

I thought about it. "Yeah, I know what you mean," I said with a chuckle.

"Well, I think I should be getting home. You have school tomorrow. You need your rest."

I think I need more than that. "It's only nine o'clock," I said, checking the clock on my phone.

Mom took her purse from the table in the foyer as I opened the door. "I love you, Mom." Emotion filled me, a knot at the back of my throat.

"I know, Bubby. I love you, too." She leaned in and hugged me. Her tender lips kissed my cheek, and I breathed her in. I swallowed hard trying not to cry.

"Thanks for having dinner tonight," she said, tucking the hair behind my ears.

Her words washed away the threat of tears. "Yeah, anytime. I'm pretty good entertainment."

"You certainly are. I know you're thinking about it."

Mom's gaze held my stare. I saw myself in her, but time had modified her stature and I wondered if I would shrink, too. "You look shorter."

"Thanks, Marjorie Jean. I believe you've mentioned that before."

"Sorry . . ."

"Damn gravity," she sputtered.

Rubbing her back, I laughed at her guttural tone. She clicked the key fob to her new Volkswagen on her keychain. It beeped. The headlights blinked in the dusky light. "I sure do like that little car of yours."

"You can borrow it anytime. It wouldn't be right to hog all the fun."

Mom slung her bag over her shoulder and gave me a wink. "Thanks again, that was some dinner."

"Night, Mom," I said, closing my sweater to keep out the chill.

"Night, my darling girl," she said.

She waved over her shoulder, and I sat on the swing as she drove away. As the taillights faded into the distance, I swayed to the sounds of spring. Voices from John's house drifted through the hedges. His father's voice deeper, sterner. I wondered if time would change John's voice, too. I wedged my foot between the floorboards of the porch when I heard my name. I contemplated getting up, but was frozen with curiosity.

"I don't know, Dad. I'm putting the house up sometime around the fifteenth of June," John said.

Distorted voices chatted just beyond the greenery between my porch and John's driveway. I strained to hear, but couldn't make out the words. I thought I heard Winston's boots on the concrete.

"I sure do like your neighbors, son."

"Me, too," John replied. "Me, too."

How much had he shared with Winston? Did Winston know about our attraction? Of course he did, Mom probably said something. A flash of heat lit up my cheeks. Who was I kidding? Nobody. Not even myself. John was the best thing that'd happened to me in a long time and I was leading him around like Chloe did Voodoo on his purple leash. I clenched my teeth. What were the damn rules anyway? I picked up my foot and let the swing sway to and fro.

Tucking my leg under myself, I shut my eyes. What was I expecting to find in John? What if I found something good? Would I ruin it? Would it take me over? Would I let it take me over?

"Hey."

I opened my eyes at the sound of John's voice. He stood at the top of the stairs with his hands tucked in his pockets. "Hey."

"I didn't mean to put you on the spot tonight, but that's how Chloe rolls," he said.

He lowered his gaze.

A thin line of agreement crossed my grin. "I know. Don't worry about it," I told him. "I'm used to it."

"We really do want you to visit us. Thought it might ease the transition for Chloe."

I lowered my gaze. "And for you?"

"Maybe," he confessed. "But it really was Chloe's idea."

"Of course it was." I stopped the swing.

"Really, it was," he said. "Bring Judy and the boys, there's plenty of room, plenty to keep you busy."

"Plenty to reel me in," I muttered. He tried to hide his grin. "I see the look in your eye, John Patrick."

"Hey, your middle naming me."

"Yes, I am," I shot back. "You're not playing fair."

His stare took my breath away. "Nope, guess not, but a man's gotta do what a man's gotta do even if it means not playing fair."

"What would your father say about that?"

"If my dad had anything to say about it, he'd hand me a rope, tell me to hogtie you and bring you home."

I raised an eyebrow at him in disbelief.

"How do you think he got my momma?" His shoulders shook when he laughed.

Standing up, I folded my arms across my chest, then stepped closer to him. He let me. "You are so full of it."

"No, ask my dad, he'll tell you. That's how he got my momma."

I narrowed my gaze.

"Damn it, Maggie," he said. "I'm not gonna hogtie you, but just come see what it's about."

Taking his hand, I held open the creaky screen door and invited him in. He switched off the light in the foyer and shut the door. I leaned into him, letting my lips graze his. His soft moan filled with sexy introspection.

"What?" I nibbled at his bottle lip. "Two can play at this game. Is this not fair?" His emerald eyes sparkled in the night. Smiling, I wrapped my arms around his waist.

"You asked for it."

I shut my eyes and waited as he drew me closer. Nothing. I opened my eyes. His teasing expression baited me. Just when I'd given up on the notion he'd kiss me, his lips covered mine.

"Goodnight, Maggie," he said with a perilous smirk.

"What?" I yearned for more.

He stroked my messy locks.

"You really don't play fair. Have you been like this all your life?" I asked.

"I've gotta get back home. If I stay one minute longer, I won't be able to stop."

"Stop what?" I asked.

John's mouth covered mine. His kiss filled me up. His hands covered my cheeks and he held me steady. My insides flipped over. Heat flooded my veins. "Oh," I mumbled.

John caressed my face with his thumbs. I nuzzled into the palm of his warm hand. "You'd better go," I whispered into his lips, feeling electricity spark between us.

"You never know, Maggie, what you just might find if you let yourself have an adventure," John whispered.

I shut the door after he left, then tiptoed through the dark hallway and into the living room. The last flame died out, red incandescent coals glowed in the dark as I huddled under the blanket on the sofa. Silence filled the air upon the last flicker. I checked the time on my phone, the wallpaper reminding me of Bradley. With the rise and fall of my breaths, I wished him goodnight even though he was miles away. Turning off my phone, I headed upstairs.

Shadows of the night made it hard to see in the dark, but after all these years, I learned to navigate every twist and turn of my sleepy house without bumping into anything or even stubbing a toe. I didn't have to feel the wall or count my steps, every creak or seam of cool wood flooring beneath my bare feet induced confident footing. Standing at the end of my bed, I stripped in the silvery moonlight that washed over me. Crawling under the covers, I waited for Montana to whisper my name.

Chapter 31

Elated to be home, I ticked off one more day of school on the calendar. I kicked off my shoes and wiggled my toes against the cool floor. Scorning the ungraded papers, I slid my book bag into the closet and shut the door. It was already almost six and I'd been sitting at my desk calling parents and wrestling with technology that was supposed to be my friend. The endless mound of work took its toll. Montana hadn't whispered to me in my sleep, but I sure thought about it all day long. The house was cool and quiet. Perfect.

I scuffled into the kitchen and opened the French doors to let in fresh air. Bones waggled out into the yard, his husky hindquarters bouncing back and forth. I expected Mom to be lurking in the shadows, but her blue Bug was nowhere in sight. I poured myself a glass of wine, grabbed my book from the counter, and headed for the chaise lounge to keep an eye on "the beast."

Bones trotted by as I put my feet up. His tags jingled. I wondered how much work it would take to train him to fetch snacks and more wine. He put his front paws up on the end of my chair and licked my toes. I leaned forward to pat his head. Two familiar sneakers sticking out from underneath the Dogwood tree caught my attention. I ignored them as I settled into the cushions. Chloe was going to have to find a better place to hide.

"Aren't you even going to ask me what's wrong?" she called.

How did she even know I was there? I opened my book, read a few words, then glanced in her direction not saying anything. Finally, I closed my book. "What's wrong?" I called back.

"Nothing," she shouted, her voice sharp and ugly.

"Okay." I opened my book again. I read a few lines wishing for the prose to suck me in and deliver me to another place and time, preferably a time approximately three weeks into the future when I didn't need to set an alarm and my days would consist of trying to find my marbles and reassemble the nerves.

"You really should check on me." Chloe persistent tone grew more agitated.

"Okay," I replied, not moving. A twinge of guilt prodded me to move as I sat trying to do my best to ignore her. I sipped at my wine and peered over the rim as I tilted the glass up. Chloe's feet wiggled then disappeared. "Damn it," I said. "Are you hurt?"

No answer.

I read a few more words then put the book down, drained my glass, and went over to Dogwood tree.

Bones followed me, his creased brow judging my actions.

I rolled my eyes at him. "Like you didn't know she was under there," I muttered.

Bones wagged his tail then sat on my feet. The soles of my feet sunk into the green grass.

I sat down, and Bones rolled over onto his back. I patted his muscular chest. "So, what seems to be the problem?" I asked, playing with Bones' floppy jowls.

Chloe didn't answer, but her feet popped out from underneath the tree.

I leaned closer to get a better view. She was lying on her back with her hands behind her head. Thin green eyes peered out at me like a cat in the night, the waves in her chest, an easy pace.

"Well for starters, Grandpa is leaving tomorrow."

Bones licked my ear. I rubbed his head and snuggled with him. "You need a bath," I said after getting a whiff of his fur. He gave a little grunt and trotted under the tree with Chloe. "You know you can't stay under there forever."

"Are you talking to me or the dog?" Chloe asked with a huff.

"Both of you."

The scent of lilacs drifted down over me as the breeze picked up.

"I don't want Grandpa to go. I like having him here," she continued. "Why can't he just stay here?"

"Well . . ." I plucked some grass from the ground and began shredding it. "He does have a ranch to get back to. I'm sure the cattle miss him."

"I doubt it," she retorted. "They're probably glad he's not there. Then they can play more, get away with stuff, whatever cows think is fun."

"So what else is bugging you?" I asked, pressing my luck.

Chloe sat up and scooted out from underneath the tree. "And I have to wear these!" she clamored, slipping on a new pair of eyeglasses.

"You didn't tell me you were getting glasses," I said, tucking her hair behind her ear.

"Maggie, I got glasses. There I told ya', now how can I get out of wearing them? That stupid *Barnyard* spent all day staring at me. She's so rude." Chloe's eyes searched mine in a plea for help.

"Sorry, Charlie, if you have to wear them, you have to wear them. Glad wears glasses sometimes," I said, trying to console her.

"Yeah, but she's old."

I scowled. "Hey now, that's my mother you're talking about. I wear them, too."

"Yeah, I know. I shouldn't be mad at her, but it's not fair.

Hardly any of the kids have glasses and besides my dad and my grandpa don't wear glasses. Mom doesn't wear glasses."

I tucked my legs up into my chest and wrapped my arms around my knees. "Maybe you won't have to wear them all your life. Later you could get contacts or have that fancy eye surgery like all the sports stars."

Chloe grimaced. "Yeah, that sounds like fun."

I chuckled at her sarcasm, then felt the seat of my pants. "I gotta get up, I'm getting wet."

"Seriously?" Chloe whined, popping up on her feet. "Can't something just go my way?"

"Excuse me?" I said.

"Nothing works out for me. I think I was born under an unlucky star," she surmised with her hand on her chin.

Chloe sauntered alongside with her hands crossed over her chest as I meandered back to the patio. "I guess I see it differently," I said.

"Of course you do. You're a grown-up. Grown-ups always see things differently. They're always trying to convince kids that things aren't so bad, but really, they should try being eight sometime."

"We were all eight at one time or another," I reminded her.

"Look, I'm just sayin'. I have glasses, my grandpa's leaving, my dad's on the phone with the house guy, and the worst of all, the teacher rearranged our desks, and now I sit right next to Hilary Barnhardt, princess of the land of evil. She stinks, and I feel like my life is over."

"Sorry to hear that," I said, hoping it would stop the rambling list of everyday life.

"Yeah, now is it registering?" she asked, squinting up at me.

"I really like those frames."

"Dad helped me pick them out. I wish Mom could have been there. She's all about accessories. She probably would have fought for me, told the doctor I didn't need glasses cause glasses were not her accessory of choice."

I grinned, grabbed my wineglass, and headed inside for a refill. Upon opening the refrigerator, I retrieved the bottle of chardonnay.

Chloe climbed up on a stool at the kitchen counter and put her head down on the speckled granite. "Seriously, Mom wouldn't make me wear glasses."

"I'm not so sure about that," I replied. "Just think how much better you'll be able to see."

"Woo-hoo," she bellowed, like a dying seal that'd been clubbed inhumanely.

"Sorry," I said, patting her head. "Want some lemonade?"

"No," she said. "Is Glad coming over tonight?"

I shrugged. "Don't know. Usually, she just shows up. Do you need to check in with someone at your house?"

"No, my grandpa's taking a nap on the sofa and my dad's in the garage. How am I going to get my motorcycle helmet on with these things?"

"Just like you did before. Or don't wear them on the bike. It's not like you're driving." I opened the dishwasher and stuck the morning dishes on the top rack.

"Someday I'll have to drive."

"But not anytime soon."

"Thought I'd find her over here," John said as he came in through the French doors.

My eyes met his with a smile.

"Come on, kiddo, Maggie's probably exhausted and we need to get some dinner. Thought we'd show Grandpa the park tonight. We can get ice cream."

"Woo-hoo." Chloe's bellowing tone became more dreadful. Bones howled at her. "Like that's gonna make me feel better."

John tucked his hands in his pockets. He came inside and helped his daughter down from the stool. Her arms and legs flopped around like limp noodles.

"Ice cream would make me feel better," I said. She rolled her eyes at me. "Just trying to help." I lifted both hands in a friendly surrender.

John made her stand up. "Get going, short stuff. I'll be right behind you. I have something to tell Maggie."

Chloe slumped forward and dragged her feet as she moped toward the door.

"I'll be home in a minute, go wash up. You get to pick the restaurant," he said.

Chloe's green eyes twitched with interest. "Really?"

"Really," John said, lowering his gaze and his tone.

Chloe patted the top of Bones' head. "Did you feed him?"

Oh, crap. She's a better dog owner than I ever could be. "No."

Chloe opened the cupboard closest to Bones' dish and scooped out his dinner. "There ya' go, boy."

"Thanks," I said. "What am I going to do without you?" The words escaped my lips without a second thought. A shard of worry dimmed her green eyes.

"I don't know," she answered.

Chloe left quietly. I silently scolded myself for bringing up the move. John watched his daughter move like a sloth out the door.

The swig of wine settled my nerves as I sat at the counter staring at my pathetic friend leave. "Sorry."

"It's okay. She needs to get used to the idea sooner or later. The house is going up on June seventeenth. Just got a few things to do to get it ready."

Disappointment washed over me. Now I was on Chloe's island.

"You're really good with her. You must be a great teacher," John said.

"It's a little different there, another playing field," I explained.

"Still, you're really good with her. Thanks."

"No problem. I kind of like her, an awful lot." I sipped more wine. The second glass of chardonnay slid down more easily than the first. And a third was calling. "So Winston's leaving tomorrow?"

"Yeah, but we'll see him soon enough when school gets out," John answered.

I finished the last of my wine. The glass tinged against the counter when I set it down. I smiled. I strained to hear, but John wasn't saying anything. I thought I heard the echo of horse hooves across the open meadows. Must have been the alcohol.

"Why don't you meet us at the park?" John asked.

"Maybe," I said.

"Please," John said, "I'd really like it if you'd bring your camera and snap some pictures of Chloe and her grandpa."

The corner of my mouth drew upward as if it was being snagged by an invisible lure. "Sure, why don't you text me when you're done with dinner and you're on your way toward the lake."

"Thanks, Maggie."

John stepped closer. Leaning into me, he kissed my right temple. I closed my eyes hoping to see blue sky smooching the snowy Montana mountain peaks. "You're welcome." Taking a breath, I listened. He touched the scar from last summer that peeked out from underneath my hairline.

"It's the scars that give us personality," he said.

I stared into his eyes. "It's the scars that remind us of our pasts."

"It's the scars that remind us that we can heal."

Chapter 32

Behind the wheel of Mom's new Volkswagen, I grinned wildly as I settled into the leather driver's seat. Mom had a new pink and orange paisley scarf tied around her neck. I stopped the car, shifted it in park, then held out my hand in her direction. She reached into the glove compartment and produced the scarf she'd given the other day.

"Hang on." I tied my hair up with my ponytail holder then tied the orange and blue paisley scarf around my ponytail. Chloe wasn't the only one letting her hair grow out.

"Your hair is getting long there, Marjorie Jean."

I grinned, ignoring the middle naming then put the car in reverse, checked behind me, and slowly backed out of the driveway. I gripped the wheel with both hands. The tail of my silk scarf whipped around lashing my cheeks. Mom propped her arm up on the door. With each day of spring, the smell of the lake drifted further into my neighborhood. Children played in the driveways and rode bikes up and down the sidewalks ushering in summer. Coasting to the stop sign, the lake greeted us. Mom glanced at me from the passenger's seat.

"It will always welcome you home," she said.

"What?" I asked.

"No matter where we go, the lake will always welcome you home."

"Yeah." I nodded. "You're right about that." I wondered if I could live without the water. I wondered if I could live without the endless horizon.

"You're thinking about it again, aren't you?" Mom asked.

I eased my way into the road. Peering left, right, then left again with caution, I veered onto Lakeshore Drive toward the park entrance, avoiding her question. A pod of lightweight sailboats bobbed in the cove just off the shore.

"If you don't go, you'll regret it later," Mom said. "I know you."

"I'm glad somebody does, cause most days I'm not so sure I know myself." I put on the blinker and entered the parking lot.

Eager to snap photos of Chloe, Winston, and John, I packed my camera in the backseat. Its viewfinder offered a veil. I could see others one frame at a time and if I was lucky enough I'd capture them in a thread of time that portrayed some sense of their true selves that provoked understanding. I unbuckled then glanced over to Mom. I hated it when she was right.

"Let's go, Glad," I said, reaching for my camera.

Mom peered over the rim of her sunglasses.

"What?" I shrugged.

"You're impossible." She shut the car door with a huff.

"People keep telling me that," I replied, knowing it was true. I slung the camera strap over my shoulder.

Chloe barreled down the pathway which led to the point that jutted out into Lake St. Clair. Her hair trailed in the wind as her shoes slapped against the pavement. Mom held her arms open and Chloe fell into her basket of love.

"Man, it's about time you guys got here. Come on." She beckoned us to follow her and tugged at Mom's hand. "My friend Autumn is here with her mom. You can meet them. Come on, we're all by the gazebo."

A voice called my name. I shaded my eyes, scanning the horizon.

"Hey, Judy," I called, waving at her.

Harry and Walter ran toward Chloe. Walter squeezed Chloe's middle and grunted.

"Easy, cowboy. I'm not a tube of toothpaste." She moaned.

"How's it going?" Judy asked.

"Same as always," my mom said, shooting me a look.

I held her gaze. "Nice," I responded. "My mother thinks I'm a kook."

"Not a kook, just a stubborn old lady," she retorted.

Judy chuckled.

"I'm not an old lady," I said with raised eyebrow. Judy rubbed my arm. "What? You think I'm a ninny, too?"

Judy squinted into the sun, its fiery orange hues close enough to sizzle on the lake's horizon. "I'm not sure. What are we talking about?"

Chloe, Harry, and Walter stood before me like a jury taking notes.

"Maybe we should discuss this later," I suggested.

"Go on, you Three Musketeers, we'll be along in a moment," Judy said, waving her hands as if she were shooing away flies.

"All I'm saying is—" Mom took a deep breath. "Don't squander any chances that involve adventure. Here's your chance to take that *fork in the road*, veer off the beaten path." Judy shifted her weight and nodded in agreement.

"I know, Mom. I know," I murmured.

Judy put her sunglasses on. "I think I'll stay out of this mother-daughter love fest. Besides, look at that."

Mom and I watched Winston as he reeled in a fish. The children squealed with delight as it wiggled. I took the lens off my camera and moved closer. Peering through the viewfinder, I blocked out the rest of the world. Zooming in, I clicked a few frames. Judy and Mom scurried ahead of me. I followed with my eyes focused on the new girl with shoulder-length dark hair, sleek as midnight and bright green eyes. She and Chloe shared glances and giggles.

"Hey, Maggie. This is Autumn."

"Hi, Autumn." I held out my hand to shake hers.

"Hi, Maggie," she said. Her crooked smile captivated me. "I'm the new girl."

"Chloe's told me a lot about you."

Autumn giggled then pinched Chloe in the arm in friendly jest.

"Nothing bad," Chloe said. "You are the coolest girl in school."

Autumn smiled. "Thanks."

"So, Chloe tells me you just moved here," I said.

"Yeah, we did."

Her smiled disappeared. I didn't press for information as the woman on the bench in the straw hat focused her attention in my direction.

"That's my mom," Autumn said. "Hey, Mom, this is Chloe's friend, Maggie."

The woman stared with a forced smile, her shoulder-length hair even darker than her daughter's, her eyes solemn, her shoulders curved like she carried a burden, but then didn't we all? I held out my hand. "Hi, I'm Maggie Abernathy."

"Hi, Sylvie Peterson. Nice to meet you."

Autumn's eyes met her mother's. Her smile flat-lined, and my instincts bristled. "I live next door to Chloe and John," I said. "That's my mom, Glad, the one putting the worm on the hook." *Ironic*. "The curly dark-haired woman is my friend Judy and those are her boys, Harry and Walter."

Autumn's mom's thin lips pressed together as I introduced everyone. "Come on, I'll introduce you. I know how hard it is to be the new kid on the block." A shadow crossed her face. She adjusted her sunglasses and walked with me to the group of chattering people. Mom let go of the hook and Chloe dropped her fishing line in the water. Harry peered into the water.

"Well done," Winston claimed as he nodded to Glad.

Mom wiped her hands on the towel that John held out.

"Thanks, Glad," Chloe chimed.

Chloe wound the line in and gave it a little jerk every few seconds.

John leaned next to her coaching every move.

Mom's words, advice, wisdom loomed over me.

"Hi, I'm John McIntyre," he said.

John nodded in Sylvie's direction. She introduced herself, and I listened.

"How many pictures have you taken?" my mom asked me then she turned her attention to Autumn's mom. "Hi, I'm Glad Abernathy, Maggie's mother. Welcome."

A thin smile crept across Sylvie's lips.

Walter tugged at my shirt. I glanced down at him.

"Maggie, that guy is huge."

Walter's awe for Winston tickled me. I stood back and snapped a few frames of Walter staring up at Winston with this dumbfounded expression only he could don. Chloe reeled in her line all the way.

"Dang. He ate my worm." Her mouth drooped.

Walter stood like a statue, still gawking at Chloe's cowboy. She poked him. "He's just a guy," she said, inspecting her grandfather's face.

"I've never seen anyone that big," he muttered. "Wow."

Judy and I laughed. "Judy, this is Sylvie Peterson. She belongs to Autumn."

"Nice to meet you," Judy said, giving a little nod. "Walter, stop staring. It's not polite."

Harry dangled a worm in front of Walter's face.

"Harry," Judy scolded. "Oh, no, here we go."

The corner of my lip curled toward the sky at the antics. "Boys will be boys," I reminded her.

"Yes, they will," John added.

Sylvie stepped back then stuck her hands in her pockets. "Autumn, five minutes. Your dad's expecting us home."

Autumn stopped laughing. "Can't we stay?" she begged with pleading eyes.

Her mom shook her head. "We really should be going."

Chloe shrugged. "Bummer."

"I know. It's way *funner* with you guys."

I snapped a picture of the two girls sharing the moment, remembering how safe it felt to be in the company of someone who understood me, someone who hung on the ballet bar upside-down with me while the others primped their tutus.

"Well, we have five minutes. Let's make the most of it," Chloe said, graciously accepting the circumstances.

Chloe held her friend's hand and the girls wandered into the grassy area away from the water's edge. I clicked a few more pictures of the friends. The girls plopped down in the grass, sat crisscross-applesauce style facing each other, their knees touching. Autumn picked a dandelion and plucked the pedals from the head one-by-one. Chloe picked at the grass. I clicked a few more photos then caught Autumn's mother's stare, wondering if I'd said something wrong.

"Maggie," Walter hollered. "Come here."

I meandered to the water's edge to see the commotion. He knelt next to a green plastic bucket. His dark curly overgrown hair, almost like an Afro, intrigued me. I smiled at Judy and snapped his picture when he wasn't paying attention. Those were the best kind.

"Look, a perch," he said, leaning closer to get a better view.

I knelt next to him. The fish swam in curious circles as its lips opened and closed at the water's surface. Walter reached in and tried to touch him. The fish slapped its tail. A splash of water sprayed me. Walter laughed.

"What are you doing?" I asked.

"Trying to pet him," he said.

John leaned over my shoulder. "That's one big perch." He wiped a drop of water from my cheek, his touch warmed me to the core.

"Hey, kiddo. Is it okay if I steal your girlfriend?" John asked quietly.

Walter smiled. "Sure, as long as you bring her back."

Walter stood up then kissed my cheek. He skipped toward Chloe. "I thought Chloe was his girlfriend."

"You sure don't pay attention sometimes. He only has eyes for you," John said, leaning against the steel railing. His eyes scanned the horizon.

I took his picture. The click of the aperture caught his attention.

"Sure is beautiful here," he said.

The wind caught the curls of my ponytail and blew them forward across my face. Brushing them away, I leaned on the railing next to John. "Sure is. I love this time of year. I'll love it more in just a few more weeks," I said.

"School's rough, huh?"

"Yeah," I answered. "I'm counting." The muscles in my chest constricted.

"Just like your students. I know Chloe has a countdown going. You seem so stressed whenever you talk about it. Maybe . . ."

I glanced over to him and grinned. "I bet I do. Just the thought makes my blood pressure rise. All the assessment, documentation, expectation, it's crazy. What happened to play?"

"You're a smart woman, Maggie Abernathy. You have a way with children."

"I love them. It's all the other bullshit I hate. There's so much more to an education than a test score. A piece of paper in your hand doesn't always equate to a successful life."

John took the camera from me. I let him. I stared out into water as a freighter drifted in the horizon. He snapped a picture of me. I couldn't see his eyes as he peered into the viewfinder, but he could see me. Our roles reversed. I smiled, then he snapped another photo.

Chloe bounded over with exuberant enthusiasm. "Let me take one."

"Sure, I think you remember how." John secured the camera strap around his daughter's neck.

"Now you two stand together," she ordered.

John and I scooted closer. He put his arm around my shoulder. When I glanced over to him, he stared through me and that's when Chloe snapped the photo.

Chapter 33

Winston shuffled up the stairs of the porch, the soles of his boots scuffling along.

I sat wrapped in a throw reading. "Chloe's inside with Mom."

His warm smile unnerved me. It was the smile of a parent, not a cowboy. He cleared his throat, and I closed my book.

"You seem like a nice person," he started.

I drew the throw tighter. Where was he going with this? Where was Chloe or Mom when I needed them?

"I just came over to say goodbye. My flight leaves in the morning. I've had a good time here."

"Well, it was certainly a pleasure to meet you. I'm glad that you were able to come to Chloe's career day. It really meant a lot to her," I said. "You're welcome anytime." The butterflies settled.

"It seems that my son is quite taken with you." Winston paused, took a deep breath, and scanned the suburban scenery. "That's not something to take lightly."

It took every ounce of energy to make eye contact with the man. What did he want from me? Damn it, where were Chloe and Mom? I let my eyes wander to the screen door. There was nothing but silence inside.

"I don't mean to make you uncomfortable," he said, taking a throaty breath. "Think about Montana. We have plenty of room. The kids would have a ball."

"You mean Harry and Walter?" I asked.

He chuckled and rubbed his chin. "Yup, Chloe sure is smitten with those boys. I've never seen so much curly hair in my life."

"I call them the Mark Spitz boys when they run around the beach in their Speedos. It's quite a sight." I kept my eyes on Winston. The creases in his skin, a roadmap to his past. He was a handsome man. He was a father watching out for his boy.

I took a deep breath. "Um, how exactly do you know how John feels?" I picked at my thumbnail afraid to connect gazes.

Winston's boots shuffled closer. His finger lifted my chin. His hands were warm, a little rough, and thick. His eyes gleamed as he shook his head. I felt like a child.

"I know you feel it, girl. Open your eyes, let yourself see it."

Sweat poured off my forehead. I kicked back the covers and sat up in panic. It seemed so real. I grabbed my phone to check the time. It felt like three in the morning, but the clock registered ten minutes past eleven. I'd only been asleep for an hour. I never had dreams like that. *Shit.*

Taking off my wet T-shirt, I tossed it on the floor. Damp shivers infested my body. I got up, opened the dresser drawer, and found a clean top. The touch of running cool water eased the hot flash. God, I hated these things. I stood in front of the mirror naked. Winston's image so real inside my head. I patted myself down with a fresh towel. Moonlight trickled through the partially opened blinds.

I padded softly across the room as if there was someone else sleeping. I reminded myself, I was the sole proprietor of this big house. I loved my house, but the dust and chores were becoming too much. Maybe I was getting too old, no, I corrected myself, too tired. Maybe I was the one who'd outgrown this place.

I tiptoed through the hallway and down to the kitchen. Tomorrow Winston would fly back to Montana. I switched on the light.

Bones grumbled from his dog bed, licked his jowls, yawned then put his head back down, and closed his eyes.

I filled a glass with cold water then rolled it across my forehead before taking a long drink. Walking past Bones, I switched off the kitchen light. My foot kicked something on the floor in the dark foyer. I switched on the tabletop lamp. There on the floor was an envelope. I didn't recognize the handwriting. Picking it up, I inspected it, then ran my fingers over the bold script written in black ink. The back popped open when I checked to see if it was sealed. Taking the stationary out of the envelope, I unfolded it. Inside was a ticket to Montana. I read the note. *Maybe this will persuade you to come see us. The offer stands. Winston.*

My breath caught in my chest.

"He must have slipped it through the mail slot," I said to myself, wondering how he snuck it past Bones.

Switching off the light, I carried my water upstairs in one hand, and Winston's invitation in the other hand. I slipped back into bed then tapped out a text to Judy. *Call me in the morning. Maggie.*

I drained the glass of cold water hoping not to have to get up in the middle of the night to use the bathroom. My phone buzzed with a return text. *I'm up now. What's going on?*

I mouthed the words as I typed. *Just received an interesting offer. Winston left me a plane ticket to Montana. What do I do with it? I can't accept it. This is crazy.* I pressed send.

The screen of my phone lit up. I opened Judy's next response. *What's crazy is that you didn't tell me that the boys and I were invited, too.*

I smiled. *How did you find out?* I typed faster. *Sorry,*

I guess I should have mentioned it. I meant to, but got sidetracked with all the commotion at the park. Besides. I have to think about it. Send.

The vision of Winston was crystal clear as I closed my eyes. My phone buzzed. I read Judy's reply. *What's there to think about? I'm in.* She was quick to make up her mind. Judy probably already had plans for all of us. I continued to read. P.S. *John told me.*

I tapped at the keyboard. *Call me tomorrow.* I put the phone on the nightstand and stared into the darkness. Ribbons of metallic light washed across my bedspread, the purr of John's Harley faint. I kicked off the covers and went to the window. John's garage light glowed behind the privacy fence that separated our yards. It faded within seconds. The almost-full moon shone in the sky, the light reflected from dense clouds that drifted overhead shaped like the Montana mountain range. In one breath, something changed. With my hand flat against my chest, making sure I was awake, a mysterious wave of clarity rolled over me. Staring into the yard, I searched for fairies. I rubbed the sleep from my eyes then went back to bed.

My alarm rang at its usual time. My face was pressed into the pillow on the opposite side of the bed. I never slept on the right side. I was a creature of habit and liked my usual space. I kicked the sheet off and wiped the small drip of drool from my lip. Zonked and dazed, I tried to wake up remembering yesterday, more importantly last night. I rolled over with a groan and cursed the week. It was only Wednesday, a regular old Wednesday. I turned off the alarm then checked my phone. Judy's texts were there and the envelope with the airline ticket was on the nightstand. Reaching over, I touched it, the foggy dream of Winston at the edge of my mind.

Bones trotted in and barked at me.

"Fine, I'll let you out," I said to him as if he would respond with "thank you".

I went to the bathroom, slipped on my sleeping pants, then shuffled downstairs to the kitchen. I opened the French doors and Bones ran out. I pushed the button on the coffee machine and waited for the aroma of hazelnuts to greet me.

Leaning against the counter, I touched the teacup Mom had given me last year at about this time. The delicate pink ribbons reminded me of my journey, reminded me of so many women's journeys, some not as lucky as me. As soon as the coffee stopped dripping, I filled the cup and went out to the patio to greet the morning.

"Maggie," the deep voice called.

I walked to the edge of the stone floor. "Yeah," I answered.

Winston rounded the corner with Bones under his arm. "I think this belongs to you. Someone must have left the gate open. Probably Chloe," he said.

I sipped at my coffee. "Thanks." His eyes connected with mine as if he really was there last night talking to me in my dreams. "When's your flight?"

"Ten. Gonna drop Chloe off at school with her dad then head out."

Tucking my hair behind my ear, I pretended I wasn't standing there in pajamas. "Want some coffee?"

Winston smiled. "You look like you need to get ready for work, not entertain some old coot in the early hours."

"I bet you're up at the crack of dawn every morning." I pictured him sipping coffee on a porch watching the sunrise as fog lifted to reveal the mountains that surrounded his pastures.

"Yeah, can't teach an old dog new tricks," he said.

I smiled as my lips touched the rim of my breast cancer teacup. Bones nudged my shins asking for breakfast then he jumped up in the chaise lounge, and leaned into my thigh.

"Have a safe trip." He turned to leave, and suddenly I felt like a fool. "Winston," I said.

The morning light lit his face as he faced me, his posture like a Marlboro Man.

"I got the ticket. That was very generous." I got up then stepped closer to him. The dewy grass stuck to my feet. His smile tugged at my heartstrings. "I don't know."

"I'm sure you'll figure it out. We all do. Thanks for being so good to Chloe."

"You're welcome."

His stern jaw softened with a thin smile. "Just remember to bring your camera, because I have lots of cattle just waiting to meet you."

"I'll think about it," I said.

Maybe Montana wasn't calling me home. Maybe it was Winston. He turned and left. The gate latch clicked. Bones and I went back inside. I fed Bones and refilled my cup of coffee. There was a small knock at the front door. *Good Lord.* I opened the door. Chloe was dressed in jeans and a white T-shirt, her hands behind her back. The Tiffany necklace from Chicago hung around her neck. I think she'd worn it every day since Brook had given it to her.

"Hi, Chloe," I said. "Glad to see you're wearing your glasses."

"Sorry to bug you, Maggie, but my grandpa said he just saw you." She pulled her hands out from behind her back. "Here, this is for you. I know what grandpa gave you. He doesn't know I know, but I know. I'm just keeping quiet about the whole thing."

She smiled, her permanent teeth nice and straight. She held out an envelope.

"I wrote this hoping it would help you make up your mind. I know you're not sure and I'm not even sure I know why, but you grown-ups sure do need a lot of attention."

Chloe took a deep breath. "But, I do know that you should come see me, us. It wouldn't be the same without you." She took another deep breath and stared through me.

Opening the creaky screen door, Chloe handed me an envelope. The girl next door had moved into my heart and had unpacked her bags to stay. "Thanks."

"Dad says that you have to want to come for yourself. I'm not sure what that means, but I'd like it if you'd come to see me. Well, I have to eat my breakfast. And you look like you need a shower or something."

"Yeah, I need something," I said, wondering what exactly was in the envelope she gave me.

"Have a good day, Maggie. Don't let those boogers get the best of you. By the way, Autumn really liked you."

I finished my coffee as I watched her head home. Bones jumped against the screen door, knocking it open, then ran after Chloe.

"Good grief." I sighed. I put Chloe's envelope on the table and went to retrieve Bones. I trotted down the porch stairs. "Bones," I called. His body disappeared under the hedges as his tail waggled back and forth with adventure. I bent down and peered through the spring greenery. Chloe sat crisscross with her eyes closed rubbing Bones' head.

"Chloe," I said.

She opened her eyes. "I just want to be alone."

Bones licked her cheeks. This morning proved that nothing good could come of Wednesdays either. "I have to get Bones back inside and I have to get ready for work," I said with a grunt as I hooked my fingers under Bones' collar. He didn't budge. Chloe always came first in his book. "Come on, boy," I said. He dug his heels in and hunched his back. Chloe sat silent, her eyes still. She was never still. "What?" Small droplets of sweat began to bead on my forehead.

Chloe started to say something, but stopped.

Someone touched my back. John held out his hand to help me up when I glanced back over my shoulder to see who was there. "Great, now everyone knows what a middle-aged woman having a hot flash in her pajamas looks like," I said as I wiped my forehead with the bottom of my T-shirt.

John laughed.

"So, you think this is funny?"

Bones disappeared into the bushes. The branches rustled as he and Chloe settled in.

"Yeah, I do," he said.

"Of course you do. I have to get ready for work. What time is it?"

John unclipped the phone from his belt. It's seven-fifteen."

A wave of panic rushed through my veins. "I have to go. I look like crap and I have to get ready. What about Chloe?" I pointed to the bushes.

"Maybe she just needs some time alone. She's got a lot on her plate right now."

"I heard that." Chloe's grunt drifted out from the bushes.

"We'll make sure Bones doesn't run off. We'll put him in the backyard while you do your thing, whatever that might be," John reassured me.

I narrowed my gaze as his eyes inspected me from head-to-toe. I bent down and stuck my head into the bushes. I brushed away the twig that caught my hair. "Chloe, are you going to be okay?"

She didn't answer.

John helped me back up.

"It's been a long time since a child has made me late for work," I mumbled.

"I heard that," Chloe said.

John smiled. "I promise, she'll be fine and Bones will make it to the backyard."

I turned toward the house then checked over my shoulder.

John shooed me away then crouched closer to his daughter. "Chloe, I'll be in the house when you're ready. Bones, come with me."

Stopping on the top step, I glanced in his direction.

Bones trotted after him.

"Geez," I whispered.

Chapter 34

Opening the door, I dropped my book bag on the floor with a huff, a familiar after-school routine. I kicked it into the closet then meandered to the kitchen where I immediately stubbed my toe on the leg of the table. Picking up Chloe's letter, I speculated the contents, then set it back upon the counter.

"Nothing good can come from a full moon."

Bones stretched while I opened the doors for him. Beckett's ugly tile floor was cool beneath my aching feet. "There, out you go," I told Bones.

The ceiling fan over the kitchen table sent welcome wisps of air through my stuffy kitchen. Opening the fridge door, I stuck my head inside. Cold air billowed out. Closing my eyes, I breathed it in. The cap of my water bottle clicked as I twisted it with rage. Cold drops squirted onto my shirt. What a long day! I leaned against the counter and swigged the chilled contents down. The plastic container crinkled as I chugged.

The letter Chloe gave me this morning beckoned to me from the counter. I picked it up, opened it, then sat down on the cool floor. She had drawn a picture of Voodoo on the envelope. It was eerily creepy. I took out the notebook paper and unfolded it. A shaggy fringe emerged, and I wondered why it never bothered students to rip that edge off because it drove me crazy. I sighed at the sight of her picture. It was a picture of me on a horse. I knew it was me because my name was jotted above with and arrow pointing to the woman. There were steep mountains in the background and a stream sketched in pencil. Underneath, Chloe's words were written in newbie cursive, the kind that isn't quite sure which way to slant. Setting the water bottle down on the floor next to me, I read her words.

Dear Maggie, I really hope you decide to come to Montana. I know you're nervous, but so am I. I'm excited to go, but mostly sad that I won't get to see you anymore.

The hair stood up on my arms, and my eyes began to well. What would I do without her? I took a deep breath and continued to read.

I know I'm a pain, but I figure you must feel the same way about me that I feel about you, cause you keep letting me in. Dad says most people would have changed the locks by now. I don't think that would be very nice, but you aren't like most people.

I felt my lip curl. The words blurred as my eyes brimmed with tears.

I also figure that anyone who can make friends with my mom is pretty special. And my dad, well, I remember the first time you met him. I thought his head was going to pop off. He was kind of mad. Do you remember? But he likes you now, too.

"How could I forget?" I whispered to no one as visions of strewn tomatoes all about my wrecked garden flooded back, no thanks to Voodoo flying over the fence and a little handy work from Bones.

Well, just think about it. It could be fun. Love, Chloe. P.S. I'm not going to beg cause that would be babyish. P.S.S. Thanks for being here for me. I love you.

I set the letter down on the floor then covered my eyes and pressed the palms of my hands into them trying to stop the leaks. She was going. Seriously, what would I do without her? I loved her, too, more and more with each passing day. I pulled my knees up to my chest and hugged them tight. My eyes burned, my palms clammy and swollen from the humidity.

Bones trotted in. He sat beside me with tilted head and slobbery chops.

"What?" I said. He let his front paws slide out from underneath him until his belly was on the floor. With a thud, he dropped down and rested his head on my thigh. I patted his thick noggin. "You're not going to know what to do without her either. It'll be pretty boring around here," I lectured.

Bones groaned and let out a hot breath of air on my leg.

"Hey, what are you guys doing?" Chloe's green eyes peered around the counter.

"You're pretty quiet," I said, swiping at the corner of my eyes.

"I'm trying to do better. It makes my dad happy."

I grinned.

She came closer and bent down. She inspected my face with questioning eyes. Bones lifted his head. Drool dropped on Chloe's letter.

"You don't look so good," Chloe said.

"Yeah, it's been a rough day." I sighed.

"You're telling me," she said, sitting down on the other side of Bones. "Did you read my letter?"

"Yeah." I folded it back up. She stared at me as I slid it back in the envelope. "I like the picture of Voodoo. It's a little creepy though."

"His eyes didn't come out right. Sorry, didn't mean to weird you out. You're not going to have nightmares, are you?"

I shook my head. "Wouldn't be the first time," I answered, trying to grin.

"You're gonna think about it, right?" she inquired quietly.

I nodded. "How can I not?" I said. "It's complicated."

Chloe tilted her head to the side. Her wrinkled expression resembled Bones' when I told him no. She fidgeted with the necklace her mom gave her in Chicago. Her nails were painted baby blue.

I started thinking, *What if I like it so much I don't want to come home? What if I get attached and your dad says goodbye?*

"I'm sorry, Maggie," she said.

I narrowed my gaze. "Why are you sorry?"

"I made you think. And by the looks of it, that wasn't such a good idea."

If she only knew. If only she understood my feelings for her dad, for her. "It's okay. People gotta think sometime. Now is as good a time as any."

"Maybe," Chloe said, biting her thumbnail.

"When did you start biting your nails?" I asked, checking out my own nubs.

Chloe shrugged. "Don't know. Mom wouldn't like it."

"Suppose not. Have you heard from your mom lately?" I asked, thinking about Fletcher Thompson. I hadn't heard from him since I rejected his invitation to Los Angeles. Figured. My instincts proved me correct about his motives.

"No, not really."

"Why were you in the bushes this morning?" I asked, picking up my water bottle for another swig, my eyes glued on Chloe as she got up to open the fridge. "You can have whatever you want," I said, fingering the picture of Voodoo on the envelope. "You're a good drawer in a weird kind of way."

Chloe peered over her shoulder at me. "Is that supposed to be a compliment?" She stuck her head back in the refrigerator. "Can I have pop?"

"I don't care. Will your dad get mad?"

"Boy, you really are in a poopy mood. I'll just have water."

Chloe shut the stainless steel door and sat back down on the floor with me. She unscrewed the cap and sipped her cold drink. "I don't want to live next door to anyone else."

I stared at her, her green eyes fierce, serious, and focused on mine. "Yeah, I doubt the new neighbors will be as good as you."

Water drizzled down Chloe's chin as she chugged. She wiped the droplets off her shirt with the back of her hand. "This is worse than I thought."

I slumped down. "Ugh, I'm sorry."

"It's not your fault. Dad says he has to find himself."

I picked at the paper label on my water bottle until it ripped.

"I didn't know he was lost," she said. "I thought we were here, with you . . ."

Cracking a smile, I knew what she meant.

"What?"

"He's not the only one who is lost.".

"I got lost once in a store. I cried," Chloe said.

"It's kind of scary when you get lost." I drained my water bottle and tossed it up into the sink then rubbed Bones' back. He lifted his head, and his pink tongue lapped my forearm.

Chloe's eyes stared through me. "Are you afraid, Maggie?" she asked, scooting closer.

"This is quite the conversation," I said, shifting my weight, my rear end half-asleep.

"Glad says you're afraid."

I shot her a look. "She said that to you?"

Chloe nibbled at her thumbnail, again. "No, I just overheard her say it."

"To whom?"

"Walter and Harry's mom."

Relief washed over me. I thought maybe Chloe repeated what Mom had said to her dad. I was safe with Judy. Breathing in, I held it for three seconds then exhaled. Chloe's bright green eyes questioned me. "I don't know." But I knew.

"Are you afraid you can't ride a horse, cause my dad and my grandpa will teach you," she said, patting my hand, her innocent eyes rimmed with worry.

"It's been a long time." In the corner of my mind, I could see Bradley on a Palomino trotting down a dusty trail ahead of me.

"We can learn together," she said.

A thin smile lightened the weight. "What do I have to lose?" My stomach turned over. Faint thuds of life beat in my chest knocking against the walls begging to escape.

Chloe touched my hair, and a shiver ran down my spine. I reached out to hug her and she fell into my arms like a rag doll. Her hair smelled of coconut, her soft hands on my neck taking me back to a time when I held Bradley at her age and somehow this didn't seem too different, her breath hot on my neck. I closed my eyes and breathed her in.

"What is going on in here?" Mom stood with one hand on the counter peering down at us.

"Man, did the Indians teach you to walk or what?" I said. Mom's eyes narrowed. "Sorry," I said.

Chloe pulled away. "Why would Indians teach your mom to walk? Didn't she have regular parents like you and me?" Chloe asked, touching my cheek.

"Yes, she had regular parents like you. Indians were just really good at walking quietly through the woods. I'm sure you'll read about it someday. Oh, never mind."

Mom held out her hand to Chloe.

Chloe grabbed it and stood up. "Great. Now, who is going to pry me off this floor? I think I'm stuck." Chloe reached out to me and planted her feet then tugged.

"Thanks," I said.

She bent down and grabbed her water bottle. Her head knocked the corner of the counter when she stood up.

"Ouch," she yelped.

"Let me see," I said, inspecting for blood, bones, or a bump. "How bad does it hurt, on a scale of one to ten?"

She wrinkled her nose, then squinted her eyes and felt her scalp. "About a three."

"Not bad. I think you'll live," I said.

Mom stroked my hair, and her fingers grazed my temple. I flinched as she touched my scar. My eyes met hers.

"Does that hurt?" she asked.

"No. Just feels weird," I answered. "My scar is sensitive sometimes."

Mom smiled at me. "Oh, you girls sure do have hard heads, I do declare."

I narrowed my eyes as she talked. I knew what she meant. "You're funny," I said quietly, waiting for Chloe to walk away.

"Sounded like you two were having a moment."

I met Mom's stare. "How much did you hear?"

"Enough," she said, taking a deep breath, "enough to know that she needs you more than you know."

I stepped closer. "That's what's making this so damn hard," I said under my breath. Mom rolled her eyes at me. "Ha, that's where I get it," I said, pointing to her.

"Oh pish, and the only thing making this so damn hard is you. Would you get out of your own way already? It's just a vacation. Get over yourself," Mom said.

"Why is it my fault?" I asked. "And we both know it's more than a vacation," I reiterated. "I don't want to get there and discover—" I crossed my arms.

"Discover? Discover that you really belong with that man and his daughter. Then what? You might actually have to do something about it or maybe you're afraid that this could actually work out."

I ignored the sarcasm then glanced over at Chloe who chased Bones around the yard. "So what? What if I don't feel like getting my heart broken again. What if?" I stopped. As much as I longed to be with John, did I have the energy to cope with an eight-year-old? I loved Chloe, but that was a lot to sign on for.

Chapter 35

The screen door slammed behind me as I stormed out. I trotted down the front steps toward the sidewalk. John came around the back heading straight for me. His brow creased when I peered in his direction.

"She's in the back with the dog. You sure, you don't want a dog?" I asked.

"Bad day?"

"Um, let me think?" I sighed, crossed my arms, then answered, "Yeah."

"What could possibly be that bad?" he asked.

"Really?" I started, my insides percolated with fury. "Let's see. First, I find out what the real numbers are for next year's salary. Thanks for the pay cut. Then I get a new student who destroys the chemistry of my class. It's the end of May, for crying out loud. Who moves their child in May? And your daughter—" I stopped, John's eyes earnest with concern. Trying to calm down, I took a deep breath. "Well, she made me think and I really don't have the energy for that right now." I closed my mouth, but the words kept on coming like tickertape inside my head. *She made me care about her more than I wanted to. She told me she loved me and I love her back and I don't want you guys to move.* "And well, my mom is being my mom. It's a little much."

"I'll go tell Chloe to stay with Glad. I was just going to take my bike out for a spin. You can come. A few bugs in your teeth will make you feel better. Maybe you should put on some jeans."

"Don't you want Chloe to go with you?" I asked.

"No," John said. "I'd rather go with you. Besides, the fresh air will do you good."

My black maxi skirt flitted in the breeze. "Yeah, guess I can't sit side saddle on a Harley," I rambled, fiddling with the material.

"Suppose not." He took a breath. "But you can on a horse."

My gaze met John's, my emotions on high alert, my heart a little lighter urging me to take the challenge, and enjoy the adventure. John's green eyes, like emeralds, bright, illuminating assurance.

"You look nice today," he said.

"Thanks. Evaluation day, always a thrill," I joked. He smiled. "In all honesty, it usually makes my eye twitch. I don't know why, but it's always so nerve-wracking. I hate it. I shouldn't worry, I've done it a thousand times."

"I'm sure you did great. You wouldn't worry if you didn't care." John folded his arms across his chest and planted his feet.

"Suppose so." I took a deep breath and closed my eyes. Twenty-something children flashed behind my eyelids looking to me for the answers. "Just tired, I guess."

"Think about Montana, girl. I'm telling you, once you get there, you won't want to come home," he said.

"That's what I'm afraid of," I replied. John's eyes flashed. "Well, that's the first time I said that out loud."

"Well, then, I guess we're making progress. Now go change," he said. "You can think about riding that horse while you're listening to the lake."

"What are Montana lakes like?" I asked, lowering my gaze.

"I'm not going to say they're like the Great Lakes. It's a whole different world out there. Now go change."

I imagined John's world. I'd never been to Montana. I'd only read about it, but I'd had an image in my mind of mountains, sharp blue skies, ranches, vast land, and mountains framing the landscapes. His fingers grazed mine. He squeezed my hand.

"You'll figure it out," he mumbled.

That's what Winston said. I wished for the faith they harbored. Opening the screen door, John followed me inside.

Chloe darted through the kitchen to meet us. "Daddy, what are you doing here?"

"Maggie's going to change her clothes and go for a ride with me on the Harley while Glad watches you, if that's okay with Glad," he answered, holding her chin.

Mom came out of the kitchen. "It's fine with me. You two have fun."

"Can I go, too?" Chloe asked.

"Afraid not, there's only room for two."

I stopped on the bottom stair and held the handrail watching their interaction.

Chloe's face drooped. "Please, Dad. I haven't seen you all day."

"How about, I take you when Maggie and I get back?"

"Fine, but can I go first?" Chloe looked over to me.

"We won't be long," I reassured her. "I have to get back to make dinner."

"I'll start dinner," Glad said.

Her thin grin made me cringe. What was on her agenda now? "You don't have to, Mom. I can do it when we get back."

She waved her hand in the air at me. "It'll do me good to make my baby girl some dinner."

"Great, can you make me some dinner, too?" Chloe asked. "You're cooking is way better than my dad's."

John put his hands on his hips and stared at her through narrow slits. I teetered on the next stair to see the outcome.

"Sorry, Dad. I didn't mean anything bad."

"I think you hurt my feelings," he said. "I'm getting better, aren't I?"

"Well yeah, but Glad's cooking is just different. That's all I meant." Chloe tucked her hair behind her ears and adjusted the glasses at the bridge of her nose.

John touched the silver heart on his daughter's Tiffany necklace.

"Come on, Chloe, let's hit the market," Mom said, heading toward the kitchen. "I have to get my purse. We can put the top down. Bones can come, too," she said, disappearing at the end of the foyer. Her voice trailed behind her.

Chloe trotted after Mom.

"I'll be in the garage," John said.

The cool wood beneath my feet simmered my nerves. "I'll be over in a few minutes."

The upstairs hallway seemed emptier than usual. Photos of Bradley and Beckett lined the walls. I guess I hadn't noticed Beckett still hanging around. I hadn't seen him in person since Bradley was here. I wondered how he was and what he was doing, but the curiosity faded with the feel of soft denim, a pair of Frye boots, and thoughts of John. I slipped on a white tee and tied my hair back.

Bradley stared at me from the photo on my dresser. His childhood seemed eons ago.

"I love you, little boy," I said, touching the brushed metal frame. "I'll come to Boston soon," I said, expecting him to answer. "I know. I hear you," I continued, placing the frame back in its spot. Leaning into the mirror on the wall, I inspected my face, smoothed back the skin on my neck, and fantasized about a facelift. It seemed like self-enhancement advertisements were everywhere nowadays. "Maybe just a clothespin at the nape of my neck would do the job."

"Do what job?" Chloe said.

I screamed. "Jesus," I yelped. "You scared the—"

"Don't say it. You're doing a good job not swearing as much."

Chloe shook her finger at me. The urge to twist it off surfaced. I swatted it away. "What are you doing up here?" The sound of John's Harley rumbled in the distance. "Dad's not going to wait forever. You'd better get down there," she advised, checking her hair in the mirror. "I like your bedroom," she said, inspecting the contents of my makeup bag.

"Thanks," I said.

"I'm surprised it's so neat," she said.

I scowled at her.

"What? I figured since the rest of your house is neat, with the exception of your desk sometimes, that your bedroom just might be a pig sty."

"Nice," I said, rolling my eyes.

"Seriously, you'd better go. Glad sent me up here to tell you to lock the door. We're going to the market now. I get to pick dinner."

"Lucky dog," I shot back, hoping I wanted what she chose. "Cereal would be fine with me."

"Although that is tempting," she hemmed and hawed, "I think I'll save that for when I'm with Dad. He can't burn that."

Chloe left the room. I followed in her footsteps and watched her inspect the photos on the walls. Beckett's ghost faded into thin air as I stepped past the family photo on the beaches of Isle of the Palms near Charleston, the last vacation when we both truly smiled and felt comfortable in each other's presence. Time hadn't stolen that memory, but it had stolen my wrinkle free youthful face. Chloe caught me staring. "Look how young I look in that photo."

"Not so different," Chloe said, standing on her tippy toes to see better.

"I think so."

"Of course you do. Grown-ups are weird that way. I don't think my dad changes either."

"I wonder if that's because you're young."

"What's that supposed to mean? You're not going to get all weird on me, are you?" she said.

"Someday when you're older, you'll know what I mean."

"Well, I don't care how you look. Those glasses on Bradley's dad are what I'm seeing. Holy moly, talk about ugly," Chloe said. "They're kind of big."

I smiled. "I hated those glasses, too." The oversized black rims took over his face.

We both laughed.

"The better to see you with, my dear." Chloe cackled like a fairy-tale witch. She scooted ahead of me as my mom called up the stairs for her.

My boots clicked on the stairs. "I got the door," I said to my mom.

Bones wagged his tail. Mom bent down to hook the leash on his collar. His pink tongue hung out of his mouth as he panted.

"Be careful on that motorcycle," she said. "Wear a helmet."

"I will." I opened the foyer closet. "Here's the disaster room," I said to Chloe, peeking around the door.

"Whoa, you're not kidding. There's stuff all over in there."

She took the handle of the leash from my mom. I nudged the stuff on the floor in the closet away from the door to close it. With my jacket in one hand and the key to the house in the other, I shut the front door, and locked it. Mom and Chloe drove off in Mom's convertible with Bones in the backseat-both sporting oversized movie star sunglasses. John rolled down the driveway on his Harley with the engine purring. His smile begged for attention. I strapped on the black helmet before swinging my leg over the backseat and settling in behind him.

Chapter 36

The warm May breeze swept over me like a lover. It was finally here. I said it once and I'll continue until the end of time. This was my favorite time of year. I sat on the rock next to John staring out into the calm Michigan lake. The quiet air between us held secrets to the future that neither of us could predict. I leaned back, braced myself with my palms flat against the cool stone and held my chin to the sky, my eyes closed, my ears listening to the water sway against the rocks. John's hand covered mine. I smiled then breathed in the perfect air laced with summer adventure.

"That's nice," I said before opening my eyes.

He wrapped his fingers around mine. "Maggie—"

"Yeah?"

"Are we ever going to *really* talk about that night?"

John's emerald eyes glistened in the daylight. I held his gaze pondering the purpose of rehashing a memory I'd tucked away for safekeeping, like a treasure not wanting to tarnish it in the fresh air. The rise and fall of my chest weighed me down. The sight of his hand in mine reminded me that I was sitting next to a person with hopes and dreams, too.

"What is there to say?" I asked, my voice weak, my insides cringing with uncertainty.

John narrowed his gaze. His expression serious, hurt in his beautiful eyes.

"I'm sorry." I stared down into the blue lake. Minnows darted back and forth just beneath the surface of the water.

"It was an amazing night."

I smiled and scanned the horizon searching for myself. Heat smoldered in my cheeks. My skin tingled as I unzipped my jacket.

"That's a mighty big smile, Maggie Abernathy," John said. "In fact, it's the biggest one I've ever seen on your face. You should wear it more often. You just might get some of these little lines like me." John pointed to the crow's feet at the corners of his eyes.

"I like those lines. They're one of my favorite part about you. Makes me think you had many good times."

I laughed. John was still holding my hand and I let him.

"Have you thought about Montana?" he asked.

The corner of my mouth curled up. "How can I not? The McIntyre family does not give up easily, do you?" I brushed away a wisp of hair tickled my cheek.

"What do you have to lose?" John's voice was deep, his words slow and methodical-his eyes dark and curious.

We were discussing more than a visit to Montana.

"Everything," I said, holding his gaze.

He shook his head at me, his eyes narrowed. That familiar ache of worry surfaced. I didn't expect him to understand. I'd already had one failed marriage, which I felt responsible for even if Beckett was gay. "I've spent most my life with blinders on." I didn't trust myself.

"What does that have to do with anything?" he asked.

A flock of geese squawked overhead. My eyes followed their path over the lake. Their flapping wings stroked the sky. The noise grew louder and pricked my ears. Behind the V-shaped gaggle of birds two geese trailed, their wings doing double time hustling to catch up. "You know when one goose gets sick or injured two other geese stay with it until it dies or it can fly again."

"Kind of like me and Chloe?" he asked.

I memorized the contour of John's strong hand that

covered mine as I swallowed away emotion. *They had stayed with me*. My eyes brimmed with tears.

"Why don't you fly again?"

I peered down into the lake. The frantic minnows disappeared beneath the rippling surface. "I don't know," I said. "It still hurts sometimes, I guess. Makes me unsure." And that was truth. Beckett may have been gone, but sometimes the memories seemed like fresh wounds, tender, raw. "I don't know why, especially . . ."

"Especially, what?" John asked.

"Now that you're here."

"I've been there. When Brook cheated, I thought my life was over. When I met her, I thought I'd spend all my days with her. And you're right, just when you think it's all good, it haunts you until one day, you exorcise the demons that hold you back from whatever it is that you're in need of."

I sighed, stood up, stretched my legs, and tucked my hands in my back pockets.

John stood beside me, his arm around my shoulders. "You're stronger than you know, Maggie Abernathy."

"I don't feel very strong," I mumbled. "I can't make a decision. As attracted as I am to you . . ." An image of Chloe flashed in my brain.

"What?"

"I'm reluctant because I love Chloe and I don't want to hurt her." John held my stare. "I don't want to lose her." The corner of my mouth lifted in a grin as I pictured her chasing after Bones.

John drew me closer. He kissed the side of my head. "If it's not meant to be, then I guess it's not meant to be."

My heart constricted at the tone in John's voice. God, what was I doing? The ladies in this small town loved him, chased him, even sent babysitters his way just to get the skinny, and I pushed him away. But wasn't it better to be friends and have Chloe than be lovers and have the inevitable fallout and lose them both? Wasn't that how these things worked?

Feeling torn, I wanted to forget about Montana. John draped his other arm across my chest and held me close. I held on to his muscular forearm. "I'm sorry," I whispered.

"We'd better get home. If Chloe doesn't get her ride, it'll be a long evening," John said with a sigh. "Send her home after you three eat."

"I thought you were joining us," I said, searching his face in hopes of reading him better.

"I don't feel much like eating," John said. "Besides, I have a lot to do. The house is going up next week."

I lost my breath in his words. "There's no chance I can change your mind." He held out his hand to help me across the rocks back onto grassy knoll. "I told you before and I'll tell you again, I don't want new neighbors. I like things the way they are."

John gave me a little jerk as I hopped from the last rock to solid ground. His mysterious eyes captured my attention. Lost in the dark pools of green, I stood mesmerized.

His brow furrowed. "Things change, Maggie. People have to move on. The world keeps spinning."

I knew he was right, but I didn't want to acknowledge it. I wanted to stay in my little bubble regardless how uncomfortable because that's what I knew and I could do that. He'd move on and I'd remain stagnate. The thought terrified me. We strolled across the park back to the Harley.

John and I turned toward the young girl's voice that drifted through the air. Chloe's friend Autumn ran behind us calling for our attention. Half bent over, resting her hands on her knees, she tried to catch her breath. Her bangs stuck to her forehead.

"Is Chloe with you guys?" she asked.

"No, she's back at home," John said.

Autumn stood up then smoothed her black hair back away from her face. John spoke while I glanced around looking for her mother.

"Is your mom here?" I asked.

"Yeah, over there," she said, pointing to the bench by the play structure.

John shaded his eyes and gave a little wave. His smile drew me in.

"Tell your mom I said hello."

"Sure thing," Autumn said as she ran back to the playground.

I smiled and waved, too.

"She's really a nice woman," John said.

Heat engulfed my body as jealousy engulfed my mind. I fanned my face hoping John wouldn't notice.

"You okay," he asked.

Out of the corner of my eye, I noticed Autumn's mom watching us walk toward the parking lot. I didn't answer right away. How did he know she was a nice woman? Sure the girls played together at school, but I'd never seen her dropping Autumn off next door. I felt myself slip into uncharted territory.

"What?" he asked.

Pissed off at myself for being jealous of a woman who always wore a hat and spoke less than a mute, I stewed silently. I chastised myself for being my own worst enemy. I chastised myself for acting the way he did when he saw the bouquet from Fletcher. "Nothing," I said. Mom's voice resonated in my head. I tried to shake it away, but she was there even when she wasn't there.

"Maggie, just say it," John said, handing me my helmet as we stood next to the Harley.

Pressing my lips together, I felt a hard line form. I couldn't help but look away. "Really, it's nothing." I had no right. I was the one digging my heels in.

"It's been my experience that if a woman says, it's nothing, it's something, and it's usually something big in her mind," he said, strapping his helmet on.

"How do you know her?" I asked.

A thin smile crossed his lips making me seethe even more. My palms began to sweat. "She's not my type. You can relax," he said, putting on his sunglasses.

He reached over and snapped the strap to my helmet, his hand grazing my chin.

"You must think I'm an idiot," I said, "cause I sure do."

"You said it, not me," he replied. "You ready to roll?"

I unsnapped my helmet, took it off, and put it on the bike seat. "I think I'd better walk home," I said as the lump in my throat grew bigger.

"Maggie," John said.

"What?" I huffed under my breath as I glanced over my shoulder at him through teary eyes.

John lowered his shades, and his gaze bore threw me. Damn him.

Chapter 37

The scowl on my face made my mouth droop. The tightness in my brow resulted in a throbbing headache, and my stomach gurgled from being empty. I couldn't remember the last time I was this angry with myself, for letting John get the upper hand. I scuffled up the front stairs. Mom's car was gone. Judy was on the swing waiting for me. I hid behind my sunglasses.

"What are you doing here?" I asked.

"Nice to see you, too," she answered. "Your mom called me and said you might need a friend."

I rolled my eyes. "Jesus." I leaned against the half wall of the porch. "I suppose you know everything, because nothing can be private around here."

"To be honest, yeah, I do. John told Glad you got mad at him and refused to get on the bike."

I rested my sunglasses on top of my head. "He was being a jerk," I said. "He knew damn well what he was doing."

"Maybe, I don't know what happened between you two."

I watched Judy shift her weight on the swing and tuck her leg under her butt as if she was settling in for the long haul. I thought quickly about my words, not wanting to be the bad guy.

"He really didn't have to say what he did. He could have just said, 'You're not an idiot,' but instead he said, 'You said it, not me,'" I exclaimed through clenched teeth. "Jesus." I covered my eyes with the palms of my hands then pressed as hard as I could.

"What happened?" she asked.

I sat down beside Judy, staring straight ahead. "Where's my mom? Where's Chloe?"

"Your mom left. Chloe is with her dad on the bike. What did you do to him? He was pretty quiet."

I stared at her, my lips pressed together. "What do you mean, 'What did I do to him?'"

"Maybe I should go," Judy suggested with a raised brow.

I held my breath then let it out slowly. "Sorry, I don't know if I'm coming or going."

"Yeah, I get that." Judy's curly hair framed her face like a baroque framed Modigliani painting.

"Has anyone told you that you look like Rhea Perlman?"

"Don't change the subject on me. And yes, I've heard that before. What's so difficult here?"

I rubbed my throbbing temples. My true feelings swirled inside of me like a tornado, sweeping away any logic. Embarrassed, I chewed on my thumbnail. "It's complicated."

"Well, why don't you start at the beginning," she suggested.

I crossed my arms over my chest. "Okay," I huffed, "I'm avoiding a relationship with John because when it doesn't work out, I'll be cut off from Chloe, too and I couldn't bear not having her in my life. There, I said it."

"Who says it's not going to work out?"

"He's moving to Montana. That's really far away. I have to stay here and work. I can't just sell my practice and move. I don't have a practice. I'm mad at him."

"Why? Is there more?"

"Yeah." Rubbing my temples, I bore my fingertips into the sides of my head. "It has to do with me, though. It's not his fault."

"Bring it on," Judy mumbled.

I scowled in her direction. "This isn't a sparring match, friend."

"I agree. He's awful. What else?"

"Oh, Christ." I slunk down against the swing. "Why does he get to behave badly, but I don't?"

"Double standard rule?"

"Yeah, I guess. I think I was overly sensitive."

Judy swatted a mosquito from her knee. "About what?"

"None of this makes sense," I said, running my fingers through my hair.

"You're telling me." Judy nodded in agreement. "Got anything to drink?"

I sat silent.

"So, getting back to John, what did he say that made you so mad?"

"It wasn't what he said, he used my own words against me. All he had to do was say, '*No, you're not an idiot.*' But no, he stood there and smirked when I became a smidgeon vulnerable." I squinted, picturing his expression in my head. "He enjoyed every second."

"Seriously, you lost me. Can I have something to drink? What did he say that started this whole ordeal?"

I closed my eyes feeling the angst settle in my chest. "He said Autumn's mom was a nice woman." I groaned at my childish antics. I peeked over at Judy. She was smiling. Her dimples framed her petit mouth.

"Hmmm. You got it worse than I thought, girl. And now he knows it."

I closed my eyes wishing I'd kept my mouth shut in the first place. Breathing in the scent of lilacs and fresh-cut grass, I opened my right eye, then faced Judy. "I am such an idiot."

Judy patted my shoulder. "Seriously, wine, beer, anything."

Judy yanked me up from my seat. She held the door for me and swatted my bottom as I went inside. "What was that for?"

"Because I can," she said. "Your mom said there were leftovers in the refrigerator. Must be nice to have a mom that cooks for you."

"And get in my business," I said like a sixth grade boy high on hormones. I opened the fridge door. The feel of the stainless steel door cooled my temper. I poked around until I found a plastic container with a note on top from my mom. I read it, letting the cool air waft across me.

Eat. I know how you are. Not eating will not solve anything.

Rolling my eyes, I lifted the top to sniff the contents. "You hungry? Looks like chicken marsala and pasta of some sort." When I turned, Judy had Chloe's letter in front of her at the counter, you know.

Her eyes met mine. "John wouldn't have relished the moment if you hadn't validated his feelings. You're all a mess," she said. "This letter is sweet. They really love you."

I retrieved a couple of Blue Moons from the fridge. "I don't have any wine, only beer." Setting the beers on the counter, I opened the microwave door. "Can you hand me that container?"

Judy passed the chicken over the counter, and I slipped it into the miracle of ovens. Opening the drawer, I slid a bottle opener across the counter in her direction. I leaned against the counter watching the numbers countdown on the digital clock.

The bottle caps clanged as they hit the counter.

"Here," Judy said, sliding me a beer.

"Thanks," I said, almost knocking it over as I reached out to grab it. Tiny suds dripped down the bottle, and I licked them off.

"Why does this bother you so much?" Judy asked.

"What?" I took a long drag from the frosty bottle.

"That they love you and want you in their lives."

I rolled the cold beer bottle across my forehead. "You don't want to know."

"Actually, I do so we can get on with life. Actually, I want to go to Montana," she said.

"Nice." I chugged my beer. "Want to get me another one," I said as the microwave beeped. I took two plates out of the cupboard and grabbed two forks then sat next to her at the counter in Chloe's usually spot. My hand stuck to the seat as I maneuvered the stool up to the counter.

Judy hopped down from her stool and served up two more beers. I popped the tops and held my bottle up to hers.

"Cheers," I said, pushing a plate of food in front of her. "You need some meat on your bones, too. You eat the big portion."

"So what don't I want to know?" she said with a mouthful of food.

I rearranged the food on my plate with my steely fork. Beckett had picked out the modern pattern when we redid the kitchen. "I hate this silverware. Remind me to send it to Beckett." Heat drifted toward my face. The steam collected on my chin and I wiped it away. "Promise you won't laugh, or anything else?"

Judy raised her hand as if she were taking the Boy Scout oath. "Promise." She slurped up strands of pasta.

"You are kind of a messy eater," I said.

"Don't change the subject."

I challenged her stare. "Fine. It's like I'm cheating on my family." She chewed slowly as I guzzled more beer. I waited for a response. There was nothing. I took a bite of chicken and mushroom. My mother was a great cook. I swallowed remorse. "Well?"

"You told me I couldn't react, so I'm not," Judy said.

Judy's dark eyes held my attention. "Say something, this is too uncomfortable," I pleaded.

"You sure?" she asked, raising an eyebrow.

"Yeah," I answered, hedging internal bets with myself.

"How can that be cheating on your family? Beckett was the one that left you. He's off doing who-knows-what and Bradley? He's in Boston. He's grown, for Pete's sake. This sounds like an excuse."

I frowned. "I just don't want Bradley to think I'm abandoning him. And Beckett . . ."

Judy interrupted with a shake of her head. "Oh no you don't," she ordered. "Beckett is over. He doesn't get a say, and I know Bradley wants you to be happy. This isn't one of your crazy classroom dramas between baby mommas and baby daddies."

My mouth fell open at her words. I raised my eyebrows at her. "You did not just say that."

"Sorry, it seems that your clientele is having an unwarranted effect on you. You have a right to be happy. You did what you said you would do and now it's time to move on. Decide which way to go now that you've finally reached your crossroads, girl."

In a quandary, I squeezed my lips together as she spoke.

"It's time to live, my friend." Judy patted my hand with hers then she touched the exposed tattoo on my collarbone from radiation treatment last year.

I twirled pasta around my fork then stabbed a mushroom.

Judy slid Chloe's letter closer to me. "Stuff like this doesn't come along every day," she said with a wink. "Oh, I forgot to tell you. I got my test back."

I held my breath. "And . . . ?"

"And, everything is normal, just like Dr. Nelson suspected. It was just a cyst."

"Yee-ha." I held my beer bottle in Judy's direction. She beamed and I made a toast. "Here's to ladybugs, healthy lives, and love."

Chapter 38

With eyes wide open, I stared at the shadows that drifted across the ceiling. Each shape-shift triggered memories that lie dormant, deep, below my everyday surface. Silvery threads of moonlight pulled at the deepest ones, the ones I'd almost forgotten. They ran like film cells through my head, the night Beckett and I learned that we would be parents, Bradley losing his first tooth when he fell off the porch stairs, my fortieth surprise birthday party that I didn't show for until it was more than halfway over, Bradley's high school graduation party. I covered my eyes with the palm of my hand then inhaled, held my breath, and tried like hell not to let anything escape.

Holding on was holding me back.

Funny how time tricked me.

Funny how time made me lose my way and warped my vision of the future.

Funny, how I lost track of myself along the way.

I exhaled and kicked my feet against the bed. The cotton sheets rustled in the silence of night as tribulations snuck up on me, tiptoed into my subconscious, and I let them in. Nothing could erase the past, but I sure as hell could change the ending of the future.

Judy's words stuck in my head. Recalling our earlier conversation, I remembered her words precisely. The sound of my breath in the midnight air reminded me just how quiet this big house was. I tossed and turned, stared at the clock, and cursed the coming day. In a huff, I closed my eyes. John's face lurked beneath my eyelids. His sultry eyes beckoned for me the way they did on that night we made love. I could feel his breath on my neck and I remembered tracing that horseshoe tattoo on his shoulder. Touching my collarbone, I could pinpoint my own black tattoo without looking. Foolish regret washed over me. I kicked off the covers and got out of bed then peeked through the slats of the blinds with hopes of catching a glimpse of self-direction. I threw on my sweater then went downstairs.

I switched on the light in the library, organized the photos on my desk, then sat down to write a list of things I needed to do. Visit Bradley was number one. I flipped open my laptop and searched for a plane ticket. I booked a flight out on Thursday evening after school. My students were higher than kites and I was hanging on by a thread trying to balance academics with survival. Opening my phone, I sent Bradley a text. My heart lightened with the hasty decision. I'd spent my life planning each step, not allowing myself to fall down. This impromptu trip to see my boy excited me.

John and Chloe's photo peeked out from the bottom of the pile of photos. I kept it there on purpose regardless of my projects or my feelings. It had been in the same place since last summer. I traced the outlines of their faces. Their bright smiles made my eyes tear up.

I placed the photo on top of the pile.

My phone buzzed with a text. Everyone I knew was in bed. The time read a few minutes past midnight. It was Bradley confirming my arrival. I sent him a short note back. *Will explain later. Last day of school is next week. Took a personal day. Can't wait to see you. Love, Mom.*

I went back to my laptop to register for a substitute. My phone buzzed again. I expected to see a reply of hugs and kisses from Bradley, but it was John. *Saw your light on. Can I come over?*

I tapped out a text. *I'll open the front door.* I heard him shuffle up the porch steps as I unlocked the deadbolt. Peering through the peephole, I took a deep breath, I felt the future swell in my chest. My heart pounded.

"Hi," I said.

John's eyes flashed as his gaze met mine. He opened the screen door and I joined him on the porch.

"Hi. You're up kind of late," he said.

"Yeah, couldn't sleep." I sat next to him on the swing as he patted the seat for me to join him. He put his arm around my shoulder and pulled me close. It was familiar. It was time. It was what I needed. "Please tell me Chloe's asleep," I whispered.

"You're such a worry wart," he whispered. "She's fine."

"Can't help it." Goosebumps covered my arms.

"You chilly?"

I nuzzled closer and rested my head on his chest. "No, not really. Can't believe the school year is almost over."

"Yeah, but I think the last month has been the longest for me with all this moving stuff."

I sighed. "I don't want you to sell your house."

He kissed the top of my head. "Maggie, I think about you all the time."

His words calmed me. "Yeah, I think about you, too." His lips were warm against my forehead. He'd grown to be part of me. I closed my eyes, blinking away the tears.

John lifted my chin with his finger. "Open your eyes."

I did. A thin smile melted the seriousness that held me hostage. I ran my hand over his chest, his heartbeat strong and steady. I kissed his fingers as they brushed messy tresses of hair away from my cheek. "I'm going to see Bradley in Boston."

"That's good."

"I need to talk to him."

We both knew what that meant.

"You're a good mom," John said.

I snickered. "Some days, I'm not so sure." I laid my head back on his chest.

"I see how you are with Chloe. Nobody can fake that. Bradley is one lucky boy."

Bradley's face filled in my mind. "I just love him so much." Emotion built in my throat. I swallowed it away with a smile.

"I know you don't want to hurt anybody, especially him. I know how that goes."

"Yeah," I said, remembering the first day I met Chloe. Her brash introduction the beginning of a heartfelt connection that I didn't want to sever.

John caressed my cheek. I stared into his caring eyes that knew something I didn't.

"At some point, it has to be about you," he said.

"You mean us."

His smile warmed me.

Suddenly, the midnight chill was gone. "You know how I feel," I said.

"I know," he said, "I think we both feel the same way."

His left dimple appeared with his grin. He cupped my face in his hands. His soft lips met mine and I kissed him. I leaned back not afraid to reconnect with his stare.

"Yeah, I'm bad at this mushy stuff," I whispered.

John's smile was contagious. "It's okay, I'm not so great at it myself."

"I couldn't sleep. It gets harder and harder to sleep. Why is that?" I asked. "You think after all these years, I'd be so exhausted that I would conk out and not get up. Very frustrating."

"Yeah, I know what you mean. Frustrating."

John's eyes twinkled in the moonlight.

"What, you can't sleep either?" I asked.

"No, you," he whispered. "You're frustrating. I'm trying

to kiss you and you're rambling on about not being able to sleep."

I grinned. "I told you, I'm not very good at this stuff."

John put his pointer finger against my lips. "Shh, let me kiss you."

My mind reeled with thoughts of Bradley, Boston, Montana, horses, mountains, possibilities that frightened me, and burdens I felt slipping away. John's tender lips met mine. His fingertips tickled my neck. A soft moan escaped me as I embraced the moment. Leaning back, I lifted my eyelids to make sure I wasn't dreaming. "I think you already know, but I've decided to see what this Montana thing is all about."

John's eyes twinkled and his smile grew. "I knew you'd come around."

Maggie's journey continues in: *Maggie's Montana*

Dear Readers,

I hope you've enjoyed the second part of Maggie's journey. I also hope Maggie and Chloe have touched your heart in the same way they have touched mine. If you loved this book and have a minute to spare, I'd really appreciate a short review on the page or website where you purchased *Maggie's Fork in the Road*. Your message to new readers is invaluable, especially for debut authors like myself. Reviews from readers like you make it possible for Maggie and Chloe to continue their adventures.

It is with much heartfelt gratitude, I thank you. Until next time, remember . . . *all forks in the road lead home.*

Sincerely,
Linda

Website: www.LindaBradleyAuthor.com

Facebook: https://www.facebook.com/Linda-Bradley-389688594534105/

Twitter: **@LBradleyAuthor**

Link to my Amazon page: http://www.amazon.com/Linda-Bradley/e/B00JUIS2FS

Also by **Soul Mate Publishing** and **Linda Bradley**:

MAGGIE'S WAY

Middle-aged, Maggie Abernathy just wants to recuperate from cancer during the solitude of summer vacation after a tiresome year of teaching second grade.

Maggie's plans are foiled when precocious seven-year-old Chloe McIntyre moves in next door with her dad, John. Maggie's life changes in a way she could never imagine when the pesky new neighbors steal her heart. With Maggie's grown son away, her ex-husband in the shadows, her meddling mother's unannounced visits, and Chloe McIntyre on her heels, somehow Maggie's empty house becomes home again.

Available now on Amazon: http://tinyurl.com/jowuly4

CPSIA information can be obtained
at www.ICGtesting.com
Printed in the USA
BVOW09s2015281117
501445BV00016B/289/P